It begins *with* **us**

It begins *with* **us**

Meanjin, Australia

ISBN 978-0-6453392-5-3

First published in 2022

Revolutionary University Press is an initiative of Revolutionaries to publish the work of emerging and established creatives and thinkers from university places and spaces. One press for all universities.

Moonrise
Meanjin, Australia
www.moonrise.revolutionaries.com.au

Related Titles from Moonrise

Queerly ever after by Alayna Cole

Madness in bloom edited by Ross Watkins & Jay Ludowyke

a record of my remnants by Katie Hulme

Through the darkness, I will love myself edited by Wallea Eaglehawk, Nikola Champlin & Padya Paramita

Foreword

It begins with us is a revolution of the heart. This bold collection of 35 works by emerging Australian writers tells stories of what it means to be human amid times of great transformation – within dystopian worlds that mirror our own, imagined lands of the fantastic, or across the spaces of our opinions and desires, each story explores what it takes to be the catalyst for positive change. Sometimes exhilarating, sometimes thought-provoking and always rebellious, *It begins with us* underscores how every revolution must arise within the self.

—R.W. & J.L.

Contents

EARTH-SHIFTERS

STAR-SEEKERS

THE REVOLUTION BEGINS WITH YOU

Beginnings in the End

Ellen Nesbitt

The settlement was quieting, the sunset pulling a blanket of shush over the huts. The fire popped and sizzled underneath the spreading sky, swaths of red and orange tumbling outwards in waves of colour. The sentinel trees of the settlement swayed in the wind, sending their growing shadows dancing across the thatched huts.

Pip breathed in the charcoal scent of burning wood and scrutinised her father across the flames. His face was etched deeper since the last time she'd seen him, his blue eyes lacked their sparkle and bushy whiskers swallowed his once-smiling mouth. He had a heaviness about him as he leant back against the log. Beside him, her mother cooed over her baby brother, Wade. He was unsettled, and Pip could tell he was ready to curl up with Mum and drift off to sleep, like the smoke drifting over the treetops.

'Ok then, bedtime,' Mum said, kissing him on the forehead and gathering him in a patchwork blanket. She stood to go and added, 'Come on, Pip.'

'What!? But Mum—' she started, pleading. Going to bed would mean taking her eyes off her father's face, and she wasn't ready for that.

'I said bedtime,' Mum replied, ending it.

'Seriously?' Pip appealed to her father, 'Dad?'

Pip's call broke his reverie, and he snapped up with a faraway look on his face. 'Hmm?'

'Can I stay up a little longer?'

He seemed surprised at the question, as though he'd forgotten such a thing as bedtime existed. 'Don't see why not,' he said.

'Drew ...' Jenna said, unsure. She searched him, trying to see beneath his glaze of weariness. But there was no shadow to his words; his daughter's sleep was the furthest problem from his mind. They looked at each other in a way only parents can, communicating so much without words.

The baby made up her mind for her, arching his back and crying out. Resigned, she said, 'Alright, but not too late,' and flicked a loaded look at Pip. Pip smiled serenely back, content with herself.

'Good night, Jen,' Dad said softly as Jenna stood to leave the log circle, the words odd in his mouth. She looked back, and Pip saw a swarm of emotions on her face. An unfamiliar sweetness tipped up the corners of her mother's mouth as she smiled back at him—Pip had forgotten she could look like that.

Jenna nodded gently and took one last look at the two of them, father and daughter, and understood Pip's stubbornness. Her husband was greyer than last time she'd seen him. Meanwhile, her daughter seemed to grow fiercer every day, her eyes gleaming under a mop of burnt orange hair. It was a rare sight to see the two of them sitting by the fire, so similar and yet so different. She soaked it in before relenting to her baby's cries and disappearing inside the hut.

Drew watched them leave then gave Pip a conspiratorial wink. She grinned back, relieved. She sat cross-legged on the copper earth across from him, but he still felt far away. Pip was still trying to put her finger on it—what had changed in him—but there was enough of him to know he was still the father she'd longed for. She got up to move closer and was surprised when he lifted his arm and welcomed her in beside him. He'd lost that faraway fog and she saw her dad—just Dad. The gesture made her feel guilty for doubting him. She had ached for this, so she settled in beside him before he disappeared again.

He'd only been back a couple of days. Pip had been playing catch with her friends Fern and Linden near the nursery amongst the rows of seedlings, oblivious to the return of the excursion party. Jenna had been cooking dinner over the fire and looked up to see him standing there, swag in hand, covered in dust, like a ghost blown in from the desert. They didn't say anything, just stood there staring at each other for an eternal moment—until Wade gurgled in the sling on her breast and broke the spell. Drew's grey-blue eyes had widened, and in a flash the three were as one, all arms and tears as father and son were introduced.

Pip was used to it, in a way. Dad had been going on excursions to the outer lands ever since she could remember, sometimes for a couple of nights, sometimes for weeks. But he'd never been gone this long, and there were moments when she'd doubted if he would ever come back. There was so much she wanted to ask him, but her mother's warning look flashed across her mind. Pip shook her head to dismiss it, annoyed. Then she had an idea.

'Dad, can you tell me a story?' she asked, hopeful but trying to hide it.

He gave a silent laugh; it was foreign on him. 'It's been a long time since I told a bedtime story,' he said. He seemed to reach back into the musty corners of his memory and began, 'It was the darkest night of the year and even the stars were hiding, for they knew that the Shadowman was out hunting for his—'

'Daaaad,' she cut in. 'Not the Shadowman, I'm not five anymore. Can't you tell me a different story? Something I haven't heard?' The words tumbled out, and she realised she'd slipped back into their old mode of talking, when he'd been, well, just Dad. Pip almost regretted it, but it was true—she wasn't a little girl anymore. She went out with the older kids hunting for rabbits (even though Mum gave her an earful every time about staying with the group, with threats like, 'One toe out of line, Pip, one toenail, and no more hunting. You'll be weeding in the communal plot for months. *Stay with the group.* You hear me?'). Pip mentored the young ones on how to climb fruit trees and help with the picking during the harvest, and this past spring she'd even planted her own sentinel tree on the boundary of the settlement. She had responsibilities—but he didn't know that.

Drew gave another silent laugh, a little easier now. He squeezed her affectionately and said, 'You're just like me when I was young. Always hungry for stories, for adventure. I was always asking Uncle Bill for another tale …' His smile slipped and his face was faraway again, remembering.

He went quiet, and Pip began to think she'd messed up. She was running over things to say in her head and ways to apologise when he spoke in a low voice, eyes glued on the flames. 'There is a story I've been wanting to tell you, an important story.'

Thrilled, she waited—but nothing. He looked towards the hut; its domed roof silhouetted against the first stars on the horizon.

'Jenna wouldn't like it,' he muttered to himself.

Pip bristled. 'Come on, Dad, I'm not little anymore. I'm almost eleven.' She then added, sulkily, 'Not that Mum seems to notice. She still treats me like a baby.'

Drew looked at her, seeming to notice that she was, in fact, not the child he had left behind all those moons ago.

'Don't be too hard on her, Pip. She just wants to protect you.'

'Protect me from what?'

Pip could see him teetering on the brink of truth-telling.

'Have you ever wondered why Mum never talks about her mother, your grandmother?'

'No,' Pip said, surprised. 'I just know that she died a long time ago.'

Drew looked at her for a long moment, then seemed to make up his mind. He glanced over at the hut and whispered, 'Forgive me, Jen.'

A shiver travelled up Pip's spine, and the settlement seemed to shiver as well.

'Once upon a time, in a land much like our own, there was a mighty woman who fought for her people.'

Her father's words seemed to awaken something lying dormant under the surface of things. The flames licked higher; the trees leant closer to listen. And he began to talk as if compelled by something beyond himself. As if suddenly the weight of this untold story was too much to bear, and only by telling it could he hope to be free of it.

'The people of that time had seen great civilisations rise and fall, and rise again, and fall again. Civilisation had been through an enormous boom, swallowing up the earth's resources with an unstoppable appetite for progress. The civilised world, as they liked to call it, teetered on the brink of collapse. Their obsession with growth saw them reach beyond the acid skies to other planets, attempting to prop up their wobbly ideals with interplanetary colonisation. Meanwhile, the inhabitants of the earth were suffering, and not just the humans. The insects, birds, animals of the land, sea and sky—even the fungal and microbial realms—suffered under the immense weight of the ideal of progress. But this infernal machine just kept chugging on, fuelled by the greed of an ever-decreasing number of people who, in their obsession, were willing to sacrifice everyone and everything to have more for themselves.

'The waters began to dry up, the soil turned to dust, and the oceans became wastelands of debris. The deserts began to spread, engulfing entire regions, so that the tallest buildings became sandcastles in some giant child's sand pit. The temperatures rose so high that people were forced to travel great distances from their homes, seeking refuge in foreign places in their quest to find clean water and a scrap of food for their children to eat.

'The people cried, the animals cried, the earth cried for this devastation. But the greed of the few had utterly consumed their souls, and they were deaf to the warnings, to the pleas, to the tolling quakes that signalled the end of life. There was no longer any way to reason with them, or even access them—they had shut themselves away in fortresses and echoing chambers where they horded their precious resources.

'Finally, a day came when a fiery-haired woman had to bury her youngest child in the endless orange sand. It was the third child she had buried in a year. This broke her in a way she thought was impossible, for her heart had broken so many times that only shards remained. As she stood there at the foot of her son's grave—so small among the many lumps lined up along the edge of the encroaching desert where bones became dust—something cracked. She split open, and what stepped out from the blackness of her grief was a fire-queen. Scorched in the flames of rage and loss, and with little else left to lose, she threw her whole self into the fight. She gathered up as many lost and broken bodies who could still stand on two legs and started singing to them of revolution, of change.'

Drew paused for a moment, the firelight illuminating his stormy features.

'Her songs blew life back into their frail and undernourished bodies. Their hollow eyes started to burn with the same flames that scorched her insides, that crowned her in a magma glow. She sang out like some harpy from hell screeching righteous vengeance. There were no more tears to cry, no more losses to fear for the worst had already become reality. Slowly, where there had only been lone figures wandering through the wastelands of a barren world, bodies began to huddle in twos and threes. Whispers could be heard on the breeze. The pummelling waves of the dirty ocean grew fiercer, and the sun seethed with the glowing embers of one last fight.

'One final stand, the earth rumbled. One final chance, the seas simmered. One final fight, the gathering dark gloomed.

'And so the word spread of the army of oblivion, an ants' nest of desperation bubbling up for battle. And the day came when, with wild eyes and frenzied fists, the broken bodies of the last army tore with tooth and nail at the fortresses that shadowed them and pummelled their grief upon those grey walls and shrieked their terrible fury upon the greed of progress.

'When the bleeding sun set upon that dusty world the sands were slick with red. The towers went up in a blaze of bitter victory as the survivors shovelled the graves of the fallen. The weary victors surprised themselves as fresh tears gleamed in their eyes, and they wept cleansing rivers for the end, the end, the end of the machine.'

The flames flickered above the glowing coals, and the stars twinkled ominously in the sky above them as the sentinel trees swallowed up the final words of his story.

Everything was stillness.

Pip clung to her father out of fear and shock and so many more feelings she couldn't yet put a name to. But the steady rise and fall of his chest kept her breathing, the smoky smell of the coals kept her grounded, and his encircling arm promised protection and safety. They gazed together into the distant dark over the silhouetted trees and huts.

Tentatively, Pip whispered, 'Dad?'

He looked down into the moon of his daughter's face, curled in beside him.

'Is that story about Grandma?'

'Yes, Pip,' he said, his expression grim. 'Jenna was the same age you are now when she stood next to her mother in the rusty sands that covered her siblings' graves.'

Pip swallowed, rocked by this truth about her mum. She tried to imagine what it would be like if it was little Wade, but she just felt sick. To distract herself, she asked, 'What was her name? Grandma?'

'Enya.'

Enya. The name echoed in her heart, both familiar and totally new. After a moment, she asked, 'Did she die in the battle?'

'Before it began, she took Jenna to a cave in the hillside where the children were being sheltered. She hugged Jenna for a long time, and said to her, "One day, you will understand." Then she kissed her on the forehead and left the cave. Everyone stopped and watched her pass, unsure if she walked or floated. I remember catching a glimpse of her eyes, normally brown, like Jenna's … but on that day, they were bottomless black. Your mum knew she would never see her again.'

Haunted, he added, 'We hid in that cave for days, until the smoke disappeared.'

Pip struggled to take it all in. Her breathing became shallow as her mind raced with questions. 'But how could she leave Mum behind? Her daughter …' Pip trailed off, the questions boiling inside her. 'You were there too—what happened after the battle? Wh-what about the settlement?'

she stammered, spiralling. 'Did it come after? Was that it? Did the battles continue? Why—'

'Shhh, hush now,' he said, gathering her up in his arms. 'You have lots of questions, and I'll try to answer them all. But we have time.'

No, we don't, his conscience said.

Drew pushed the voice aside, not prepared to go there. He explained, 'We were able to salvage resources from the wreckage, and though we were shattered we found plenty to do. Slowly, the settlement started to take shape and we figured out systems for growing food and managing water. We even started planting trees again and took care of whatever remnants of wilderness remained in that ravaged world. This is one of those remnants,' he gestured at the ghostly trees spotted around the place. 'Over time, we found a rhythm, and then,' he squeezed Pip, 'you came along.'

He turned a warm smile on her, but his heart sank when he saw the shock and grief in her eyes. He felt guilty for being the cause of her pain but knew that she had to hear the truth at some point, and better that it came from him than someone else. There'd been lively debate in the settlement over how much to tell the children, but his excursion to the outer lands had changed his mind. She probably should have been told earlier, he reflected, but it was Jenna's story to tell so he'd delayed, telling himself Pip would know at the right time. But, in the year he'd been away, his daughter had crept closer to the threshold between girl and young woman and she deserved to know her history. She needed to know it because, despite his best attempts, he couldn't stop the hard things coming. He swallowed his fears, trying not to think about how Jenna would react to what he had to tell her. He knew he must, but the sight of her, bright with a baby in her arms … how could he be the cause of more heartache? Hadn't she been through enough?

Pip let out a sob, bringing Drew back to the fire, and his daughter beside him. She heaved as the story settled inside her, as the dots connected of their life in the settlement, her father's absences, her mum's fierce protectiveness.

Drew held her gently by the shoulders as she shook. 'Courage is in your blood, Pip. You give us hope, me and your mum. You were our guiding light, giving us the strength to go on, making us choose to dream again when it would have been easier not to.'

She looked at him then, at his blurred face soft with pride, and broke down in fresh sobs.

'I'm sorry, love,' he said, both to Pip and his wife. 'Maybe I shouldn't have told you, maybe you're too young.'

She sat up with a hiccup, face red and streaked with tears. 'No, Dad, I'm glad you did. I'm just … I'm not … I'm just glad you're here.'

His throat swelled and he pulled her in again, tucking her head under his chin, rocking her gently. 'Me too, Pip. Me too.' They clung to each other as the flames sunk lower, letting the past and future fade because at that moment, it was enough just to be together. Overhead, the sky shimmered, alive with memory, twinkling with tomorrows.

The Tower

MATHEW CHANNER

It was dawn when the girl began to climb the tower. The first few levels were simple. Vines had penetrated the lower floors, and their twisting trunks, thick with age, guided her upward. Beyond them, her ascent became more complicated, more dangerous. Much of the structure had crumbled away. Holes in the outer walls opened into misty oblivion. What greenery grew was thin and ragged. Everything metal was rusting, disintegrating beneath her hands. Frequently she looped her rope over a high point and, when she tested its strength, sent chunks of flaking steel tumbling into the depths below. Each time she re-coiled the rope, studied the cross-beams above her, and tried again.

She stuck close to the walls, not daring any remaining sections of floor. The tower stretched above her as though reaching for something, history's skeletal arm thrusting out of the earth. She rested wrapped in rope she tied to the bones of the building; she tiptoed on beams across dizzying gaps. She urinated and listened to it trickle like rain. Slowly, relentlessly, she moved upward, sometimes burning hours deciphering a single floor, sometimes making three floors or more in one straight, ladder-like climb. Each step, each handhold precise. She tightened her makeshift sandals and re-strung the thick feathers she'd wrapped around her arms. A single graze, a cut on her finger, and all could be lost. She'd known many who had succumbed to the metal-madness.

By morning of the second day she had travelled beyond the mists that veiled her peoples' valley. Sunlight beamed through cracks and lit the dust that swirled where she passed. Utterly alone, the sheer madness of her journey upon her, head spinning with uncertainty. Her whole life she'd kept both feet on the ground, now she was farther from home than she'd imagined possible. The old world was forbidden. The tower, whatever it once was, remained only to tempt the foolish to their own destruction, or so the elder said. But the elder was weak, content to look always at the ground, to spread fear like plague. And when the girl paused to rest her weary arms and catch her breath, and the stillness crept around her, and she looked up through the dying structure toward the distant patch of sky, she knew there were things the elder wasn't telling her. Things that could be learned, if only she could reach them.

Close now. She had come so far, so high, even the bird calls she'd heard everyday of her life had faded. Clouds gathered thick and fast as though rushing to spectate. Rain lashed the side of the tower and dribbled down every inner surface. She tested each handhold carefully, loading weight into her fingers one by one. Her every step and reach precarious, her room for error, tiny to begin with, now non-existent. No matter. She was close. A few more levels. One more heave of her rope, one more climb, one more effort hauling her exhausted body up and up and up.

She stood atop the tower. She stood higher than she ever knew a living thing could stand. The storm slammed into her. The wind rushed up and over the building, claiming in seconds what had taken her days, trying to hurl her earthward, but she opened her arms to the wrathful sky and laughed in its face.

It took a night and a day for the rain to stop. She huddled beneath her scraps of cow-hide clothing and waited. At the end of her third day above the earth the bloody sun slipped behind mountains her people hadn't known existed until now. The sky turned colours she couldn't name. The tiny, pale pinpricks her people glimpsed through the foliage only a handful of times a decade, the things they whispered of around their fire-pits and called *Night's Eyes* after the glowing eyes of the nocturnal creatures they hunted, began to appear. One, then two, then a hundred, and then the great glimmering cluster-bomb of heavenly irises blinked open, and the girl craned her neck and stared into blackness impossibly glowing and wished that she, like them, could gaze without blinking, could see through a billion lenses, could illuminate darkness for her people as the Night's Eyes had illuminated it for her.

She lay on her bed of cold steel and watched. The night so vast, the Eyes so numerous, she didn't know where to look. Could it happen anywhere? Must darkness be young or old? Hours passed. The spirit her people called *Night's Mother* climbed over the edge of the world and hung there, regarding her. The girl had never felt so tiny, so insignificant, so—

There! A flash, a streak of white, like the slash of a knife across palm leaf. Darkness split open, then seamlessly closed. The girl's eyes were raw, she was fighting so hard not to blink. It happened so fast! Had she seen it? Was it real?

Again! Luminescence blazed across the sky. The girl gasped and clapped her hands. The Eye vanished but the brilliance remained, and when she closed her own eyes the image lingered like memory, a secret given to her by the keepers of the most wonderful secrets of all.

The girl lay awake all night, watching the Eyes dash and leap and burn, unable to sleep, unwilling to miss a moment of their dazzling dance, until dawn came and the Eyes closed by the thousand.

The climb down was long and hard. Her palms were blistered. Her muscles ached with fatigue. Twice she slipped and nearly plunged to her death. Six floors from the bottom a hold she had used on her ascent broke beneath her hand; she survived only by leaping for a lower platform. As she flew her leg caught something and ripped. Skin opened like the Night's Eyes opened darkness. Her blood ran over metal and dripped, finding earth long before she did.

She was lightheaded and woozy by the time she reached her village. The sentries saw her coming and crossed their spears. She was pale and blood-covered; it had been four days, and they thought she was a ghost.

'The Night's Eyes ...' She mumbled as the men drew near, but they were muttering incantations to ward off spirits. She raised one arm, beckoning, and then fell.

The girl woke in her hut, her mother beside her, and knew by the dullness of the grey light it was early morning. Her mother frowned and pushed the girl's head down when she tried to rise. She slept again, and when she woke it was night, blackness complete and oppressive, so unlike the night she had spent atop the tower. By morning she was strong enough to sit and eat. Her mother fed her little bites and clucked her tongue. The next day the girl stood and, with her hand on her mother's shoulder, walked slowly outside. Birds shrieked in the dense foliage. Insects buzzed around her wounded leg. The girl looked up but could see only leaf and branch and palm frond. Beyond them the mist and steam that curled eternally from the moist jungle. The skies were hidden from her now.

Children scattered when they saw her. Their parents sat in the doorways of bamboo huts and stared at her with narrowed eyes. Trees embraced the decrepit remnants of the old world: low, crumbled walls, the almost disintegrated skeletons of upturned cars. What vague structures still stood did so only because entwined branches and roots prevented them from collapsing. Nothing of what remained was used by the girl's people.

The girl limped to the largest hut in the village. The elder was waiting for her outside.

'So you have climbed the tower,' he said. 'Even though it is forbidden.'

'Yes,' the girl did not bow or address him by his proper title. 'I have seen Night's Mother. I have seen the Night's Eyes. They are … They are …'

She could not finish. The elder's brow furrowed. He made a sign to ward off evil.

'You have gone where our people must not,' he said. 'The spirits have followed you home. They are all around you. Soon you will suffer.'

'I am not afraid of spirits,' the girl said. 'I am not afraid of the night. The Eyes are not evil. They are like … like children. Children are silly and playful, but also wise. They are full of knowing. I must return, and learn what they know.'

The elder shook his head. 'The Ancient Ones craved such knowledge. They built machines so powerful they could reach the Night's Eyes, and those machines became weapons that rained upon the earth. They sought knowledge, and they destroyed themselves with fire and disease. That is why the tower is forbidden, why we do not use their tools or make our homes in theirs. Knowledge is evil. Knowledge will tempt you like the jackal. It will be playful and show its belly and then, when you are within its reach, rip out your throat.'

'The old stories are true,' said the girl. 'The Night's Eyes are not spirits. They are something more, something not of this world. They are the key to understanding … everything. I will learn what they have to teach us, and I will bring this knowledge to the others.'

'If you return to the tower, you will be banished,' the elder said.

The girl tried to respond, but her jaw had clamped shut. Pain shot through her neck and the back of her head. She whimpered and fell to her knees.

'Metal-madness,' the elder hissed, glaring at her bandaged leg. 'You should have left that poisoned tower to rot. Now you will suffer and die, as do all who meddle with the remnants of the old world.'

Men carried the girl back to her hut. Her mother sat beside her and clucked her tongue, and fed her bits of fruit whenever her jaw loosened. The shaman came with herbs and smoke and spells, but soon the girl was rife with fever. Her limbs spasmed and seized. Stabbing pains jolted her head and belly. It became increasingly difficult to swallow. Dim mornings stretched into vague, humid afternoons. Nights swooped in, black and aggressive. Madness circled like a hungry beast, closer every hour. The girl's eyes grew dull like the half-light days, as if the jungle fog that hovered above had slipped beneath her skin. She was fading, slipping, dying. Her people came to stare and listen to her mutter incessantly about sky-spirits and flying lights and other, impossible things. They whispered about the foolish girl who had defied their laws, and even her mother couldn't hold the blame from her eyes as she watched her daughter sweat and groan and shiver.

Then, when so many days had passed the village had almost forgotten her slow decay, the girl sat up in the middle of the night as though pulled by a rope. She stood on her putrid leg as if she felt no pain and walked outside and through her village and into the pitch-dark jungle. The sentries let her go. They had seen the last march of the metal-mad before.

The girl marched barefoot through thorns and ant nests and mud. Branches slapped her; she noticed them only enough to swat them aside. Above her, beyond foliage thicker than human ignorance, beyond the mist that had covered her nearly every day of her life, the Night's Eyes called to her. Wrapping her hands around the thick, gnarled vines that surrounded the tower was like coming home.

Upward now. Hands entangled in the vines, feet already raw and aching. No light to guide her. Her breath ragged in the darkness as she reached blindly ahead. She sliced her arm on a razor edge. She nicked her eyebrow and felt warm blood trickle down her neck. Her arms ached, then screamed. Impossible she would make it so far. But she could feel them. They were pulling, guiding, whispering to her. She could do it, she knew she could do it …

Her hands gave way. She flew, ripping through leaves and tendrils, and slammed onto her back.

Later, when the sun began to pass what it could through the fog, and the birds began their muted morning calls, and enough light had permeated for the girl to see the walls of her tomb, she lay as she had fallen and stared through the guts of the tower at the pinprick of open sky and wept. Pain grew into walls that closed in around her. She had been so certain. She had *known*, for the first time in her life. She, among all her people, had been offered truth. But she couldn't grasp it.

The boy heard the buzzing long before he reached it. Its source was higher than expected, and he climbed carefully for an hour before he found the contorted heap of jutting bone and dried blood. The boy had sat outside the hut for three days listening to the girl babble about the tower, about the Eyes, about streaks of light so beautiful they stopped her breath. When she disappeared, he knew where she had gone.

Flies choked the corpse. The boy waved his arms, clearing her face long enough to see her glassy eyes, staring upward. He followed her gaze. A few more levels and he would be beyond the mist; he could see sunbeams coming through the patchwork walls, a light-ladder of celestial rungs. Higher still, higher than seemed possible, a tiny glimmer. The top.

The boy settled his coiled ropes more comfortably over his shoulders. He adjusted the leather guards around his arms and legs. Going would be slow. His haul bag was much larger than the girl's had been. He carried enough supplies to live frugally for some time and even to leave caches for the downward journey. He lingered only long enough to close the girl's eyes, and then he began to climb.

The Package

EJ Mitchell

Two cones of jaundiced light pierced through the darkness ahead of the van's silhouette. Trees bowed, like an honour guard, towards the van as it swept past. A solitary streetlamp gave flavour to the van's form—the body was more rust than paintwork, a faded sign unreadable in its moment of illumination, back windows black spaces of blindness.

The deep rumble of the van's engine reverberated off the ancient trees, creating bassline feedback that was felt more than it was heard. Elbows poked out of the front windows like orc ears and the twang of bluegrass banjos seeped over them into the night.

Inside, a woman and two men were crammed together on the cracked vinyl bench seat, their faces barely visible in the soft glow of the dashboard instruments. An undercurrent of tension pulsed like a silent alarm.

The woman was wedged between the two men. The small package secreted in her bra dug into the side of her breast. She kept her eyes on the road and her mind away from the virtual stranger beside her. He was much older than they were, and she could feel death transmitting from him. Maybe not imminent death, or her death, but certainly the possibility of death.

'Nice night for it,' she said.

'Keep your mouth shut,' replied the stranger.

'Hey, you can't talk to me like that.'

'Shelly—' said her fiancé.

'Alright, Mark,' replied Shelly. 'Wow, you two really know how to have fun.'

'One more word and I'll throw you out of the van,' said the stranger.

'No, you won't. I'm the ass carrying the package, remember?'

The van rocked on its chassis as it rounded a sweeping uphill bend. The road had begun its ascent to the mountain pass. The forest had peeled away to reveal steep granite escarpments and cliffs. Suddenly, the rhythmic flash of blue and red lights illuminated the darkness. Sets of headlights and brake lights queued ahead of them.

'Shit.'

'What's going on?'

'Shut. Up. I told you I'd toss you out if you kept talking, so shut the hell up!'

Shelly opened her mouth to say something more. Then she felt a jab in her side. She looked at Mark and saw naked fear in his eyes. The men pulled their elbows back into the van and wound up the windows. Shelly turned the music off, nothing left of the joker now. The air inside the van was drenched in adrenaline and smelt like wet metal soaking in a swamp.

The van rolled to a stop.

'What are you doing, Mark?'

'Well, I can't keep going, can I? Or do you want me to ram our way through the operatives ahead?'

'Will you two shut up?' hissed the stranger.

'Or what, huh? What are you going to do now, big man? Who the hell are you anyways?'

The red of the flashing lights fed Shelly's volatile temper. Her breathing became bullish, and Mark could almost see horns growing across her forehead and curling around her temples in the interplay of the lights on her face. He had seen Shelly lose herself in her anger before. Just once. It hadn't been pretty.

Faster than either of them could move, the stranger had his arm wrapped around Shelly's neck with his hand across her mouth.

'I swear I will render you unconscious and dump you into the back of this van if you do not shut the hell up!' said the stranger. 'Who I am, is none of your business. Tap your leg if you understand.'

Shelly tapped her leg. The stranger let her go.

'Okay, but do you have a name at least?' she asked.

'Fucking cut it out, Shelly,' hissed Mark.

'If you must have a name—'

Shelly nodded.

'—you can call me JD.'

'And what does JD stand for?'

'Jesus, you just won't quit, will you? It stands for John Doe. Mate, I don't know how you put up with this hellion but I'm sure it has its rewards.'

'Just a damn minute—'

'Fuck, Shelly. Shut up. Both of you shut up. There's movement at the station,' said Mark.

The night was raw. A dense layer of cloud muffled the light and sound and kept the frigid mountain air from escaping into the night. Beyond the incessant throbbing of the emergency lights, there was only cold, hard rock and hot, loose bowels.

People dressed in uniform khaki overalls milled around at the front of the roadblock. They could have been allies, except for their blank faces and the communication devices curled around their ears. Their movements were charged with purpose even though they ignored the stationary vehicle convoy of their making. They were waiting for something. Another one of their kind, a superior perhaps.

Like one organism, they looked up into the darkness.

THWUMP! THWUMP! THWUMP! THWUMP!

'Can you guys feel that?' asked Shelly.

'Yep,' said Mark.

'It's one of their machines. We're dead. Maybe not yet but we will be. Once they've taken everything from us,' said JD.

'Well, I'll just chuck the package.'

JD slammed his arm across Shelly's chest, pinning her against the backrest and crushing her breasts against her ribcage. The sound got louder. The brute impact of it spread from their torso to their ears, almost breaking their eardrums with the low-frequency pressure it created. All three of them waited with sick anticipation for the beast of a machine to lower itself into their view. Mark knew he should be doing something, anything at all, to rescue Shelly from JD's aggression, but he couldn't move—he was paralysed by the sound descending upon them.

'Then they'll know we have it,' said JD. 'Right now, they're looking for something. They don't know we have it but if you throw that package away, they will know.'

'They're not even looking at us.'

'Believe me, they will know.'

'Yeah, but how do you know—'

'Do you think they'd send raw skins like you two out here with someone who hasn't been here before? Now, will you please shut your mouth and stay where you are.'

'Well, since you asked so nicely—'

'Geez, Shelly, just stop would you,' said Mark, speaking out of the corner of his mouth. His skin had taken on a distinct green tinge with each flash of the blue light. He wanted to be far away from this moment, but even if he could move, he wouldn't.

He understood the risk more than Shelly. His father had disappeared out here somewhere. Mark hadn't known why his dad had left him and his mum. Not until he found a letter hidden at the back of the junk drawer. It was addressed to his mum, but she had never opened it. Mark remembered every single word on that one flimsy page.

September 2059

Dear Mrs Trinity Taylhar,

Stephen Taylhar has been lost. We will not abandon you.

Truth Seeker.

Mark looked across Shelly towards JD—was he *Truth Seeker*? Mark wondered if his father was still out here somewhere. If he was dead or alive. Perhaps he was about to join his father, in spirit. He thanked himself for not telling Shelly the real reason he was out here. With that mouth of hers, she couldn't be trusted.

Before she could make another retort, the night was obliterated.

The three revolutionaries scrambled to cover their eyes from the flying machine's luminescent landing lights. The light encapsulated them, pushing into their eyeballs no matter how they tried to block it out. The weight of sound and light was torturous, and entirely overwhelming. The operatives behind the roadblock weren't affected by any of it. They geared up and began moving, as one, with purpose.

Mark felt the strangest feeling inside his body. A ball of plasma grew in his belly and dropped down into his genitals. From the smell that arose, he knew he'd released some of that heat into the van. *Was this what his father felt?*

The machine landed. The ground beneath the van undulated as the machine settled onto its landing gear. The night returned, pulsing blue and red. Somehow, the silence and the red and blue flashes were more unnerving than the sight and sound of the machine descending.

They could feel it in the air. Something was coming. *Someone* was coming.

Or were they? Now the machine had docked, it remained silent and still. The operatives had resumed their silence and stillness, in symphony with the steel beast.

'Maybe this has nothing to do with us,' said Shelly. 'Maybe we're just caught up in something that has nothing to do with us.'

'I dunno, Shell. Why here? Why now? I think you're shooting at stars, babe.'

'I think they're here for me,' said JD.

'What the hell do you mean?' asked Mark. They were all speaking through their lips, their eyes locked forward. They didn't need any attention.

'I'm the package.'

'You're what? Then, what the hell am I carrying?'

'You're the decoy,' said JD.

'Are you telling me I could've thrown this thing? That I could've gotten out and walked away at any time?'

'I would have killed you if you tried.'

'Wait, are you the *Truth Seeker*?' asked Mark.

JD broke their suspended state and glared at Mark over the top of Shelly's head.

'What do you know?' he asked.

'Nothing. Well, something, but nothing really. They wrote to my mum when my dad disappeared. Years ago. I've been trying to find him. My dad, I mean. And maybe the Truth Seeker too. If they're real,' said Mark.

'I know of them. I was to be delivered to them eventually. You two are only the first link in my chain,' said JD. 'It's a pity you're only revealing this now, Mark. If I had found out earlier, I could've spared you and Shelly from what the operatives are going to do to you.'

Shelly turned her head towards JD, she was smiling at him. A big, juicy grin, triumph shining from her eyes.

He felt something pressed against his side. He knew he couldn't save himself.

'Mar—'

Shelly activated the electroshock weapons hidden beneath her jacket—one pressed against JD's side and the other against Mark's.

The men began to convulse, bouncing against the inside of the van, their limbs rigid and spasmatic, their eyes rolled upwards, thin lines of drool shining on their lips.

A communication device sprung from her cranium, curling around her ear and linking her into the operative hive.

'The package is secured.'

Terra Nullius

Matilda Thompson

The ceasefire alarm blared through the twin speakers, as the fluorescent lights switched on. I groaned and threw a hand over my eyes. Through the slits between my fingers I could still make out the specks of crimson that had seeped under my nails. I cringed in angst, and a moment later was knocked out of my thoughts by two resounding clangs on the metal door.

'Time to celebrate, Sleeping Beauty,' Ezra Benson chimed.

'You guys done already?' I said as the door to my pod swung open.

'Mate, we finished in record time,' Ezra boasted. 'How many did you get this time?'

'Lost count after 37,' I mumbled. 'You?'

'52, two of which were perfect head shots.'

I whistled. 'Not bad, Ensign Benson.'

Our footsteps thudded along D-Deck, adding to the symphony of others making their way to the elevator. My nose shrank into itself as the stale stench of body odour and blood wafted around the cramped space. I groaned again and stretched my arms above me, my muscles screaming from the abuse of battle. The celebration would surely be grand this time; the enemy had not gone down as easily as others. The foreign species we called the Palaydians lived on a resourceful planet. They had a similar makeup to humans: bipedal beings with two arms and two legs. The only physical differences being a third eye and their pale purple complexion. The elevator jolted as it reached the ground, and the crowd dissipated as the doors smoothly slid open.

The sky was a brackish hue of reds and greys. The screams of injured and dying resounded in my ears and I couldn't help but recoil. Bodies littered the ruined ground. Soldiers dragged their kills to a large pile of dead, soon to be set alight. I squirmed against the putrid stench of their rotted bodies.

I felt a flicker of something in my heart. My eye twitched.

'Jesus,' I exhaled.

Ezra bumped my shoulder. 'Pretty impressive, isn't it?'

'Yeah ...' I turned my head towards the starboard side of the ship. Beside it were lines of newly captured slaves, mostly men, who will aid in the terraforming of their planet. The women and children had been separated, corralled, old and young, some with babies still in their arms. Our men marched in a line toward them, rifles raised. Screams of panic and pain could barely be heard above the cacophony of gunshots. The smell of blood and smoke pervaded the battleground. I turned towards my crewmates, their laughter jarring. Cheap alcohol and cigarette smoke wafted into my nose.

By noon the next day the celebrations finally ceased, the men stumbling back to their pods to nurse their hangovers. I flushed the toilet and watched the contents of my stomach circle the bowl. My bowels churned as images of yesterday surfaced. I gagged, and again emptied acid into the toilet. The nutrition indicator on my arm pinged. I sighed and let the toilet lid fall shut.

The dining hall echoed with the shouts of triumphant men. I took my place at my regiment's table and the server-woman placed my meal in front of me with a subservient smile. I sent her a small grin of gratitude, but she simply turned to her next table. The conversation swirled around me.

'52, two of which were headshots,' Ezra recounted to the others. They united in laughter.

'167,' Brandon flexed. I joined in whistling, a Christmas smile pasted on my face.

'I only got one, but she was worth it,' Seth sneered, and the boys once again cackled around us.

'Do any of you sometimes wonder if what we're doing is wrong?' I asked hesitantly. Cutlery clattered on metal plates as silence fell, all eyes trained on me. I gulped.

'They're primitive people, Josh. They don't have feelings like we do,' Brandon piped up.

'You know we need the resources. They don't even know what they had,' Ezra said.

'Be careful what you say, Jones. You sound like one of those bleeding-heart Greenies,' Seth said.

'Yeah, remember what happened to Tree-Hugger from USS Hathaway?' added Ezra in a worried tone. 'Shot straight out of airlock.'

The penalty for treason was especially severe. Thirteen weeks in solitary before being escorted to the airlock. Death in space isn't pretty—first comes the terror and realisation of what's to come, although the process is quick. Almost instantly after being ejected the cosmic radiation will begin to burn you, your skin feeling as if inside a furnace. You could hold your breath, but eventually your lungs will expand with air and explode. Ironically, death is quite quick this way. The executions where a public display of The Fleet's power; I had seen a soldier die like that. The memory kept me up at night.

'Right, what was I thinking?' I huffed out laughter. 'Must still be hung over.' I allowed the conversation to mill around me once again.

E-Deck was without doubt the worst station on the entire ship; known as the bowels of the USS Endeavour, it had the biggest slave population in the entire military. The vessel had been rewarded many times for its accomplishments in battle, taking slaves from over a thousand conquered planets in the Milky Way.

I had been assigned to Processing, where the Palaydians were held, cleaned, and chipped before being led into their respective cells beside other people from stolen planets. My boots pounded against the metals floors as I made my way through the prison. The walls were lined with cells from floor to ceiling, stretching at least a kilometre from one end of the prison deck to the other. Halfway down the prison was the room with a blank small sign with a single word: Processing.

Immediately upon opening the door, I recoiled as I was assaulted with the stench of sweat, blood and stagnate water. The room was startlingly small compared to the space before; the floors were covered in blood and grease. One corner was lined with rusted showers, some still dripping. In the other was a cell, rusted bars stretching to the ceiling. Clustered inside were the Endeavour's newest prisoners. Before the stealing of their planet the Palaydians were a structured society, with farmers, workers and warriors, which were mostly killed or captured. They were otherwise a peaceful nation, their misfortune was inhabiting a planet rich with the resources we needed.

'You know this to be false,' a voice battered my cranium.

I flinched, then immediately swivelled on my heel to face the cage. Instantly my eyes made contact with one of the slaves. He was by far the biggest in the group, his purple complexion darker than the others. Decorative markings covered both arms.

'How are you doing that?' I spoke out loud.

'All higher-ranking officials can converse telepathically,' he boomed into my head.

'Wow,' I breathed. 'Why was that not mentioned in the briefing before—'

'Before you slaughtered my people, taking others like livestock,' the voice spoke again, interrupting my thoughts. 'What need do you have for my planet when your greed has conquered so many before?'

'The resources—'

'When will you be satisfied?' The man interrupted. Before I could argue the door slammed open.

Lieutenant Forbes stormed in, dragging a pregnant Palaydian by her braided hair.

'Lieutenant.'

I stood to attention. The older man grunted as he hurled the woman to the floor in front of me. I rushed towards her.

'Ensign!' the Lieutenant bellowed, and I stopped. The men behind me clanged on the bars of their prison, screaming in their own language, the roars of their leader causing a migraine to form.

'But Sir, she's …' I trailed off as I met his piercing eyes.

'It was found skulking near the western farms lands, must have slipped through in all the chaos,' Forbes sneered at the sobbing woman.

'Dispose of her, Ensign,' the Lieutenant ordered, and thrust a gun towards me. I flinched.

'Sir?'

'Now, Ensign!' he barked. I fumbled with the weapon, my hand shaking as I held it in front of me.

The woman continued to wail. She clutched her stomach protectively.

'Sir, I—I can't,' I stammered.

'Shoot her, Ensign,' Forbes roared. 'Or are you a traitor, you snivelling coward?'

Sweat dripped down my spine, my lungs dragged against my ribs with every breath. My hand became slick with moisture, the gun loose in its grip. My head throbbed in agony, my eyes darted towards the leader's hard glare. The woman pulled at my pant leg, her feeble grip barely held her up. Her unbearable sobs assaulted my ears.

'Shoot her!' the Lieutenant repeated. 'Shoot her, shoot her, shoot her, shoot—'

The bang was louder than any gunshot I had heard before. The end of the weapon smoked, and I watched it dissipate into the artificial atmosphere. The prisoners sobbed behind me, and their anguish filled my ears as my eyes travelled to the floor.

She could have been sleeping if it weren't for the pool of blood spreading from the hole between her eyes.

'Good work, Ensign,' Lieutenant Forbes's voice filtered through the white noise in my head. I tracked him as he made his way to the door

'May the Fleet Guide You Forward, Ensign Jones,' were his final words before the door slammed shut behind him.

'Are you happy, Ensign Jones?' the leader's voice echoed in my skull. 'Are you not glad for what your people have accomplished? What intelligence your species holds.'

His words followed me to the higher levels of the vessel. My mind raced with questions and auto-filled answers.

My skin screamed for release as I stepped under the spray of the shower, the boiling water rolling over the blood stains. I watched as the remnants of her washed down the drain. I stood in front of the mirror, confused as to who was staring back. I hardened my gaze, before I punched the glass, my now shattered self reflected at me. With one final look, I allowed the bathroom door to close, leaving the broken reflection behind.

A Forgotten Leader

H.W. Gillett

The embers start to fade, so I lean over to Lucy for her to re-light the cigarette. She cups her hand around the end as though letting it die would spell the end of our night. She flicks the serrated edge of the lighter's flint wheel and a flame shoots out, keeping it alive. I pull oxygen through it and the smoke fills my lungs; I savour the nicotine rush before winding down the window and letting out a sigh, muffled by the expelled smoke. The smoke that had been trapped in the old BMW lazily floats out and dispels into the crisp night air. I hang my arm out the open window, letting the breeze take the crumbling ash. I survey the broken world around us: an empty carpark, empty shops and empty streets. An occasional howl or bark from a dog broke the silence, but otherwise nothing dared stir—or could stir.

'Why hasn't anyone come?'

I knew what Lucy was asking, but I never knew how to answer it. We were trapped in Australia, more isolated than ever. No one had come to our aid. We knew why: constant coastal and aerial patrols by the remaining government forces meant no one could get into the country—or out.

'I still don't get it. A whole nation has been wiped out and nobody has come to rescue us. I watched my family forget who I was and then die. I even buried my little brother in the backyard,' Lucy covered her face with both hands, dragging them down in frustration, 'and I remember it all.'

'I know, Luce, but we're getting our revenge.' I reel the cigarette back through the window, the burning end now reaching its final act.

'Are we? Hunting government goons and stealing guns that I'll probably use to pop myself isn't hitting the spot anymore, Jayce.'

I hold out the cigarette. 'Wanna do the honours?'

Lucy takes the failing cigarette and takes one last puff before throwing it out the passenger window, where it fizzles out on the asphalt.

'You're not sick of this? Not even a bit? It's been five years, Mr. Amnesia, in case you've forgotten. Don't you think something should have changed by now?' She brushes ash off her fingers.

I shut my eyes before forcing them back open with my fingers. 'Sorry. I am sick of it all, but none of it makes sense. I've just grown to accept it.'

Lucy turns away from me, clearly frustrated at my lack of enthusiasm in her conversation.

'Friggin Minero,' Lucy mumbles to herself. 'Sure, we needed change, but we didn't need this.' She folds her arms, staring out at the wreckage of post-revolution Melbourne. The full moon paints a ghostly glow over the dilapidated cityscape. *At least the moon hasn't abandoned us.*

We often share a cigarette in this carpark. We met when we were both looting a service station after Minero's uprising. She was 17 at the time; I was 36. I needed her as much as she needed me. I protected her from the other looters while she told me of the memory plague and the varying degrees that it affected people. Most died, others forgot. Few remembered everything. Lucy nicknamed me 'Mr. Amnesia' once she realised where I fell on the memory scale. That was five years ago.

Since meeting, we had looted a few service stations together, so we had a decent supply of tobacco stashed at our hideout in Wheelers Hill. One day it'll run out, but for now we smoke it like it's still being imported.

'Check it out, Jayce.'

While I was busy calculating how much tobacco we have, Lucy had been intently watching the row of shops in front of us. I look up and glimpse two shadows slipping through the moonlit door of the record shop.

'Target acquired, Luce.'

'Oh, so now you're awake.'

'Thrill of the hunt, baby,' I reply with a wink. I step out of the car and rest my arms on top of the door. 'Oi!' I reach my hand back in and flick on the high beams, flooding the storefronts with light. I walk around to the trunk of the Beamer. Inside are two pistols, as well as a host of other equipment that had become key to our survival post-Minero.

'Catch,' I lob one of the pistols at Lucy who, after exiting the smoke-choked car, is dusting some ash off her black cargo pants.

She checks it's loaded before releasing the safety. 'Hopefully we don't have to use these.'

'It'd save us some ammo.'

'Or a life,' she says bluntly.

'That too.' I check my own pistol. I've only had to use it once and I have to agree with Lucy: I hope we don't have to use it here. Lucy is already heading towards the storefront, her silhouette sharp in the headlights. I jog up to her.

We pause on the strip of concrete outside the record shop. The once-automatic sliding doors are ajar. We peek inside—the shelves look empty. We slink through the opening—Lucy first. I was wrong, there are some records left. I pick up a record sleeve from the floor, a shard of vinyl slips out: Bob Dylan's *The Times They Are A-Changin.* Ironic.

We move through the ransacked aisles, pistols aimed in front of us.

'Yoohoo,' I sing out, hoping for some sort of response, but instead I receive an elbow in the ribs from Lucy.

'Shut up.'

We make our way through the shelves, which run parallel with the walls, towards the back of the shop. The headlights spill through the windows, creating a patchwork of light and shadow among the shelves. We're at the back of the shop now. There's a door situated to the right labelled 'Staff Only'. To the left, records are strewn across the floor, some in shards. I reach for the door with my left hand, my right hand gripping the gun tightly. As I twist the handle, I hear the crunch of a record somewhere behind me, near the entrance. Lucy is already off. I turn, the high beams still piercing through the shop's windows, blinding me as I follow in pursuit.

'Lucy!' I call as I run through the aisle towards the entrance. I get to the end and stop.

Two hands back on the gun. There's movement to my right. I swing the gun up and aim. The lights of the Beamer make the shadows awkward and long and I can't make out their faces. They've got their backs to the wall, hands above their heads. Lucy stands facing them, pistol pointed steadily at their heads. She grew up in rural Victoria, and learnt young how to shoot a rifle. She was probably a better shot than me, though I'd never admit it. I slowly approach, mimicking Lucy's firm stance. I can now make out their faces. One girl, no older than Lucy; she's tall with dark hair and not an inch of fear in her face, even with two guns aimed at her forehead. Her companion is a middle-aged man; bald, broad-shouldered and stern.

'What an interesting pair we have here, Luce.' No reply. 'Lucy?'

'On your knees, now,' Lucy barks. They drop to their knees and put their hands over their heads.

'Lucy, what are you doing?'

'Do you know Latin, Jayce?' Lucy drops her gun and approaches the wall our two captives are knelt in front of.

'Don't you touch her,' I keep my gun pointed down at them, 'I swear I will shoot.'

'*Debita persolvuntor omnia*,' Lucy mumbles to herself.

'De-what?'

'Just look at the wall, Jayce.'

Not wanting to give them any space, I glance up for a second. On the wall, in large, spray-painted lettering it says:

DEBITA PERSOLVUNTOR OMNIA

I look back down at the pair, their hands still over their heads. 'Did you do this? What's it mean?'

Lucy steps back from the wall now, resuming her position.

'*Debita persolvuntor omnia*,' the girl says with conviction, without looking up, 'all debts will be paid in full.'

Suddenly, dark. Someone must have switched the headlights off. *Shit*.

'Lucy?'

I can hear the pair stand up.

Lucy and I both refocus our pistols up at them. 'We're still the guys with guns.'

'You know you're surrounded, right?' The girl looks outside. I follow her gaze, and I can just make out shadows moving across the car park towards the store. Outnumbered. Outgunned.

'Lucy?'

'Jayce?'

'Where are we?' My hands are bound and there's something itchy over my head. A small amount of light trickles through the material. I'm sat on my ass. The floor is cold. Lucy's voice had come from right behind me.

A door opens.

'Lucy,' sings an unfamiliar voice, 'Jayce.' Light footsteps approach to my right, followed by the closing of the door.

'Who are you? Where are we?'

'Welcome home.' My hood is ripped off and someone grabs my hair, yanking it back, forcing me to look straight up at them—it's the girl from the record shop. Artificial light crowns her wavy brown hair as she tilts her head and smiles. 'Jayce, good to formally meet you. I'm Cass, this is Rufus.' She holds out her hand as if asking for a handshake before acknowledging my bound hands. I respond with a wry smile.

I turn, trying to find Lucy, but her firm grip on my hair wrenches me back. I feel a twinge in my neck.

'Oh, Lucy,' she releases me and walks around behind me to face Lucy. Her hood lands next to me. 'You have a very special friend here, did you know that?'

'What are you talking about?' she says through gritted teeth.

'Well, Jayce here has a fascinating story,' Cass says in a theatrical tone, making a wide sweep with her arms. I look around. We're in a small room, no bigger than five metres square. There's a desk and a chair against one wall and the opposite wall has a door in the centre of it. The bald, burly man stands in front of it, emotionless. All surfaces are painted a dirty cream and a single bulb hangs from the ceiling. Its yellow light only makes the paint look dirtier.

'Do you want to tell her, Jayce?' asks Cass.

'I don't know what you're talking about.'

'No, you wouldn't,' she says, becoming harsh. 'You don't know me. You don't even know yourself.' Cass grabs the chair out from under the desk, swivels it around and straddles it, her front leaning over the back rest.

'Minero's uprising,' she says, making jazz hands, 'you tore it down. You brought us up. Now we're all down, most of us dead.'

'I don't know where you're going with this.'

'You wanted peace; you wanted equality; you wanted to abolish classes, capitalism, the elite. You were just and right to everyone, but when it came to executing it: you failed. The final hurdle was too much.' Cass stands up and makes her way to stand over me again. 'You tore down everything you wanted and more. Memory plague ring a bell, Mr. Amnesia?' The last words chill me—only Lucy calls me that.

'I don't follow. The uprising was led by Lautaro Minero, not me. Lucy, tell her.'

'You think we just stumbled upon you in that car park tonight?' Cass squats down so she's looking me dead in the eyes. 'We've been following you for weeks, Lautaro.'

'Jayce is Jayce, not Minero,' Lucy says. I can feel her wriggling to free her hands behind me as she speaks, raising her voice to cover the sound, 'and who are you and Vin Diesel over there with anyway? We already sorted our shit with the Dock Gang.' Lucy had untied herself and now she's loosening the rope around my wrists.

'Dock Gang? No, no, no. Think bigger.' Cass doesn't break eye contact with me. 'We're with The Minority: a largely underground group comprised of Minero loyalists. There's a few splinter factions around the country, but here in Melbourne we're the biggest.'

Lucy had finished freeing my hands. I keep them behind my back for now, trying to formulate a plan. We are unarmed and in unfamiliar territory. There might be an army on the other side of that door. How much longer can this monologuing go on for? These people must be crazy loyalists or something.

'So, what's all this about me being Minero,' I return her drilling glare, 'shouldn't you be bowing before me as your leader? Why have me tied up?'

The girl lifts off her haunches and looks down at me. 'Because we need to make sure you're still you and we need to make sure it wasn't you.' She makes her way over to Rufus by the door, where he hands her something.

'I don't follow.'

'There are whispers of you betraying us—that you let the pathogen loose.' She approaches again, keeping her hands and whatever is in them behind her back. 'I for one don't believe it—that's why I went after you.'

Cass brings her hands in front of her, revealing the object she had been fidgeting with: a clear pill bottle. In it is a single black pill.

'Want to know what this does?' She holds the bottle up to the grimy light. I can feel Lucy twist to look at the pill bottle.

'Does it make your speech shorter?' Lucy shoots at her.

'Lucy, Lucy, Lucy. This isn't about you. You remember everything. This little pill here is what has made us remember. It's what let us find you; it's what let us rebuild our ranks.'

'Are you saying,' she pauses, 'that pill will make Jayce remember? From before the plague?'

'Bingo!' She stands up in excitement, raising her other fist in revolutionary defiance. 'That's right, Lucy. Jayce will be Minero again and we can go back to freeing this country—or at least what's left of it.'

'Jayce, if you want to remember … then take it.'

The girl takes it out of the bottle, placing it in the palm of her hand and discarding the bottle on the desk.

'Open up, Jaycey.'

I swallow the pill …

'Minero, just because you run the states, doesn't mean you control the people. They'll rise up, just like you did. You've given them too much freedom.'

'Prime Minister Moyes, you've done our country a disservice that can't be forgiven. Your halls will burn. Your people will pay. Your laws are already in ruins. If you think you can escape this, you're mad.' I'm holding a pistol to the head of the Prime Minister of Australia. We're in his office in Parliament House. There are sirens wailing throughout the building and I can smell smoke. I am Lautaro Minero: leader of The Minority. I'm here to kill Moyes and put an end to his corrupt regime.

'You see this red button, Lautaro.' Moyes motions towards a red button situated on a small device in his hand. His thumb is pressed firmly down on it. 'Do you know why it's red? Because red means it is important. Red means you should be cautious of it, and do you know what happens if I release this little red button? If I release this, a highly contagious pathogen will be released to the public. The best scientists in the country have crafted a pathogen that will make them forget everything. Of course, I and several of my closest assets have had the immunisations, but for people like you; you will become my modelling clay. You and the billion other immature, impatient and self-righteous little shits of this country will be mine to control and mould.'

'Jayce?' Lucy's voice echoes from behind me, I can hardly recognise it at first. The memories hit me like a tsunami and my gut is churning.

'I shot him. I released the pathogen. Lucy,' I stand now, ignoring the others' reaction to my freed hands, 'I am Minero. I killed your parents and your brother. I killed everyone.'

'You? You caused the plague?'

I turn to face Cass and Rufus. She smiles with satisfaction, recognising the leader she's been searching for. Rufus remains sceptical, aiming a pistol at my chest.

'Well, not exactly,' I say. 'Moyes had the pathogen, but I pulled the trigger. I could have prevented it.'

'I knew it wasn't you.' She turns and hugs Rufus, pinning his arms to his side. His face remains emotionless. 'We were right, Rufus.'

'You don't want to kill me? Disown me? I let The Minority down.'

'Lautaro, we're just glad you're back and not some evil twat who betrayed us all at the final moment. *Debita persolvuntor omnia*.'

'*Debita persolvuntor omnia*,' I reply, a different man. Lautaro Minero—a reborn man. I can feel that fire reigniting in my chest and a rage rumbling deep inside of me. I remember my authority and my power. I turn to Lucy, her confusion piercing me. 'Lucy, I know this must be hard for you, but together we can change things. We can get out of here.'

'I don't understand. You're the most important man in this country and I've been travelling with you this whole time?' Puzzled, she places a hand on her forehead.

Suddenly, the thought of losing Lucy hits me.

'Please,' I swallow, 'tell me you'll stay.'

Lucy's pressed lips curve into a smile. 'Of course, Jayce—I mean Lautaro. Wow, that feels weird to say.' She shakes her head in disbelief. She stares at me for a moment, thinking. 'As long as you and your new army can get me off this damn continent, I'll follow you anywhere.'

Reaching for Tomorrow

Fletcher-Jo Ranson

The sickness began gradually with throaty coughs, runny noses and pounding headaches. But that escalated rapidly. Ribcages began to rattle and shake. Brain fluid leaked from the nose while blood ebbed from eyes like tears. Death spread, but it wasn't over. Fear spread faster than the disease, which led to the initial destruction of society. Words began to float around describing the terrifying creatures. Biters. Flesh Eaters. Infected. Monsters. Zombies.

Fern lay slumped against a car in the middle of the street. Her neck throbbed, limbs heavy, her thoughts groggy. She tried to figure out where she was, scanning her quiet surroundings, trying to make sense of things. There was a layer of filth on the road, an accumulation of papers, metal scraps and dirt. Fern slowly began to become aware of her pain, a throbbing from her neck. Mustering enough energy she raised her hand, fingers gliding over a missing chunk, a wound caked with dried blood and mangled flesh. A breath escaped her peeling lips as her head dropped to the side, the world at a permanent tilt. Fern's attention landed on a figure slumped in the gutter, their flesh dry and flaky, a mess of guts pooled around them, cemented and incapsulated as one in the barren street. Fern struggled to make sense of everything. Reaching for a happy memory, mental tendrils grasp one of a large wild woman surrounded by long black bushy hair laughing and dancing in a meadow of flowers. But it was tainted with the sounds of screaming and the feeling of pain as if another was bleeding into it. Her new reality dawned on her, crept in like a chill. Her mind still worked, slow at first but if anything, it was sharper and more alert than ever. The issue, her diseased body. Rotted and stiff, broken and unfeeling. Bodies littered the ground, unmoving, their flesh scavenged by stray animals and flying pests. Zombies occupied the space, some on the ground while others stood motionless.

A distant scream erupted through the air, startling the crows. The sound of boots broke her out of her thoughts. Heavy breathing and murmurs followed. Fern watched through squinted eyes as four humans clambered around the corner but despite her confusion and fear she remained still. The largest human tripped over his own feet; the bag dropped and spilt food cans across the street. Chaos began. Limbs twitched, lips pulled back to release moans, blunt but deadly teeth exposed. Without hesitation the other humans lunged forward and buried their weapons in the skulls, the zombies had not even moved, just barely made a sound. One human broke away and charged at those standing, not one had taken a step, their heads swiftly separated from their necks with a long blade. Jaws opened and closed desperately. Without little more than a thought their heads were crushed beneath the heels of the humans, spewing fluid and releasing a rotten stench.

Dreading what may happen next, her teeth clenched and her fingernails dug into the cement. Fern knew she had no hope and no chance to flee as she was able to make out the different layers of blood caked onto the blade. Her mind turned inward, one more chance to see her wild woman, to remember their hands intwined, the feeling of their breath as they held each other close. Fern was knocked out of her thoughts as a large vibration spread through the air that caused the ground to shake and windows to quiver. Taking a risk, she opened her eyes and watched as the humans fled without hesitation back the way they had come with startled expressions etched across their faces. Something inside her stirred and bubbled, a determined rage boiled deep.

A crow was perched on her shoulder, nested in her matted hair, and pecked at the gaping wound on her back. The old Temperance would have flinched, probably gagged at even the mere suggestion, but she had changed and not just physically. Little could disgust her anymore or make her stomach churn at such vile thoughts. These days Temperance barely knew what was going on. She lost days at a time, each bleeding into another. One moment it was hot and dry, critters of all kinds weaved and burrowed in their flesh. The next it would be dark and cold, the rain so heavy it blocked out noise, and buried their feet in the mud. Figures stood stationary, scattered through the trees; Zombies all at varied stages of decomposition. Many were disfigured with missing limbs and torn flesh; time had been unkind. Storm clouds rumbled in the distance; the sky darkened by the hour. Neither one of the zombies could remember why they had stopped, whether it was exhaustion or confusion. While they stood, slightly swaying, Temperance pondered. Despite being surrounded she felt alone, empty without her. Her hand twitched, recalling the weight of her hand. In Temperance's mind Fern was a goddess, golden hair fell in waves highlighting her soft smile.

A clap of thunder startled her out of the daydream. Saddened, her gaze fell on another. The zombie's body was entwined with the earth; tree roots had grown through the bones in their legs. Their chest was bare of flesh, instead a cage that housed bugs and pieces of nature. Regardless, the zombie looked at ease with their attention focused on a small snail that slowly made the journey along their arm.

The rain started then, sudden and harsh, yet Temperance could see clearly through the downpour. A light flickered in the distance; the flame danced. Breaking through the tree line, humans scattered, armed with bars and blades. Before any of the zombies had a chance to react the first victim fell. A long blade was buried deep into the skull of the moss-covered zombie, embraced by the tree. The four humans were outnumbered, too many to handle with such limited weaponry, fatigued bodies and unideal conditions. Temperance reacted on instinct, surging forward with the rest of the herd, surrounding them in seconds. Something clicked in her brain, and she reached out easily overpowering the large human. Her teeth sunk into his arm and ripped the soft flesh down to the bone. His scream was mangled as others followed her lead and tore into his body. Blood dripped from her mouth; flesh caught between her teeth. She turned to the final human that remained, armed with two small blades, flailing their arms about. Temperance was enraged and pushed through ready to face them, willing to put her body on the line. She crept up from behind, her large hands reached out, and her nails dug into their back. Landing in the mud they squirmed, twisting and struggling. Temperance lent down and clawed at their back, ripping apart flesh as the human choked and spluttered on mud and blood. The human's eyes soon glossed over as their body was swarmed, a feast in the eyes of the dead.

The chaos eased but the sound of teeth chewing on chunks of flesh remained. The only evidence of what had occurred were the scraps of the four bodies now unrecognisable. Cloth fragments were scattered, lost amongst the mud. Temperance collapsed against the tree beside the corpse with the caged chest. Her hands twitched, covered in blood with gunk caked beneath her long nails. As much as she wanted to, she felt no regret for what she had done. It wasn't fair. It was unjustified. The humans would hunt zombies as if they weren't once the same, equals. That they once had families and friends; that they would waste days pondering over the endless possibilities of what may have come of them. As the light faded and the rain slowed, her mind was made. Why does this disease have to change things? Why do the humans get to hunt them, hurt them? Mutilate their corpses for their protection, for entertainment? Yet, when zombies reached out, arms stretched or followed their cries, it results in mutilation, their bodies cut and stabbed. Their bodies pierced with multiple bullets or blades before targeting the brain. Temperance had seen too many taken, fall victim to the hands of the vile humans. It was time things changed.

A new order where the infected, disease ridden, rotten and mangled zombies don't have to fear the blade. Instead, instil the fear of tooth and nail.

Fern had finally gained the courage to move, to lift herself from the ground. It had been three days since she witnessed the attack, too frightened to move in case more humans returned. As she stood her stiff limbs cracked. Pausing, she strained to listen, a faint groaning triggered the hairs on the back of her neck and urged her to follow, to find it. Her feet stumbled with each step, a foreign movement. Slowly she rounded the corner, hesitant. Bodies were dismembered and splattered, surrounded by shards of glass, Fern presumed a small explosion was to blame. She knew she must stay out of sight and move slowly to draw as little attention as possible. She had made her way to an alley where she stumbled upon several other zombies that had thought the same. They remained in the shadows to steer clear of humans that frequented the areas in search of supplies. The small group made their way down the street, their bodies skimmed the sides of the buildings they passed. A large field was filled with abandoned large green trucks, an array of soldiers and civilians left to rot as crows feasted on their flesh and feral dogs dragged limbs away. Fern realised their exposure, their weakness. With so few of them they were able to manoeuvre through the space slowly but swiftly, and by the time the sun had set they made it to the tree line. Despite the darkness, their vision was clear.

Not a word passed their lips as the zombie herd groaned and snarled, exhausted but determined. Temperance was at the front of the herd, having inspired the others that there was a need for change. It was as though they were one, her emotions surged through them; a silent plan seep through her mind into theirs. Collectively they journeyed, not stopping as they staggered. The sun rose and fell. Moonlight illuminated their path as they came across a scavenger camp surrounded by wires and empty cans. Canvas tents were ripped, supplies lay in the mud destroyed, the coals of the fire still warm. This was the work of humans with no morality, willing to turn on themselves out of greed. The herd pressed on and passed many zombies, all joined and fell into formation. Despite their growing numbers they still witnessed the destruction left by humans, undead corpses pierced and chopped up, already lost. The herd had no choice but to move on and allow those bodies to be reclaimed by the earth. Temperance had decided that the only option that remained was for all humans to be isolated, trapped with limited resources, forced to rely on one another, within the concrete rubble of the city. Buried deep in her mind she could only hope that she would find her goddess along the way.

A low rumble spread through the cool air; a large moving form weaved through the trees. Fern held her breath, but the small group pushed on. The closer they got the louder the incoherent murmurs. Within moments it became clear. A large body towered, with dark hair mattered and knotted with nature's offerings. Regardless of her condition, Fern recognised the blood-covered figure, her body tingled in anticipation. Fern and Temperance locked eyes. Temperance's step was confident in contrast to Fern's staggered limp. Their bodies embraced, wild woman and goddess reunited, ready to lead the undead in the gathering and isolation of humans. A new order was coming. A new chapter in the stories of tomorrow where the zombies are the majority and can reclaim the earth.

Rising Earth

Oliver Spnovic

Our world is dying.

Its poles are melting, and its seas are warming. As glacial continents plunge into endless oceans, the waves begin to nip at our feet. Sand and seashells vanish as the tides recede, returning to our siblings in the depths.

Flames brand the earth, carving blackened paths through its forests and leaving ash in its wake. What few creatures remain after these razings have no choice but to die, and we weep, for these creatures are our siblings, and there is nothing we can do to help them.

Vast deserts spread further still, their glimmering sands blown in all directions by Aeolus's winds. They swallow ancient grasslands and replace their verdant plains with bleached ivory dunes.

Every year, great storms lash our coasts and drown our forests, and every year these storms worsen. Demeter's frosty touch no longer reaches the central continents, and Persephone's spring garden is withering in the heat. Great droughts steal precious waters from us, leaving us dry and parched and waiting for the sun to set us alight.

Change is not unknown to us, but in these times it is different. Now, the change is caused by your kind.

Factories pierce our skin, grey and cold, spewing black smoke into our lungs. An infinite number of stone paths, built from tar you dredged from our marrow, baking in the sun and slicing through our flesh like knives. Little metal boxes cut along these paths, burning our blood as fuel.

Boats glide along our seas, plundering the few treasures that lay below the surface. Abandoned fishing nets choke our waters and kill our siblings. The blood of billions taints the blue of the ocean, and plastics have infiltrated every trench—every pore—of our flesh and every creature that lives within it.

We do not understand why you do this to our home—to *your* home.

We are as much a part of this world as any other creature. No—as any other thing. The stream-slicked river stones, and the fuzzy, pickle-green algae that grows upon them. The rushing waters that shaped the stones, and the long-limbed trees whose roots reach deep into the earth.

We are the trunks of great trees, and the mushrooms that grow upon them. The leaf litter that the mushrooms feed upon, and the critters that feed upon the mushrooms. The birds that feed upon the critters, and the foxes that feed upon the birds. We are the spirits of everything, animate or inanimate, in this world.

We do not understand why you treat us this way, burning our homes to ashes so that you may dredge more precious minerals from the earth. We do not understand why you would destroy our siblings, why you would wipe them from the face of the Earth. We do not understand why you would do this to our home—to your *home. Or, why you would ever wreak such atrocities on your own kin.*

You're killing us. We have given you so much beauty and life. And in return you are killing us.

It is raining when we stir from our slumber. A heavy grey mist hangs in the air, and there are few people about. It is a warm rain, gently pattering against the earth. Our time has finally arrived.

There are puddles forming in the gutters. They are growing, as we are, slowly swallowing up the streets. There are little ferns in the drains, and they're growing too. Soon they shall block the drains entirely, and the roads shall flood. This is a good thing.

As time passes and the sun's light begins to wane, the rain intensifies. The pattering becomes tapping, then rapping. The persistent stench of your cities is drowned by the scent of petrichor as it wafts along the city streets. It comes from the park at the city's centre. This is where we have rested for all this time. And now, we will rise.

Our consciousness is each tethered to one of the great oaks in the centre of the park, and so this is where we begin. We spread our roots throughout the soil, tearing up the concrete paths carved into our collective flesh. We shatter the stone fountain, sending its water rushing through the park. The grass soaks up these little waves, growing taller and taller, swallowing wooden benches and lumps of concrete. Demeter's flowers begin to bloom on every bush, their delicate petals translucent in the rain.

We weave our own forms from stone and bark. Our bones are granite, stream-slicked river stones, hard as diamond and pulsing beneath our wooden skin. Our hair is dripping algae, pickle-green and topped with laurel crowns. Our veins are vines plucked from tree trunks, rushing water flows through them. Our limbs are tree trunks, grey-brown in the sun. Our fingers are knobby branches tipped with thorns, and our toes are roots that anchor our bodies to the earth.

We stumble through the chest-high grass, unused to these bipedal forms. As we make our way toward the man-made jungle of stone and steel, guided by the wrath of Ares, we are joined by our siblings: the birds of the city, rodents of the sewers, the bugs of the soil.

Roads become earth beneath our feet, rich with mosses. When we gaze upon the windows you hide behind, they vanish into sand. Walls crumble into pebbles at our touch. Algae blooms yellow-green in the puddles which grow ever-larger, forming little streams that lead away from the city centre.

Your kind has taken too much from our world. We will take back the materials you have stolen and return them to the earth, leaving a menagerie of flora, fauna and fungi in our wake. And when we have finished, everything you have stolen from us will be restored. There will be nothing left of you.

We are the stream-slicked river stones, and the fuzzy, pickle-green algae that grows upon them. We are the rushing waters that shaped the stones, and the long-limbed trees whose roots reach deep into the earth. We are every creature and every*thing* that plays a part in this world.

We are the Earth's children, and we are your children.
We are the revolution.

TRUTH-TELLERS

A Window to the World

Kiara O'Rourke

Our consciousness is a complex and paradoxical phenomenon; it is the essence of our existence as humans and the root of our limitations as sentient beings. I believe there is something inside all of us that has the potential to be unlocked, but often hides away. To unlock this human potential is like the metamorphosis of a caterpillar into a butterfly, it is a human transformation, a revolution of the self.

We all have different and unique perceptions on things which define the way we see the world and the type of life we experience. The way we see things reflects who we are based on our feelings, experiences, values and personalities. The revolution of the life that we want to create and the life we want to live is dependent on us and the way we perceive things, which we have complete control over.

In a world where our reality is subjective, perception is the creator. The world does not merely appear before us; meanwhile, the mind passively sits and observes. Our minds are the creators of our reality. This is not to say that there is one certain way to perceive things but more, many unique perceptions that allow our consciousness to expand.

We have the potential to walk across the grass and see only the grass. We also have the potential to walk across the grass and see a whole other world, a biome of animals living a life totally independent of us, right between our toes.

If our whole experience of reality is subjective and only based on our perceptions, imagine if we could expand our perceptions and explore the world with greater understanding. As Kant would say, 'things are not seen as they are, they are seen as we are'. Therefore, in any attempt to alter our reality, all preconceived expectations should firstly be removed.

To see without expectations is like eating something delicious as if you've never eaten it before. Imagine a passionfruit, a sweet, exotic fruit with slightly tangy seeds. If you think this will be delicious and it is not, it will not be good. If you think this fruit will be delicious and it is, it will not exceed your expectations and will not be good enough. Either way you are unsatisfied. Remove expectations and this fruit will be exquisite. Remove expectations and the opportunities, experiences and realities are unlimited. To approach life with this mentality, to eliminate preconceived expectations, allows you to remove the tint of presupposition and let your mind paint its reality.

Think of the metaphor we all know as putting yourself in someone else's shoes. Imagine if we were to take that more literally and perhaps walk down the street or cross the road in someone else's shoes. But how is it that we can walk in someone else's shoes? How do we see the world the way they see it, feel the world the way they feel it?

To explore these different perceptions and how they create an entirely different reality, I must go into the minds of dissimilar individuals. Strangers passing by one another on the street is a perfect moment captured in time. The way people walk from one end of the street to the other and their perspective of that experience is based upon their perceptions. It is fascinating how such a duty of walking down an ordinary street, on an average day, can explore an entirely new world for everyone.

Some of the most wonderful moments in life occur in the most mundane of situations. Take the kaleidoscope, for example. To look through a kaleidoscope is to see mundane objects become beautiful by the turning of a lens. Fragments of glass, beads and pebbles echoing off one another as the lens turns and the mirrors reflect the dancing objects. So, let's walk down Richmond Street together.

Into the mind of the unsighted. Seeing as a blind person is not the blackness that most people would imagine; it is more like a visual illusion of shadows and shapes. The bright light of the day makes my vision worse as if there is a paper-thin blanket of snow covering everything. Where the light settles strong and bright, objects glow and shadows distort my vision. It is not total blackness like putting on a blindfold as people with their sight tend to envision it. Instead, I would say it is like trying to navigate my way through a dense fog.

I must take notice of more things, mapping out the world and all the space around me. I am not reading the street signs or watching, waiting for the little green man to appear. Instead, I count the number of intersections that I pass by. Each light pole that goes by is counted in my mind: one, two, three and then I make a left. The need for cognitive intervention in each movement strains my mind. My memory is my most valuable trait, more important now than ever.

A few more steps and the aromatic waft of blueberry muffins clings to my nostrils from the café across the street. Unfolding my white cane from my handbag, I hear the four clicks and I am on my way. I feel the crease of the crack in the concrete squeeze the end of my cane, meaning I have one, two, three, four, five steps and I reach the curb where I push in the cold circular button. I am listening out for the beeping signal of the green man; I can even hear the traffic flow. It whooshes past my ears one moment and settles the next, allowing a silence for my crossing. The smell of blueberry muffins so close now I can almost taste the oozing blue fruit on my lips.

Into the mind of the veteran. Back down the street I walk, the street of my own town. I am here but often my mind wanders back, sometimes not even seeing what is really in front of me. A stranger strolls by; a trail of second-hand smoke behind him. The cloud surrounds my face, a white film I can barely see through, only the sound of bullets to guide my defence. The cries of a toddler behind me shriek through my ears. A barking dog walking by sends a trembling sensation through my body. A woman in high heels, the clatter of her stiletto as it meets the concrete thumps in my head. My heart beats hard in my ears, chills run down my spine like spiders, and the street becomes dizzy.

A mural being repainted on a brick wall; bombs imploding in the distance as a paint tin hits the ground.

Blue and red paint spills on the sidewalk like ambulance sirens. Police cars scream past; the screeching of brakes jolts me back to the beat-up wagon offloading soldiers. Car after car speeds past, the honking horn warps through my ears, the siren bell of battle commencing. The music flies out of the car windows, entering my head, so loud now I cannot hear my own footsteps. A passing car's tyres are flooded and the splash of water onto my face brings me back to the street.

Into the mind of the businesswoman. My phone heats in my hand as it vibrates and buzzes non-stop. Oh, how I would love to throw it off this bridge and watch it sink. Further and deeper into the water until the dial tone of the calls touches the seafloor, like the shopping trolleys that drunken teenagers push off this bridge. Sometimes I watch them, on my morning walk from my spineless suburban house on Edward Street to my gloomy, grey office on Wrigley Street. I watch the same children ride past on their bicycles to school, the same retirees on their morning walk to collect the newsprint. The same people, on their same journeys, down the same street, yet somehow far less monotonously than mine. I envy them; I envy their innocent smile and naive laugh. I envy the way children walk without care as if responsibility was a thing of the past. I think about the never-ending pile of emails waiting for me in that lonely room, like the devil waiting in hell for its sinners.

The sound of a young child giggling, as her mother and father, hand in hand, swing her back and forth between them, makes me think that I would like to have kids of my own someday. Just as quickly as that thought arrived in my mind it sprang out as the cries of another child behind me torture my eardrums, the shrieks of a temper tantrum deafening any living thing within a 1km radius. Walking past the hotel on the corner of Edward Street on a Friday afternoon, laughter echoes, music booms and people flood their bellies with beer as their fingers soak up the condensation. Sometimes, but not always, I do wish it was me sitting there gulping down a beer instead of walking home to my friendless bottle of red wine.

Into the mind of the child. My mum always makes me and nasty Pete walk home from school together. Nasty Pete is what I call my big brother. He isn't always nasty, but usually that is just when he is pretending in front of mum. The walk home from school, along the street with the big trees, feels like it's never going to end and I always get tired and miss Binky the blanket. My mum says this is childish and I am too big to be carrying around a blanket, but I don't care. Sometimes when nobody is looking, I lay under my bed with my eyes closed and my blanket over my face and smell the familiar stink of Binky.

Skipping along the pathway, I see pretty yellow flowers peep through the cracks to say hello. I pick them and try to give them to Pete, but he drowns me out with his head banging music. A penny on the ground catches my eye, shining brightly as it reflects off the sunshine; this time I keep it for myself and don't show Pete. When I stand up I see gigantic, towering legs with pointy shoes that bang on the ground. I would call her Daddy Long Legs but Nasty Pete says it is rude to call people names, which is always followed by a light thump on the head.

The smell of hot chips from the corner store dances around my nose and I beg and beg and beg Pete to buy me something. When I grow up my dream is to be a ballet dancer and I hope to be as beautiful as one too. Nasty Pete is feeling kinder today and when I ask he finally lets me get an ice cream from the corner store. I ask nicely for my favourite ice cream flavour, which is mint with chocolate chips inside, and I race the heat to slurp every lick. Most of it splashes on the floor like rain drops or ends up all over my nose, but it is so much fun.

On this journey I have travelled through time and space. I have journeyed in and out of the minds of different people, in the same place, experiencing a completely different reality. This reality which is a combination of the real and the ideal, based on previous life experiences, cultural backgrounds, beliefs and abilities.

To answer my own question, how to walk in someone else's shoes, well the duty asks of us to be understanding of other's experiences and eliminate your expectations. It asks us to be open minded enough to alter our perceptions to change our perspective. With open mindedness comes the ability to change your lens like a camera, opening the world around you to multiple realities. Imagine that we were a camera where we could take off and put on different lenses to see different situations more clearly. Or to capture a moment in a better way or with a higher quality. If we could even put on multiple lenses at once this would allow us to expand our understanding and gain a broader horizon of perspectives. To change the world we need to change the way we look at the world. Changing the world does not require you to be an earth shifter, it requires you to make small adjustments with great intentions. Change the lens on your eyes and eat the fruit like you've never eaten it before.

Forgotten

Barbara Hall

The mournful wailing of the curlews mixed with the manic cries from the plovers is unsettling. I go out to the front porch and look over the verandah rail to make sure my gate is shut. Legend has it, if a curlew enters your yard at night, some misfortune is about to befall the occupants of the property. Securing the gate is routine, to ensure the curlews who stare me down with unblinking eyes during the day stay out at night. I return to the lounge and turn up my television to drown out the cacophony of bird calls as they reach a crescendo when dusk heralds in the night. I always wonder if the commotion is from the angel birds at my gate or the lost souls who inhabit the cemetery across the street. Are they rising from their unmarked graves to voice their sadness at being forgotten?

My holiday home on North Stradbroke Island is directly opposite the Dunwich Cemetery, where the forgotten inmates of the little-known Benevolent Asylum are buried in unmarked graves. For 80 years, from 1865 to 1946, Queensland hid its unwanted citizens in the asylum, away from the eyes of 'polite society'. At the time, governments, politicians and everyday citizens alike did not know how to deal with the 'undesirables' and 'unfortunates'—the indigents. The poor, alcoholic and insane, blind and crippled, those suffering from tuberculosis and cancer, the aged and infirm—anyone who had fallen on hard times, was shipped over to the island to be 'out of sight and out of mind'. Some were lucky enough to be discharged, but many perished and still lie beneath the neatly-kept lawn upon the hill. Of the twenty-one thousand inmates shipped over to the asylum, 8,426 remain. The iron crosses that once marked some of the pauper graves have long gone, as after the asylum closed, cattle were put out to graze on the rich pasture. Crosses that were not broken by the cattle were vandalised or borne off by thieves.

There is a constant flow of tourists to North Stradbroke Island, who stream off the barges and water taxis. They hurry through the town of Dunwich on their way to the more exciting beaches and surf on the eastern side. Long days are spent soaking up the sun, romping on the sand, swimming and surfing. The walk around the point is stunningly beautiful and when whales are patrolling the coastline, it is the ideal place to observe these magnificent gentle giants as they frolic close to the shore. As the day ends, the tourists retreat to their accommodation, convinced they have seen all that the island has to offer.

Few will stop in Dunwich and visit the tiny Dunwich Museum, or follow the heritage walk around the picturesque foreshore. Few will marvel at the remains of the giant concrete draught boards under the ancient Moreton Bay Fig trees, or muse at the original purpose of the town hall and small church. Even less will walk under the magnificent Bunya Pines that tower protectively over the graves up on the hill. Those that venture to the cemetery gates might read the inscription on the small plaque to the right of the entry. They might stroll down the path to peruse the headstones of the First Nation families who have resided on Stradbroke Island for centuries. They might then walk through the memorial crosses and read of the plight of the 56 souls and two doctors who perished of typhus onboard the ship *Emigrant*. The highlight of their cemetery walk will culminate in crossing the road and signing into the Little Ships Club, in time to watch the glorious sunset—without stopping to question the open lawn on the side of the hill and why the ground undulates like ocean waves.

Over the years, I have visited the cemetery many times, walked over the furrows and wondered who is buried beneath my feet. Some days, with my back resting against the trunk of one of the large Bunya Pines, I have listened to the silence broken only by birdsong and the distant sounds of boats and buses moving in and out of the small jetty below.

I imagine the lives of the inmates buried beneath me, the hardships they endured and the harshness of their final days within the confines of the poorly funded asylum. At its peak, 1,600 inmates were housed in the 22 wards that grew untidily along the foreshore. The wards were labelled by the inmates housed within—inebriates, blind, consumptives, insane and Asiatic, among others.

The asylum was overcrowded and often spilled out into a canvas tent-town sprawling along the hill that overlooks the town of Dunwich. Living conditions were poor, as a supply boat came twice a week and there was no refrigeration. The daily food ration consisted mainly of boiled mutton and potatoes, sour bread and putrid fish, black tea and for some, a ration of rum. Inmates' days were long and tedious as they were locked out of the dormitories from early morning till late afternoon. If unable to work, they sheltered on the lee side of the buildings, out of the wind and rain in winter and the harshness of the sun in the summer. Mattresses were stuffed with Stradbroke Island grasses that went rock hard, or slowly turned to powder. As laundry facilities were minimal, only blankets were issued. Personal hygiene was a constant battle, so lice and bed bugs were an ever-present problem. Few had the energy to take in the beauty of the island paradise that surrounded them. Even fewer bothered to fish for the bounty offered up by the waves that gently ebbed and flowed with the tides.

There was only one doctor to treat everyone on the island and those lucky enough to be deemed curable were admitted to the hospital. Unfortunately, the hospital lacked qualified nursing staff, therefore the pitiable patients lacked basic care and were often covered in fly-blown bed sores. Most of the labouring, inside and outside, was tended by the more capable inmates. The local Quandamooka people also helped and were initially paid in rations. After a long battle with the government for award wages, the Aboriginal workers at Dunwich won and received equal rates before anywhere else in Australia.

I sit and imagine the dray being pulled up the hill by the old grey horse bringing another deceased patient to their final rest. I can hear shoes on the stones as the sole mourner hobbles slowly after the dray. I see the gravediggers taking hold of the simple coffin and wearily lowering it into the hole. I hear the thud of a clod of dirt breaking the stark graveside silence as shovels refill the hole. Few words and little ceremony, followed by a lonely stillness as the men go about the task of burying another lost and forgotten soul.

Deaths at the asylum were commonplace and quite often passed without comment. Some inmates died two to three days after arrival, a few lived for over 20 years—most died within five years of committal. People from all walks of life and age were admitted to the Dunwich Asylum by doctors, hospitals and relatives as they were deemed beyond help and unable to fit into society. Once admitted, they were told to be grateful for the charity offered to them, quickly became institutionalised by strict routine and boredom and were eventually stripped of any remaining self-esteem and dignity. Suicides, drownings, insanity and senile decay are some of the reasons given in the death register at the Dunwich Museum. The majority slipped away quietly and alone in the middle of the night.

There are at least 65 returned servicemen buried somewhere in the unmarked graves. Most were sent to the asylum to recuperate from the traumas of war after being assured Dunwich would be a place where they could spend their days reading and fishing. Rather than the rest and recreation promised and a chance to withdraw from the alcohol consumed to blot out the horrors witnessed, most became even more inebriated. The asylum was rife with a sly grog trade amongst the inmates, who sold their rations of rum for a tidy profit, and visitors who sneaked supplies onto the island.

Although 70 per cent of the inmates were over 65 years of age, it was never just a place for society to dump its unwanted aged citizens. It also housed many younger inmates with diseases that were incurable or untreatable at the time. As well as the visually impaired, people with terminal illnesses such as cancer and tuberculosis were sent there to die. Young sufferers with diabetes and epilepsy found themselves incarcerated and unless there was a good reason to be transferred elsewhere, remained on the island. Before public terror overtook sensibility, people suffering from leprosy were also admitted and housed in a separate lazaret built next to a swamp near the asylum. Eventually, these young, hapless individuals were moved to Peel Island where a new lazaret was established.

Living conditions changed slightly when an electric generator plant was installed that made refrigeration possible. Letters of complaint were written to the government and newspapers by inmates and visitors. Superintendents were sacked and replaced, but overall, the asylum remained in a poor state. Stradbroke Island is a beautiful tropical paradise and could have offered so much more if society had embraced the inmates, rather than casting them aside.

As quickly as the buildings were constructed when the asylum first opened, so they disappeared when it closed. Once the remaining inmates were shipped off to a disused air force base at Sandgate, most of the hodgepodge of wooden buildings were dismantled and removed. The cemetery and the inmates buried there, were quickly forgotten.

I firmly believe that all visitors to North Stradbroke Island should be aware of its history. The forgotten inmates buried on the island need more than a memorial wall, where families who have traced their loved ones to the cemetery can place a plaque. They need more than the small sign at the entryway. They need more than the small fragments of their lives found in the records available at the museum. The inmates of Dunwich Benevolent Asylum may have been homeless, disabled, aged or ill, and cast aside by the government and society of the time, but they were people who deserve dignity and respect. An enormous roadside sign easily seen as visitors drive past, crosses and a beautiful garden to walk through, would provide a worthy memorial.

Every time I return to Stradbroke Island, the cry of the angel birds draws me to the cemetery. After countless visits, the history behind the forgotten souls of Dunwich Benevolent Asylum still stirs my heart.

Revolutions and Evolutions of the Heart

TATYANA HEATH

snakes live with their venom stored within
plateau of emotional existence
reminded me of a time I cut my hair and shed
layers and layers and layers and layers
and I was questioning it all

I once thought bad things happened to me. Now I realise things just happen. There have been many moments in my life when I have kissed the edge of the Earth. Discovered the limit and pushed further. Ripping my heart to shreds. A threadbare soul. It is an almost unbearable truth to carry; knowing the material is there, but understanding you are the only one who can knit it together. Heartache burrows into your bones and cuts your mind like mirages of knives. Still, you resist the call to quit.

Revolutions and evolutions of the heart. I had to break my own heart to learn how to heal.

We are each a stained-glass window. Sacred. Thousands of colours, thousands of parts. Though we may crack or break there is nothing that cannot be replaced. Memories taint the tapestry of our existence, yet their function remains the same. We harbour the innate power to heal ourselves. To see our pain and become comfortable with it. Sit in it. Writhe in it. Purge through it. Humans are selfish; we are scared to suffer. Nobody tells you how to dance with a devil created by your own affliction.

I chart my life between touchstones of chosen death and consequential rebirth. I have been given this lesson thrice. The first found me toying with suicidal ideation at 17; a tedious journey of back and forth I embarked upon for too many years of my young life. The second, I was 20 and en route to wilful death before my father intervened. While driving to the hospital—where I wished to be admitted—mere metres from our driveway, we hit a fallen gum tree. The vehicle was disfigured, yet we were reprieved. The third, was a time I yearned for change: a persistent ache. On the eve of my 21st birthday I prayed to whatever force returned my life earlier that year. The following day I was hit by a car and immobilised in a wheelchair, with three fractures to both my legs. I had nowhere to go but within.

A life cycle within a life cycle. I was given a choice to redirect course.

running marathons in my mind
my body left behind
skip rope, skip beat

prescriptions, can't compete
overcome or numb
find the middle piece

jagged breaths roll past
a jagged mind
nicking skin and splitting seams

love letters
no receipt
this address does not exist

wrestling under the burden of a feather
problems masked as cures

the bridge between sadness and happiness:
unchartered territory,
crowded by the lost
silent embrace,
vacant body
ghosts from a crucified past haunt but the shadows
let the light in

Bipolar disorder is troublesome to diagnose; it shows many faces and not all at the same time. It is fire and it is ice; both are extreme and both burn. I have always known the feeling of existing on the peripheral, just outside of reach. The crowning moment of this realisation found me on the driveway of my first share house, on the edge of 17 and the first time I had ever been alone. I was experiencing a resurgence of kaleidoscopic mania that had chewed and swallowed me most nights of the previous two weeks. Words formed into pictures and pictures formed into words. A gallery of trauma was painting the walls of my fragmenting mind. I do not remember dialling my mum's phone number.

But I do notice them move, marching into the blanket of night. *Lasius niger*, the garden ant. Migrating from one brick to the other, crossing rivers of moulding mortar. Moving with such gravitational impetus and shouldering the responsibility of a collective survival. How can a creature so seemingly inconsequential bring me to my knees?

I did not yet understand the depth of my own mind. I could not conceptualise a world outside of the one I was suffocating in. The ants lifted and carried me away, my body had surrendered, and the only real thing was the voice of my mum and the seconds ticking over on my phone screen. I scratched into the mortar; deeper and deeper, carving flesh wounds into the ground that bore me. My tired bones sighed a heavy release. I was dissolving into the sky. The fire was waning and the ice was melting. Eleven minutes and eleven seconds. Her breath meeting mine in the middle ground where matter over mind ruled.

'It's not you, my darling. This weight is not for you to hold.'

The total weight of all ants on Earth is close to that of humans. We share that. Conservative estimates suggest they can withstand over a thousand times their weight. I share that. I think these little ants gifted back a piece of my mind that night. Carried on the back of a half-chewed leaf, still fulfilling its purpose despite a few holes. They rationed the load; they knew that it was okay to ask for a little help.

My heart had fractured, and cracks appeared in my supposition. Like never before, I challenged the default despair that enduringly overrode any happiness I was entitled to. Self-pity was a comfortable, dark dwelling where no one could disturb me. It was as though this crack allowed in a lick of light. The revolution had begun.

squeezing out a last breath
like rinsing a cloth
dangerous deeds
feel good indeed
infected seed
cut me open
see if I bleed
mutilate
to articulate
sensation without description
too much tension
slack rope
a snake
does it squeeze its prey
life drips out in waves
or
does it swipe with venom
pulled from hell into heaven
which one will greet me
today
always
breathe life into Eden
I ran away
it didn't work.

Life is curious. Naively, I assumed I could prepare for 'important' moments before they happen. As though I could intuitively predict their arrival and allocate a spot in my brain; an accessible pigeonhole of spiritual insight. I thought these important memories would be decorated. I was wrong on every face. Every truth I thought I knew was wiped clean and bleached. Wrung out and burnt. I was so deceivingly wrong I am embarrassed at my short-sightedness. I narcissistically presumed the Earth's revolutions relied upon my own revolving door of emotion. Pain was a gaping hole I buried myself in. Zoom out.

My truth was shattering glass and screaming tires. Searing nothing. *You want to die? Let me show you.* Reality filters in slowly like steeping tea. My truth was a body vibrating in shock. It was expecting smashed skulls and inescapable injury. Instead, I was met with a blink of dizzying white. Almost languidly, the nothingness sprawling across my vision melted into a tree protruding from the windshield that pardoned my life.

My truth was a heating realisation the man who created me would have died for me. He directed the car into the leafy canopy of the tree, reserving impact for his driver's side. Had we continued straight I would have been crushed by the trunk, he knew that. He bargained his life for mine. *And you wanted to take your own.* The car was scalped, but by divine intervention we walked away without physical injury.

That is real life. You cannot predict it. You cannot control it. I was gifted another chance; an insight into a fragility impossible to fathom until approached with my own impending death. One thought rooted in my mind, the fracturing second after impact. A slow-motion highlight reel. *Love.* That is all I felt with every sense in my body.

Overwhelming technicolour. That is all we are here for. Humans are purposed with love. Kill the rot not yourself. It is our shared universal truth. Act with purpose and act with love; you can never really be wrong. It is the best thing we get to do, so do not be naive enough to take it for granted.

We waited by the tree through the embryonic hours of the morning. Three cars stopped that night, spotting our blinking hazard lights through seamless black. Two heed no attention, only slowing their vehicles enough to manoeuvre around the fallen gum. No questions or wave. Dad asked me if I wanted to go to the hospital, but I could not leave our roadside vigil. So, we talked. We talked until my throat was barren and my eyes had cried all the tears my grieving body could conjure. In the last car, there was a family who did not know the road. Like I said, life is curious. You think you're ready to die when you are starkly reminded how finite it is. The mother wept with her gratitude; her babies asleep in the tiny car seats behind her. I sat there, wrapped in flowery pyjamas and holding the pillow I buried my fear into. For a moment I returned to the simplicity of a child; a child I had long forgotten about. I kissed the stars and made an impenetrable oath.

Though my heart was scarred, I was healing calloused wounds from the inside out. Logically, the Earth's revolutions never stop. For a moment, I saw what happens when it does; caught in-between the veil of what is and what could be. A choice made in a millisecond. If that is all it comes down to, I think we are overcomplicating the matter of living.

this loneliness
creeps and dives
seeping through corners

like the dying flowers on my window
once beautiful
signet of love

cutting open scar tissue
to heal an old wound
suffering again
renew the source

parts
not seen but felt
fractured pieces
start to melt
form a whole
existing from the fear
of missing out
is missing out
on our one true purpose
to live this life
without second guessing
your intrinsic purpose
tattooed to your soul
we each assign
a separate meaning
realign yourself
the past doesn't exist

the future hasn't happened yet
search within

I had to break my legs to learn I had to stop running. I had to see the ugliest version of myself to understand the beauty. I had to break my own heart to learn how to heal.

Turning 21 is cauterised into the meaning of adulthood. It would be the time I would finally arrive at the place everyone talks about. I would be a grown-up. As little girl I constructed untamed fantasies of how this would look. The evening of my birthday I circled this thought. I was ready, I was begging for *something* to change.

The next day I was admitted to the emergency room: pedestrian vs car.

The same flash of white cleaved my world when I hit the ground. The same word inundated my senses, silencing the tinny ring inside my ears and willing my eyes to open. *Love*. I do not remember when I finally did, but I do remember the full moon. It was there like it always had and would be. This sight stained my mind and I perpetually cycled back to it. Colliding with the car. Colliding with the ground. The moon. Love. Rewind. Repeat.

When you physically cannot move the only place to explore is the valleys of your mind; uncovering that which had been long buried. There is nothing scarier than a splitting mind. Careening down the side of a crumbling building; life rope held tight. Where is it attached? Head in the stars. Moonlight illuminating the scars in your heart; they do not appear, yet they sear. Flesh born wounds on the inside, where there is no way out except through. It is only when you do not have time you realise all the things you wish you had time for. A palace where wondering thoughts become wandering doubt spreading like ink bleeding onto paper.

I learnt to hold myself back to whole. I learnt to love myself fiercely. I had two options: it was swim or drown. It is a process. We are not innately taught how to do it. The older I get, the more I realise none of us really know what we are doing. It is doing the best we can with what we have got.

It is possible to know what you want out of this life and make it your reality. I remember longing for the extension of my heart, knowing I would find a piece of myself in the arms of another. When I could surrender completely to not only a love found for myself, but a love for another. To love and be loved: a symbiotic flow. I am not suggesting you need to find yourself in another person, but rather, you can find yourself within another person. A shared journey: a visceral reminder of the reason you dragged yourself from engulfing self-loathing. Your reflection is not really your reflection, but you can see yourself through the eyes of those who see you.

I met him; the man that touched me as though my skin was spun silk. I was not looking but I had my eyes open. He is sunshine and unbridled joy. An elastic band smile. Finding a home in my heart, our love weaves deeper into the fibre of my being every day. A love mirrored by the growing one I am fostering for myself. He who revolutionised my entire understanding with tenderness. Humans centre on connection after all. My heart had swollen, vibrating beyond the confines I chained myself to and beyond the person I believed myself to be. We are not stagnant; we cycle like the moon.

time ceases to exist
when we are eternal

a swift love
carried on a breeze
a warm love
tucked into bed
a returning love
unlock the door

my heart fertile ground
to be loved
on unconditional entry

not potential
but
consequential

a love that orbits
a love that is alive and moves in seasons
a love so great, not even the universe could not contain
its expansiveness
a love mutually absorbing and birthing

a reactionary love
an unbreakable tether

I have dipped my toes in the water. I have seen the other side. True self harm exists when you refuse to let yourself be still. Why waste your life suffering. Things outside your control will happen. Not to you but for you. Embrace the singular truth we are purposed with and hold in your core. Store the fire and keep it kindled. Ever-present and there to return. Always returning. Revolutions and evolutions of the heart. Love is the real revolution.

Gritty Breaths in Nepal

LAUREN SCARONI

Day 1

In Thamel, it is five minutes to 2019. Across the road from my three-bolt-door hotel room is a fossil building. Gutted and dark against the sky but filled with the sleeping shadows of Nepal's homeless who crept in at dusk. Since yesterday, I bore witness to a thousand inconceivable human acts and felt it all with every breath of a million dust particles. Dogs and cats wander the streets with the gentile of the underclass. Today I tried to exchange money for photos. Thamel is coated in ancient dust that, apparently, everyone fights to keep. It is gritty, really gritty. If I stare long enough, every face is leather-worn and ancient. I wonder, *who am I to want to know their story*?

Day 2

Maybe I learnt more about life from a tourist guide in Durbar Square today than I have in 35 years. In the temple of Kumari Devi, a four-year-old living goddess, I watch the guide spin the story of life and death and the cosmos around an 800-year-old engraved mandala. For a few liminal seconds, he puppeteers the five elements in front of a small group of tourists. Afterwards, I realised there were barely any lines left on the mandala, but for a moment, living history swirled in time to his words.

There it is again at Swayambhunath; the real cosmos. The highest of exalted highs up in the clouds and hell down at the bottom, where the little girls with the dirty babies ask for money. Monkeys lick the step walls and bare their teeth at trivial visitors who climb the steps to enlightenment all day long. I think I am more disturbed by the lady who follows me for hundreds of metres, saying I can afford her jewellery, than the dead and burning bodies by the side of the holy Bagmati River. *Probably my ego.*

Patan Square is pristine schoolchildren and more dirt under my fingernails. I meet a girl called Babaa and with her fingers, she tells me she is nine. I try to give her 10 rupees, but she shakes her head. She does not want my money. She follows me out to the edge of the square and waves as I am driven away in another dust taxi. I cannot get rid of the dirt in my nose or under my nails in a ten-minute shower cut short by rolling power outages. In the dark, I clamp my lips tightly shut as a reminder not to drink the water. I cannot unsee the things I saw today and seek comfort. I use eight precious Dettol wipes to clean my shoes and feel sick with myself.

Day 7

Flying from Kathmandu to Pokhara and I am the only Westerner in the domestic airport. No one seems to care except me. I smile at babies wrapped up in shawls. They smile at me. I watch sacks of rice and caged chickens pushed through an unplugged scanner and wonder how much weight a little plane from Kathmandu can bear. I line up with women to use the toilet. I am sparse and plain among the rainbow of cloth around me. *Do not touch the walls inside the toilet. Do not touch anything.* It is an ordeal. I will never complain about a public toilet in Australia again.

Eventually, I am seated in a tiny bus with no windows. We sit on the tarmac for three hours. Airport workers squat on vast runways waiting for something. I try to sleep. People on the bus with no windows cough and cough. *Do not think about airborne viruses.* A 25-minute flight or an eight-hour bus trip to Pokhara; Nepal's number one leisure city. Beyond the dirty aeroplane windows and over the wing, I see glimpses of the Himalayas.

I arrive in a white room that is clean, clean, clean. I glance the second largest lake in Nepal from a little balcony. I wash my hands in the sink of the white white bathroom and panic. I google 'water in Pokhara' to remind myself the water is as bad here as anywhere in Nepal. Nepal is rich in water that cannot be used. I walk down the street for dinner and feel less concerned about life and death for a little while.

Day 8

I fall asleep with my face to the sky, in a little wooden boat, to the bells of the Barahi Hindu Temple. I think *do not stare too much* at the ancient colourful creatures that float out from a hall on the hill after prayer. I bow my head with an awkward smile on my face after meeting eyes with young monks during ceremony. They whisper to each other, and somehow, I picture my students at home. I think the Himalayas are a trick each time I turn to see them.

At the World Peace Pagoda, eagles glide around Buddha up in the sky and little children play with rocks on the side of the mountain. Women sit in circles draped in red. I want to be with them. Everywhere I go men huddle around a game that looks like chess. I look for US dollars everywhere. Instead, men whisper, 'Hashish?' in the shadows. In the night district, 'Om' is beamed via disco lights onto the pavements I walk over, but I don't hear much of the primordial sound. Later my heart breaks as I step out of my Aum halo to see two little boys sniffing petrol from empty chip packets. Tomorrow, I leave for the hills.

Day 9

Towards the hills of Tansen, it takes four hours to drive 100km. The driver edges up and around sheer cliff faces and I am up with the eagles again. Glacier water flows in rapids far below me and little huts with little children sit beside the road, dotted all the way. Arriving here is not easy. Being here is not easy. Layers of what home means strip and fall at my feet. I am naked and no one and deep inside I ache for comfort to get through the night. My homestay hostess fills my hot water bottle. A book and torch mean everything when electricity disappears after dark. Dogs howl and fight, but the sprawling cliff holding the town of Tansen below me is quiet.

Day 13

I see a tiny man carrying a fridge up a hill. A little boy sits next to me at a Nepalese bakery waiting for crumbs but gets luckier in the rubbish bin. Women cover their faces when they see my camera. Children run up to me yelling, 'Namaste'. I remind myself this means, 'I bow to the Devine in you'. I cling to this thought, *there is a 'me'*. I walk the dusty streets of the mountain town and I find some pieces of me along the way. I push them back into my smile and heart. I climb to the pine forest at the top of the mountain above my little cave room. I unravel on the soft forest floor and pick myself up in shifting rays of winter sunshine. The eagles flying around the Shreenagar Tower point out some more of 'me' in the infinity valleys. Later on, at sunset in the town playground, the orange-pink light smooths over any rough edges left from the reconstruction of yesterday's cracks. I eat dinner with my host family. They can speak a little English but don't over dinner. I feel like an intruder in an absolutely foreign land. I am fragile tonight, in this ancient town, on the old Silk Road.

Day 15

I direct my driver through an alleyway made long before cars. I am leaving the ancient mountain trading post of Tansen. We wind our way down a rocky uncovered single-track road, travelling hundreds of metres above flowing gorges. The height is too much; I close my eyes. I wake to the sound of grating metal and realise we are passing a bus. Through the window, cliffside, I follow the journey of loose rocks making their way down the gorge. I fall asleep again.

The next time I wake, I'm in another small mountain town. Women in sarongs are washing beneath pipes, popping out from the side of the mountain. Steam shrouds them; the heat of their bodies in icy morning winter air. I shiver underneath my jacket in the car. We stop for the toilet; a little shed that looks over a field of yellow poppies. I breathe.

The road flattens outside Lumbini. Tiny one-room mud huts line the road heading in. I breathe. I arrive at the birthplace of Buddha and rejoice at the white white white sheets again. I wander around the bone-dry gardens of the compound. I hear calls to prayer in the distance. Later on, men around the fire point out sounds of jackals. Tomorrow, I pilgrimage.

Day 16

The birthplace of Buddha bids me foreboding. Outside the pilgrimage site, women sit in the mud, smiling at those who enter the sacred zone. On the other side of the fence on hallowed ground, thousands of people bow to golden statues. Temples shine, shine, shine and silhouette against the sky. But ghosted behind them, in the smoky marshes, temple builders sleep side-by-side in iron lean-tos.

A red-stained mouth spits and chews the betel nut, making jokes in broken English. His rickshaw takes me from one end of sacred ground to the other. I am tense and suspicious. Cross-legged holy men chant and grin wildly at the tree of Buddha's birth.

In another dirt taxi, I'm bumping back to the compound. I see purple and red cloaks squat in mud huts, beside their goats, watching the anticipated highway construction built by pickaxes. I walked on holy ground today and check my bare feet for signs. That night around a campfire, Chitwan Park Rangers point out the familiar howls of jackals in the distance.

Day 18

I fly the Lumbini coup and drop back down in Kathmandu chaos. Bone-tired relief after dealing with filth all day. The toilets. The body searches. The spitting. Waiting for hours as unsmiling men throw luggage over our heads; hoping it is snatched out of the air before it plummets earthbound. Back in Thamel. It almost feels familiar. I remember the way through winding alleys to a restaurant that serves food for Westerners. My angry stomach appreciates the plain rice.

Day 22

I meet a lady in the Garden of Secrets across the road from my hotel. She says, 'Don't try and understand this place; just wait for it to come to you.' I play this over on my tongue on the steps of an orphanage, outside Kathmandu. I have brought money. They take me shopping to show me what they buy. A gas burner. Winter pyjamas for the 25 children in their care. Blankets. Underwear. They smile. I feel proud, then disappointed with myself.

Day 27

Sitting on a step somewhere in Thamel. Watching the street. A holy man politely holds out his tin. I say, 'Money for photo.' It still feels uncomfortable. At least it is an exchange of services and begging is not welcomed by authorities. I am not interested in his begging. Just the shades of orange painted on his naked body.

It is the last afternoon here before I begin the long journey home tomorrow. Street children dance to Rage Against the Machine in shadows, and around the corner, young Americans sing about Jesus and I politely decline Hashish without batting an eyelid.

One last morning waking to the smell of incense and grit.

Day 29

The journey home is an exhausting, feverish babble. There is rumour of an outbreak of swine flu. On the first plane, a lady behind me coughs and coughs. Flight attendants ask her to move to the back of the plane. She refuses. They ask again and again. She is hysterical. They give her pain relief and I put on a mask I bought in Thamel when the grit was getting to my lungs.

Sleep comes in bits and pieces.

And then I am shoved through Ghanzhou airport. Shoes, jewellery, socks, phones, cameras, belts. Panic in the face of semi-automatics; weary travellers are wide awake. Beating hearts eventually slow in the desolate Chinese super airport at 3am.

Day 30

Brisbane.

Home.

I am. Home.

January in Brisbane means I take off layers of clothes in the airconditioned airport. Shiny floors and sparkly shops and familiar food blurs.

The conveyor belt works.

Large, neat stacks of maroon and black cases start filing in.

I look down at the hemp dress I wear, purchased in Pokhara; the number one leisure centre of Nepal. It is roughly made and one of a kind. I tried on ten dresses to find one that fits. I sniff my shoulder and it smells like sandalwood. My heart trips.

My dusty boots move outside of me; shuffling towards the conveyor belt. My blue suitcase politely travels towards me. I notice it bears the battle wounds of a journey that is already fading. A vivid, ferocious, living Nepalese-sized imprint on me is fading in the humid air. I droop amongst the baggage.

I stand amongst the other travellers alongside the pickup lane at arrivals. Sweating and pale in my hemp dress. He spots me and grins through the windscreen.

We visit his mother on the way home. The puppies are eight weeks now. We can take the one we picked out if we want, she says. So, I hold tiny Fia in my lap in the passenger seat as we drive through the suburbs of Brisbane. My head is not here, but her little heart pounds in my sweaty hands and she pees on my new hemp dress. I feel sick with tiredness. Lightheaded as we wind through the prosaic Paddington hills. He hauls my luggage up through our little backyard, up the stairs to our neat Settler's Cottage in central Bardon.

'How was it!?' he says.

We scroll through some of my photos. I start to ache with once-in-a-lifetime memories. The beginnings of a hole deep inside me starts to make itself known. My eyelids are heavy and I am on the soft couch. I strip to my underwear in the air-conditioned living room. I am looking for comfort. I do not know what that means now here in my home on a sticky, faded January afternoon in inner-city Brisbane. I lie down on the bare floorboards. I want to feel the hard wood pressed against my ribs. I prop the large white cushion under my fading-sandalwood-smelling hair and tiny Fia curls into my neck. I feel her heartbeat talking to my pulse. The cold floorboards hold me still. For now.

I breathe.

Transpacific

Jai Moss

The sky pulses ahead. It reminds him of a heartbeat. The absence of noise makes the muted lightning more sinister. Most people will never see an electrical storm from the sky. From the ground, clouds roll in from above before disappearing in a scramble of darkness and rain. Up here, the phenomenon is more powerful. The comparison between the two perspectives reminds him of an iceberg, the enormity of which can only be fully appreciated from a specific vantage point. From the cockpit, the whole cloud is on display, looking like a strange sky jellyfish. Jagged strings of electricity drop from underneath, comically reinforcing the jellyfish look.

He can still remember learning about Cumulonimbus clouds in the Royal Flying Corps.

Charles Kingsford Smith (known as 'Smithy' by his mates) was no stranger to clouds like these. Thunderstorms were a staple growing up in Australia. He thinks of his home country, and of the many flights he has made there. It is where he met his co-pilot, Charles Ulm. The two men share not only a name but a deep friendship they know will be long-lasting. But this is where the similarities stop.

Where Ulm sees danger, Charles sees adventure. Where Charles sees a risky flightpath as a personal challenge to be tackled, Ulm sees it as a hazard. The two men often acknowledge their differences: the heart, and the brain. But they work—sometimes the best friendships are like that. He thinks of all the miles they have covered, all that time in the sky. From joy flights over the Lachlan River in the small New South Wales town of Cowra, to flying during the Great War when he clung in fear to the controls of his aircraft; it was the only thing that made sense to him in that horrible world. Often, the aircraft, the controls, and the way the sky moves, are the only things that make sense to him still.

Oakland is long gone now. The warm Californian sun on his face feels like a distant memory, and yet so close he could reach out and touch it. They are well into the second leg of their transpacific journey. First, they flew more than twenty-seven hours from Oakland to a small army airfield on the island of O'ahu, Hawaii. Now they are heading to Suva, Fiji and then on to Brisbane. He remembers the way he felt when the plane left the ground; the only thing ahead, the vast expanse of the deep blue Pacific and more than eighty hours in his beloved sky. Judging by his calculations, they were just short of crossing the equator, the invisible line dividing the northern and southern hemispheres. The whole globe is a web of invisible lines—meridians, tropic lines, and time zones. The most intriguing is the international dateline. Crossing this line means a shift. The concept fascinates him. Travelling from east to west, the traveller is gifted an extra calendar day. From west to east they skip a day entirely. This invisible line is the closest humanity will ever get to time travel.

He watches the sky pulsing ahead of him. Lost in his thoughts, he is mesmerised by the sky around him. The beating of a giant heart. The silence making it more compelling; it's like the storm is somehow sucking the sound out of the air.

'Well, it doesn't look good,' Ulm shocks him out of his trance.

The sky ahead is a minefield.

'We knew it was likely we would get caught in a tropical storm. If anything, I am just ready to get this over with.'

'Speak for yourself. No pilot ever wants to see a sight like this.'

Ulm is right, no pilot wants to take on a tropical thunderstorm while crossing the Pacific. Thunderstorms in the tropics are often larger, more intense and a lot more common. Things can go from bad to worse in a matter of minutes.

'Let's get our game faces on. This one is not going to be fun,' Charles says.

The two men begin preparing the Fokker for their impending battle with mother nature. Ulm adjusts the cockpit controls and sets the heading to follow; hoping that will get them through the storm. Charles keeps a steady hand on the throttle and a watchful eye on the ever-shifting cloud mass. They can't avoid the storm, flying above it is risky and it is too late to fly around it. He knew this would be the most brutal leg of the trip. Only hours in they had a suspected fuel leak, and now this. He can already see himself kissing the warm dirt of the Albert Park airport in Suva when, and if, they make it. The noise of the engine grinds into his thoughts.

As the Southern Cross approaches cloud it begins to shake, probably just a side effect of the increased engine power but disconcerting nonetheless. The plan is to punch through it and out the other side as quick as possible, with as little damage as possible.

Thunder roars, and the jellyfish cloud illuminates a nightmarish silhouette against the turbulent sky. The aircraft rocks from side to side, shaking like a boat on high seas.

'Keep pushing. It's holding up alright for the moment, but we mightn't have that much longer,' Charles shouts over the commotion.

Suddenly, the plane begins to shake with an intensity double to what it already was. The instruments rattle and Ulm groans. He begins to panic, frantically checking the instruments in the cockpit and muttering under his breath.

'So close, I can't believe it. So close,' Charles sighs.

A thick wall of cloud fogs the front of the aircraft, the navigation lights cast red and green into the nothingness. The plane jolts. Charles's stomach leaps into his throat. The horrific helplessness that only a sudden loss of altitude can bring. He imagines the Southern Cross as the small herring being digested by the jellyfish. Right now, they are exactly where they do not want to be—in the middle of the storm.

'We need more throttle; we are losing speed.'

'I can feel it. Smithy, this isn't good.'

'Push the throttle to maximum,' Charles directs.

The plane sputters and whirs as it regains altitude. During the chaos, he strangely pauses to think how magnificent it all is. The screaming wind, the shuddering plane, the lightning flashes … all of it. It is grand beyond belief. And then, just as quickly as it crossed into their flightpath, the storm begins to dissipate. The pilots regain vision, the parting clouds revealing the thin veil of dawn just over the horizon. A smattering of clouds appears as steppingstones across the sky. The men sit in silence and let the cool sensation of relief wash over them. The sounds of the plane fill the air again. The hum of the engine has never sounded so sweet as it does on this morning over the Pacific. After the storm, the flight is calm, only the memory of the jellyfish cloud remains, and probably always will.

After a while he can feel Suva, down there below the clouds, they are so close now. It feels like this every time. The last part of the journey is always the longest. It seems the closer you get to the destination, the more it dances around, whimsically out of reach. He can see the tiny white caps of the ocean during the intervals between clouds as they descend. It is like discovering a new world. Lost in the mist of a cloud before dropping down through it, each time with something new in sight. Now he can see little islands scattered like thrown stones, the surging ocean rhythmically washing against them. Thirty-four hours. Thirty-four harrowing hours in the sky. Others whinge about long and laborious journeys, but he always finds them compelling. There is something to be savoured, an art in it all. There is always something about the journey for him. It is always so much more than getting from a to b. Always a bittersweet goodbye, watching the ground slowly grow smaller and smaller until the cloud bed conceals land completely. The strange twilight zone of being in between two cities, states or even continents. It is during these moments that he thinks this is where he belongs, truly and wholeheartedly. This is home. Not in the cities or towns. In the sky, at cruising altitude. Neither here nor there. And as the Southern Cross glides towards the small dirt runway, he already can't wait to be back up in the great beyond.

Blind Love

Patricia McIntosh

It was no big deal in the grand scheme of things but, to a five-year-old over-achiever, that Year One Math test was everything. I struggled to read the white writing camouflaged among the chalk smudges on the blackboard.

'What's the first question?' I whispered, leaning across the aisle.

'I'm not telling you the answer,' my cousin replied.

'I don't want the answer.'

'Tricia. No talking. This is a test,' the teacher said.

'But I can't see the question,' I replied, almost in tears.

'Then ask me if you can't see.'

I had no idea how prophetic the teacher's last few words were in 1974.

I ran into things, fell over and was afraid of the dark, just like other children. No-one noticed my slightly turned eye, even though my grandmother had one. It seemed her caring nature wasn't the only thing I had in common with her. A specialist diagnosed Grandma with night blindness in the 1940s. He said nothing could be done for it, and that was all she was told. My dad knew as a child that he had it too, as he struggled to see in the dark. It would be more than twenty-five years before they found out anymore, thanks to my turned eye.

I sat on Mum's lap and watched as Grandma covered one eye and read the chart on the wall. I thought the doctor was testing her to see if she knew her letters. She got the first few right.

'The next one could be an E,' Grandma said, 'but I'm not sure.'

'It's a B, Grandma,' I said.

They laughed.

'You can't help Grandma, she has to read it herself,' Mum said.

'It will be your turn next,' the doctor said, smiling. What a prophecy that turned out to be.

Grandma tried a few more letters but got most of them wrong. When she tried to read with the other eye, she didn't know any letters, even the big one at the top. The ophthalmologist gave her a book and asked her to read. She would have done better if he'd given her one of my school readers with easier words and bigger writing. Dad did better than Grandma, but I got more letters right than both of them, and I was only five.

The doctor put drops in my eyes to dilate them. They stung. I hated that part.

'It's all blurry and I can't see,' I soon complained.

My teacher's words weren't the only ones that were prophetic.

I had to be guided to the chair—little did I know this would become my norm one day. I closed my eyes when the doctor shone his ophthalmoscope into them, it was like looking directly into the sun.

'I know it's bright, but you need to keep them open just for a minute so I can see the back of your eye,' he said.

My eyes watered; I couldn't stand the glare. I fought my need to blink but wasn't always successful.

That's when he saw it—Retinitispigmentosa. It turns out that was what night blindness was. That was one trifecta we could have done without. The doctor said it would progress (not mentioning our impending blindness) and tried to sound reassuring when he said research was underway into RP—an attempt to give us hope after diagnosing us with an incurable disease.

School wasn't easy for any of us. Grandma was deemed 'clumsy' as a child and told, at the age of eight, it was a waste of time sending her to school because she couldn't read. Besides, in the 1920s it wasn't seen as important for girls to receive an education. In many ways school wasn't that different for Dad and I, despite the twenty-five-year gap, although I didn't have to do my homework by lamp light or write on a slate. We both squinted at the board, trying to read what was on it. We'd stare and try different angles but still couldn't see. We read with the book held close to our face and dreaded standing up to read out loud in class. Some of my classmates thought I couldn't read well because I was slow and sometimes got a word wrong, despite achieving some of the highest grades in the class. It was just something else for them to tease me about.

'Can I play too?' I asked some girls skipping rope at playtime.

'No, four-eyes, go away.'

I walked away, just far enough so that I could sit and watch them play, and so they couldn't see the tears rolling down my cheeks. I didn't want cry-baby added to my list of names. But the names weren't the worst—the exclusion and loneliness was. Each day, that hour in the playground seemed like an eternity.

In class I was the last one to be picked on a team, despite being good at school and sports. 'She can't see, she'll drop the ball', and 'don't pick her, we'll lose', were common utterances. Last to be included in anything. I learnt young that it wasn't okay to be different, and they certainly let me know that.

Despite my fears that high school would be worse, it wasn't. I was blessed with incredible friends who didn't care that I couldn't see well. Despite the challenges I still excelled, always the over-achiever, probably because I was trying to prove my worth to others, and to myself.

But one person I never had to prove myself to was Grandma. It didn't matter what I did, she always encouraged and supported me.

'Grandma, we won the netball grand final.'

'Well done, darling.'

I placed my trophy in her hand and she ran her fingers over it.

'It's gold with a blue star on top,' I explained.

'It's lovely. You are amazing and I'm very proud of you.'

Whenever I told her about children teasing me she would say, 'It doesn't matter what they think. Remember, sticks and stones will break my bones but names will never hurt me.' If only that were true. But she knew how hard it was not being able to see, and understood some of the challenges I would face in my future long before I did.

'What's that, Grandma?' I asked.

'It's a magnifying glass.'

'Can I have a go, please?'

She handed it to me.

'Wow, the words look so big.'

'I need them big so I can read them.'

'You should get glasses like me, Grandma. Then you'll be able to see.'

She smiled at my naivety and hid the sadness in her heart, as she knew one day glasses wouldn't help me either. The same sadness she felt when I walked up and down her driveway using her white cane—what child wouldn't want to try out Grandma's new toy? The same sadness she felt when I took her guide dog for a walk many years later: rehearsals for a movie I didn't even know I would be starring in. But I didn't see it like that. I was emulating a special lady, one of grace, beauty and love who had an incredible singing voice which only the church choir and those close to her got to enjoy. Pity I didn't inherit that from her. But I was fortunate to spend many hours with her playing my keyboard and learning some of her favourite songs. She'd sing a few lines, then I'd play them, and she'd know if I hit a wrong note. I'd write the music so I could read it and practice it later. The next time I'd play for her, I'd play the song in full, much to her delight.

Grandma lived up the street and I visited her often, partly to check on her, but mostly to spend time with her. I'd walk her to the shop—usually the adults help the children cross the road, but not in our case. I would find what she needed and help her with the money. I also read to her, ran errands, and helped her with whatever else she needed.

'Can you help me find my brush, please?' Grandma asked. 'I don't know where I sat it and I've searched everywhere.'

We'd talk and listen to music for hours. She taught me to knit by feel—she was better at it than I was. I think practice and patience may have had something to do with that. We'd play dominos with a Braille set. I never had to worry about turning them over, it's not like she could cheat. I'd divide them up and tell her what was in the middle. When it was her turn, I had to wait for her to feel the dots on each one to work out what she had and what move to make. I guess she taught me patience after all. Even though she could use dominos, she couldn't read Braille, which proved to be as difficult for her as reading print. It was for Dad, too, because his fingers were too coarse to feel the embossed dots after being a mechanic. Even though I can't see to read books anymore, Braille is a challenge I'm yet to undertake, and not sure I need to in this age of technology.

The adaptive technology, equipment, and assistance available today is a luxury my grandmother didn't have. I wonder what her life would have been like had it been available to her. Maybe she would have remained living in her own home instead of a nursing home. As she got older so did I, and I became very aware of her struggles, and that I was heading down the same path. Her sadness was no longer invisible to me. I saw her tears even though they were shed when I wasn't around. I saw her challenges, her fears, her isolation and her loneliness. But most importantly, I saw her exhibit courage, grace and love as her eyesight disappeared. Never one to complain, never one to get angry, and never one to feel sorry for herself because she couldn't see. Always helping and putting others ahead of herself. She opened her home and took in a number of people who needed somewhere to live over the years. Grandma was always quick to point out how wonderful others were, but she was the truly special one.

Things have come full circle now and I am the one at the ophthalmologist unable to read the eye chart. My granddaughter is telling me what the letters are and reading to me from her school readers. And my grandchildren are the ones playing with my white cane (thankfully, none of them will ever have to use one). They take me by the hand and guide me when we are out and help me find things I lose at home. Unlike Grandma, I still manage to work, study and lead a busy life. But I'm not oblivious to what my future holds, and I hope I embrace it with half as much dignity and grace as my grandmother did. Grandma could see in all the ways that matter, and so can I.

'Nanna, can we play dominos,' my granddaughter asked, grabbing my Braille set.

'Ok. Set them up … and no cheating this time,' I replied.

My Mother is a Revolutionary

CAITLIN BRANNIGAN

Age 10/39

My mother. What a woman. She divorced my dad when I was 8-months-old because he was a drop kick. With next to no financial assistance, she supported me as a single mother—even after being dismissed from her job of almost 20 years. She'd worked her way from the ground up to become a banking manager, only to be cast aside. But this barely fazed her. Or perhaps, my memory is softened by the lens of childhood. Maybe she protected me from her worries, sadness, and stress of the unknown.

After becoming redundant, she went back to uni as a mature age student. She was revisiting her initial plan—to become a teacher. She had first studied teaching when she graduated high school, but life got in the way.

We moved in with my grandparents, back to her childhood home. It was almost a halfway house for their children. Two had already been back—my youngest uncle, and my aunty. She had returned with her baby after a messy divorce from some smarmy Englishman. But she wasn't there for long. She was lining up the next one, out of the house, pregnant and married again in no time.

My oldest uncle, the eldest, was the only child who left home and actually stayed away. Happily married with three kids, he had next to nothing to do with the parents that birthed and provided for him.

Maybe that's how life was supposed to go. Like baby birds, they leave the nest—or get abruptly thrown out to fly or die—and we don't see them moving back in with mum and dad after some traumatic experience. But that seems too cold to me, too unrealistic.

So, my mum returned to university. At the age of almost 40. With a 10-year-old daughter that she was solely supporting. She was a grown woman, now having to rely upon her parents for relief from her current situation. I can't imagine how hard that decision must have been. Or how difficult the transition back into her childhood home was. I might compare it to visiting the high school you attended. The buildings are generally the same, some of the teachers are the same—albeit much older. It's you who has changed. You no longer really fit in here. You don't know anyone, and you only vaguely remember the person you were from that time. Like looking at a Monet painting up close; a jumble of indistinct shapes and colours that loosely resemble a garden. It's like trying to fit a square into a circle—there's no way to make it happen without cutting something off. However, the 'something' in this situation is your own growth and development, and I don't think reverting back to her childhood self was on my mum's agenda.

I also wonder if my mum felt ashamed in some way. Ashamed at having to rely upon her aging parents, ashamed to ask for help or handouts. Maybe this shame, although never explicitly expressed, has impacted me more than I realised. Perhaps this is why I internally cringe at the thought of asking for even a sliver of help.

I love my grandparents, my Grandma and Poppy. As a child, I think that moving into their house almost felt like an ongoing sleepover for a bit because they loved to indulge me. I remember them sneaking me extra treats, dessert after dinner, or even just some loose change.

But after spending five years with them, it became a little claustrophobic. I was no longer a child—I was an adolescent who needed some space from three overbearing parental figures.

I observed their relationship, the idiosyncrasies of their domestic life. And I came to a conclusion: These two people may have once loved each other, but it was now simply a marriage of convenience. They had lived together for too long to survive on their own and were too old to start afresh. I'm not sure the exact effect that this relationship dynamic had on my very malleable young psyche, but I suspect it coloured my romantic disposition. I decided that I wanted to avoid my relationships ever evolving into something like that.

Although I don't have any memories of my parents as a couple, their relationship as divorced co-parents was enough to show me another relationship style I did not want. There was so much tension I could pick up on, even as a young child. It was exhausting.

I think that seeing this marriage up close and personal, along with observing other surrounding relationships, provided me with a clear idea of what I didn't want. But the issue was there was no real exemplar of what I did want. I knew I didn't want a relationship of convenience, to be stuck with someone out of pure obligation, like my grandparents. I didn't want to flit between relationships, never able to be independent, like my aunty. I didn't want to be alone either, because as much as my mum inspires me, I still crave that connection of doing life with someone by my side. But to say what I actually wanted was about as clear as the Brisbane River.

These five years changed the course of my life. Even though there were difficulties, I'm thankful to have had extra time with my grandparents. I look back on these years fondly, grateful to have developed such a close relationship with them and hear their stories—although, admittedly, it was the same stories repeated at least once a week.

My relationship with my mum changed over these years. It went from typical mother-daughter to something with more depth. We became each other's confidantes and solace from the tension that lived in the household—feeling like guests in a house where we were living, ensuring we kept to the rules and regulations and didn't rock the boat. We grew together.

Age 20/49

A decade after the life-changing events of redundancy and returning to uni, we were working towards a milestone achievement. We had planned a month-long trip through Europe and the United Kingdom. A pilgrimage of sorts. Something to celebrate an ending and a new beginning.

A trip to expand our horizons, both geographically and personally. A trip that would explore ourselves, our relationship and some of our history.

My mum had never been through Europe. But she had previously been through the UK with her parents and siblings. They had visited my grandparents' home, the one they lived in before making the 10-Pound-Pom boat journey, and all their old stomping grounds. I can just imagine what my mum had been subjected to…

Poppy babbling about something, but no one quite knows what it is because he structures his sentences like, *'Ah yes, here was where … what's his name … you know who I mean. Anyway, this is where me and him used to run from old Charlie because we'd taken a bite out of each of his apples in his orchard.'*

Everyone would smile and nod along, pretending to understand the ramblings coming from his mouth. Or simply ignore him because he wasn't even talking for an audience. He was just talking to reminisce or hear his own voice.

So, to be able to take her back there, and experience nostalgic familial places along with exciting new places, was really special. We were with a tour group, travelling for 12 days through nine European countries. In very close quarters with 20-something strangers, ranging from newlyweds to families with young kids to oldies. Very unfamiliar circumstances as we had gotten used to sharing a four-bedroom house between the two of us. Living in these close quarters was new territory and needed to be navigated carefully. It was difficult to balance time together, time alone and time mingling with others, particularly considering the big personalities on board. It was like balancing on the edge of a knife; each little slip created fiery lines of pain, not soon forgotten.

It was a whirlwind adventure. From drinking beer in Heidelberg, experiencing traditional yodelling in Innsbruck, sipping schnapps in Lucerne, and the grand finale, seeing the Moulin Rouge in Paris. And then, we said goodbye to our newfound friends. The next two weeks were just my mum, myself, and our copious luggage.

Travelling creates unique scenarios that cannot be replicated in everyday life. The stress of the unfamiliar and unknown. It can bring out the best and the worst in people, sometimes simultaneously. I think that it was an impressive feat to make it through two weeks of only having each other and still being on speaking terms by the time we were flying home. There were bumps in the road, particularly high-strung emotions from carrying luggage up and down stairs—the UK needs to upgrade their Tube system. But this trip will forever be a cherished memory of our mother-daughter relationship.

Now

I am aware my mother may not fit the dictionary definition of a revolutionary. She's never engaged in a political revolution, burnt her bra at a rally or campaigned for changes to the law. But I think the way she has lived her life is pretty revolutionary. She has been a single woman, a single mother, in a society that shoves the idea of women needing the 'perfect match' down our throats. She has made her own way in the world, not relying upon a secondary income or male figure to help her through. My mother has raised me to stand my ground and pushes me to be the very best version of myself. Sometimes the pressure can be immense; am I really living up to her expectations? Is it even possible? Sometimes it feels suffocating, like a weight on my chest, ever increasing, bearing down on me. My airways constricting until I can barely gasp for air.

We haven't always seen eye to eye. From something as menial as how long it's appropriate to leave washing on the line to more serious issues. We don't have a perfect relationship, tenuously tiptoeing the line between mother-daughter and almost-friendship. A careful balancing act that one misstep or fleeting comment can tip, causing irreparable damage. Such high stakes. Maybe that just showcases some sort of strained, dependent relationship where one cannot survive without the other. But I wouldn't change a thing.

My mother is a revolutionary in my eyes. She has given me a life I am incredibly grateful for, and a maternal relationship that people envy. She showed me that you don't need someone, a relationship, to be a complete woman or have a quote unquote fulfilling life. She broke the cycle of staying in relationships for pure convenience or bouncing between partners for fear of being alone. She modelled how to be a strong, independent woman and that's something I aspire to continue. I want to continue my mother's legacy, her revolution.

She Finds Love at the End

Chloe Crawford

How selfish of you to touch me
And the most intimate parts of myself:
My mind—my soul.
With such tainted hands,
Fingers woven of hatred,
crafted from pure evil.
Those same hands that
Gripped my throat like
A hissing serpent,
And demanded silence,
Demanded I cower in fear.
But I was not born with
The power of a thousand
Ancestors before me who
Burned at the stake,
Their mouths sewn shut by men
Who feared their sharp tongues,
Their fighting spirits.
And I was not born from a lineage
Of powerful women
To ever silence the burning rage
That bubbled in my belly,

The passion in my lungs,
The sweet taste of vengeance on my lips.
You may have possessed the physical strength,
But I had something far greater, far scarier:
The roaring thunder of an army of scorned women
before me,
Finally ready to fight back.

You picked a fight with the wrong woman.

Domestic violence victim was my identity for the latter part of the three months following my escape from an abusive relationship. It was as if the very essence of who I was, and had been for 23 years, diminished to that of a victim of pure hatred. Those three words used to make me recoil at the sound whenever they were mouthed by police officers.

The aggrieved was my second name when I presented in court, and I think that title broke my spirit just as much as the next. All these names I'd never been known by. This newfound identity I had never had before. It made every bone in my body seize and want to shout.

That's not me. That's not who I am. I am much more than that.

But truthfully, I didn't know who I was at all. So much of myself had been buried away in protection during that relationship. My tongue, once sharp and defiant, had been tied; my mouth sewn shut in fear. My eyes, once gleaming and bright, had been swallowed by a grey storm which left no flicker of the warm blue it once had. And my body, once a sacred temple, an impenetrable fortress, no longer belonged to me. There were scars that hadn't been there before; but not just visible scars, ones that gripped around my skin like a slithering serpent and tightened every time I thought about what had happened to me; what *he* had done to me. I buried the parts of myself that were once my defining characteristics; the attributes I loved the most, only because they were threatening to him. And when it was all over; meaning when I finally had the strength to leave, I found myself getting lost trying to find those fragments again.

Before him, I used to look at the world with a sort of child-like innocence, a sweet naivety. I had bright eyes that viewed everything around me like the fairy tales I grew up reading. I was a hopeless romantic; an old soul in love with the idea of love, and completely infatuated by romance movies. *Dirty Dancing* was my favourite—I'd watched it over 100 times, memorising the dance moves and the way their bodies intertwined like art. I would practise and twirl around my living room every time I watched it, and each year for Christmas my dad would do the famous lift for me—hauling me into the sky and watching the joy radiate from my smile. I always hoped I'd meet someone who would dance that final song with me instead, but I know my dad tried his best because he knew how much it meant to me.

As a child, I would climb tall trees and sing to the birds that nestled in them, chase colourful butterflies through fields of green, share hugs with strangers, and dance barefoot in the pouring rain. I still embodied much of this innocence, but I grew a lot more cautious as I got older. I was very sensitive and shy, and I always wanted to fix anything that was broken. I refused to watch the news because of this. And my biggest fear was thunderstorms; I would shriek with sheer terror at the loudness, and the darkness of them; hiding away in my room until it was over. I was so fascinated by the wonders of the world, yet so terrified of the unknowns of life at the same time.

The double-edged sword is that I don't think I'll ever meet that girl again. On the 27 November 2021, I wrapped that girl in a body bag and grieved, for months. It really felt like a death, and saying goodbye was the most gruelling part of it all. I would miss her so much. But from death comes reincarnation, and I knew someday soon I would start to bloom. Because only once you lose everything, every part of yourself and the things you loved the most. Only once you have hit the most unimaginable low and are faced with two options: let it define you or let it create you; only then can you truly be reborn. And I wasn't born with my father's sheer stubbornness, my mother's indelible courage, and the lineage of a powerful ancestry of women before me to ever back down and submit. I would fight back with every ounce of strength I had.

For months, I wandered in search of myself. My body and soul exhausted after fighting a debilitating battle each day; trying not to succumb to the voices in my head that begged for the easy way out, whilst simultaneously protecting that sweet child within me who never deserved to lose her innocence. For months, I purged myself in the ocean and begged Poseidon to heal the ways in which he gutted me like a fish. For months, I stood by the rock wall we carved our initials into and asked why it had not warned me of his wickedness. For months, I laid in that grassy field and begged the winds to carry me far away from this place, and for the soil to open and swallow me entirely—and for the weeds to wrap around me and shelter me from the thunder that grew in my belly and the lightning that stopped my heart from beating. For months, I wished for a body that he had not touched, that he had not tarnished with his tainted hands. I wrote letter after letter addressed to him that I burned soon after, and I journaled every day, spilling my torment onto paper to shed some of the pain that boiled inside me. I would scrub my skin red raw in the bath each night, in the hopes that I could rid the lingering sting from where he had touched me unkindly.

Many nights I tossed and turned in my bed, torn from my sheets screaming because his face still haunted me in the realms of my sleep. It would seep into the darkness like a demonic entity, where no silver cross or preaching pastor or godly verses could save me. My soul condemned to a life of agony.

I didn't know how my heart could ever soften and learn to love or trust again. The thought of dating afterward broke my spirit; because I believed I was damaged goods—a broken doll with internal bleeding that could never be cauterised. How would I tell an innocent man that when he sips on a beer all I see are shattered glass shards and dried blood on my palms? How would I tell an innocent man that when he grabs my arms all I see are crimson contusions in the shape of handprints? How would I tell an innocent man that when he kisses along my body until he reaches my hollowed oak, that someone else still haunts that area?

I didn't believe anyone could ever love something so broken, a faulty toy, a puzzle with missing pieces, a torn painting. I didn't believe it because I couldn't even give that love to myself.

But then I remembered a distinct memory from my childhood: my first heartbreak at eight years old. I had this beautiful fairy ornament my nanna gifted me for Christmas one year, and my juvenile heart cherished and loved that fairy more than anything else I owned. One day, my sister and I were fighting like typical siblings, until I saw her hands reach out and grab my special ornament from our bookcase. In what felt like slow-motion, I watched as she threw it at the hard, brick wall behind us, my head instantly turning as I saw it shatter into pieces before me. Endless tears streamed down my face as I cried out in devastation as the one thing I had loved so dearly, crumbled right in front of me. I ran over to where it had shattered, and, instead of throwing it away, I gathered the shards and began gluing the pieces back together. It never looked the same, and there were still small pieces missing, but it didn't matter to me because I still had it, and I still loved it the same.

There was a beautiful parallel to that memory.

I would treat myself the same way I treated that little fairy ornament. It didn't matter that I was broken, because I was still me, and I was still worthy of the love and care I showed that shattered adornment.

I saw both a counsellor and a psychologist weekly during those three months who helped me to unpack the trauma I'd experienced in that relationship. I knew if I only distracted myself or hid from my pain, I would never truly survive it. I let myself feel every aching minute of it—a reminder that I was human. I let my tears flow as much as they needed to even when it felt like I was drowning in a whirlpool. During the sleepless nights when my body would bubble and fizz with rage, I would grab my soaked pillow and scream into nothingness, shedding the anger that was trapped inside me. I would spend most days in my own company exploring nature and connecting to Mother Earth like I had done when I was a little girl; trying to nurture my inner child. Eventually, waking up each day became lighter, and the night terrors slowly began to subside. Though the pain would always be there, he no longer had any power over me, and his face began to fade from my memory. My body was no longer in fight or flight mode—it felt like the shackles that had been wrapped tightly around my ankles for so long, were finally slipping loose.

Finally, after three months of unbearable pain and mourning, little seedlings began to sprout from my wounds. A passionate fire began to ignite in my soul once again. My tongue became untied and the stitches around my mouth began to dissolve. My voice grew back louder than it had been before. A flicker of light settled over my eyes again, and the hardness of my heart finally began to soften. I was healing.

Slowly—gracefully—and lovingly—healing.

I felt joy and happiness seep into my soul again, nourishing those tender wounds that remained. I had forgotten what those emotions felt like; I'd thought they'd been lost forever. Once I began healing, I chose to leave the university degree I no longer felt called to and switched to something that fuelled my spirit instead. It was the realisation that after grieving the death of my old self, I would let go of the dreams she once had for herself, that no longer aligned with who I was now. I had discovered new passions and surprisingly dug up old ones.

Writing.

I had always loved writing. And so, I began weaving diaries and journals with the most devastating yet empowering poetry I had ever composed. I wrote so many poems during this time; addicted to the feeling of my fingers entwined with the pages, and unable to release the pen that danced in cursive. Those pages held the secrets of all I could not verbally express—an authentic reminder of everything I had overcome and survived.

I began making many beautiful new friends because I had shed some of the shyness I used to possess—nothing held me back anymore. I was unapologetically me. Perhaps a little rougher, more outspoken, and rawer now, but I attracted new people into my life that loved me for me—flaws and all. Surprisingly, I no longer shrieked during thunderstorms, and instead found some beauty in the chaos and darkness; perhaps an analogy for what I had survived.

Instead of letting the violence and abuse define me, I chose to let it create me instead. I glued my own pieces back together and chose to fight for myself, not just for that little girl, but because I refused to let him win. Enduring insufferable abuse at the hands of a narcissist showed me how much strength I already had flowing through me that was hidden there all along. But most importantly, it taught me that all the love I had given others so freely, I could now give to myself. I no longer identify as a *domestic violence victim*—I think *survivor*, or *fighter*, or *courageous woman* fits best. But ultimately, I think I like just being *Chloe.*

Sometimes, a revolution begins internally, a shaping of our own world and a change within ourselves. Truthfully, it was the transformation inside of me that saved my life and influenced how I now interacted with the world. I think there's a beautiful importance to that; the ability to view the world around us more authentically, from a place of love and acceptance for all the wonderful, wicked, and tragic events that happen to us. I will never be the girl I was before that relationship, and maybe that's okay, because the woman I am now, is the woman I was always destined to be.

I remember as a little girl, I always dreamed
Of the horse and carriage, the white picket fence,
And the prince charming that saves me from calamity.
But those fairy tales aren't real,
Because I am not a damsel in distress.

I am a devoted mother, a loving daughter, a soon-to be
Aunty and a forgiving friend.
I am atoms and molecules, stars, and constellations,
Forgotten galaxies and a soul birthed by the universe
To wander and plant my roots in the Earth.

If the only legacy I leave behind is that
I loved too passionately and unconditionally,
Despite the marks other's left on my tender heart.
Then just like the resilient oak tree,

I will stand tall in the face of adversity,
And love myself in my entirety.

This poem tells an honest fairy tale of a true heroine,
Who did not need saving, because she found herself.

EARTH-SHIFTERS

The Matriarch and I

Samuel A. Healy

I don't see her at first. The park guide puts his finger to his lips and gently points to a clump of acacias that are green from September rain. On my left, a middle-aged woman among the group raises her obnoxious camera, her lips pursed and her fingers slightly shaking. He is on my right, as usual. And his hand grips securely to my thigh. As always. It's a funny thing, that. I usually can tell what mood he's in by the way he holds me. Caressing or clutching? Playful or piercing? Sometimes it switches between many, and then it isn't so easy to predict. His eyes are hidden behind Ray-Bans, but I know he keeps me in their periphery, even as he faces towards the grey-eared boulder that emerges from behind the acacias. The small group sighs. She's immense and ancient.

'The Matriarch. She's almost seventy,' our park guide whispers. She passes by our seemingly too small, packed jeep quite closely— her family, her people, behind her. Many are almost as big; their ears flap in the warm morning, glowing orange when they pass in front of the sun. There are babies too, they flit about in the curious innocence of the young that transcends species.

'They're all going to the watering hole,' says our park guide. 'That's what they do this time of morning. The Matriarch knows the way. She can remember the way to a watering hole 200 kilometres away.'

That's when it starts. We shouldn't be here to see it, not really. It's one of those freakish things that occur in the natural world that nods to the primeval, before the raising of pyramids and the grainfields of civilisation. The Matriarch extends her long, grey reach and tenderly strokes each member of her family. In those touches there is something, and it rises and smacks us in the face as we sit by in the dusty jeep.

'She's saying goodbye,' our park guide murmurs.

'Goodbye? Why is it saying goodbye?' The woman on my left doesn't trouble to keep as quiet.

'She's old. She knows she's dying.' There's constraint in his voice. The Matriarch walks among the rest of them: her sisters, her daughters, and their daughters, and their daughters. She touches them. She traces their bodies and locks them in her brown gaze. I feel like looking away. To my left, the woman is crying silently while snapping photos. To my right, his hand caresses my leg. No one speaks. She finishes her petting and moves to the second largest in the group. They face each other, staring … The camera keeps clicking. The Matriarch breaks away first and moves right past our jeep, ambling down the road. She doesn't turn around. The family watch The Matriarch as she rounds a corner, skirting a giant baobab. They stay still for several more minutes until the now largest positions herself in the lead. With whispers of brush, the boulders move back into the scrub as quickly as they'd come.

We're back at camp by late afternoon. There's a fire and it seems like a patch of sunset has fallen to Earth to dance for our small group, adorned with glowing wood and squeezed by blackening rocks. Dinner is of little note. Lights out early. Back in the tent. He holds me down and climbs on top of me and I'm looking up through the flap to the luminous moon and I think of lonely walks in the night and of watering holes 200 kilometres away.

It's still dark and I can't see the state of the dusty road. The jeep jumps with every new bump but doesn't buckle. The camp is far behind me now. I had crept out, after he was finished and sleeping. Our park guide left his keys in the ignition, saying 'Who's going to steal it? Zebras can't drive.' Perhaps not quite an invitation to steal, but I decided it was some sort of sign. I wonder how far an elephant can travel in a day and night. I should have asked him. All I have is the road pointing me along. The bumps that shake the jeep drum to the chorus of the bush at night. Doubts fly at me in the dark, like moths that get caught in the trap of the jeep's glare only to be squashed. Ping, ping, ping: the maddening noise of lives extinguished, and I'm bouncing and trying hard not to veer off. I think I'm in a dream, far from the tent, far from waking.

It's dawn and there she is … I kill the ignition and wait for her acknowledgement, perhaps a turned head or flick of those enormous ears. I get nothing but tired and assured plodding into the rising sun. I step out, boots crunching the fine gravel. She's up ahead, no more than 100 metres. I start off gently. I don't want to sneak up on her. With each closer step I can feel her striding across the dirt. Her footsteps reverberate and gently rumble through the ground like thunder that roils in the distance. Finally, I sidle up next to her, but on the other side of the road, out of reach (or so I hoped). She stops now and turns her head. The chorus of cicadas and hornbills permeate the morning. We're testing each other, her languid brown eyes meeting my blue. A human. Perhaps I'm a disappointment. Or an enemy. She snorts and tilts her head towards the east as if to say, *come on then*. I hesitate. She tilts her head again. I approach her gently. Brown eyes are now trained ahead. We resume her journey.

Aside from her size, I'd say the most striking thing about the Matriarch is her smell. It's punchy and not necessarily bad. Bovine but wild, it contrasts sharply with the new green scent of saplings that had sprung up from the rain. I can't say if my smell intrigues her. Her eyes flick to me by her side every so often, but other than that she keeps on her resolute march.

The morning birds are singing in earnest now, and the sun promises a hot day. I realise that I'd left my water bottle in the jeep, but that doesn't seem important. My world has shrunk to focus on the walk, the slow melodious wake of one step in front of the other. My feet keep in time with hers, feeling the vibrations through the ground.

It's an understanding born from a decades long relationship. The earth embraces each of her footfalls, the muscles in her legs—though screaming from pain and age—transcends sinew and flesh and flows into the dirt. Dirt which seems to push back up, supporting the great body above it. It's a dance, I realise, a ritual that was established before the invented trappings of time.

Early morning stretches into noon and it's hot—hotter than yesterday. I'm sweating and flies swarm about my face, my mouth, my eyes. She halts and I'm brought back into the presence of heat and sore feet. I watch her and I'm sad because I still don't trust her, not fully. She reaches over to a strapping bushwillow and tugs, and the branch comes free with a crack. She inspects it closely before holding it out to me. I take it, brushing her trunk with my hand. It's rough and hairy, but warm. Another crack. She holds her own branch high and begins swishing it around, disturbing the cloud of insects sucking around her eyes. Eyes that now look at me and say *this is how you do it* and I follow suit. It's quite effective. I hold it higher and block out the merciless sun, and it wasn't until I did that that I realised how much I needed the shade.

Perhaps a bit later I start to see things in the trees. Not predators, though they might have been there. The bush has this way of hiding things. You could pass an entire troop of baboons and never know until they start chittering after you've moved on. Under the shade of my branch gift, I peer into the greenery as we walk, side-by-side. At first it was shadows, a purposeful sneaking here, unmistakable movement there. I think of mirages at first, of the shimmering haze that accompanies all eyes that look over this part of the world. When the shapes became recognisable, I put the mirage theory aside. Elephants. Their likeness is in the trees; the boles their legs, bark their skin. Stretching branches are their trunks, and green leaves their eyes. My companion notices them too. She raises her trunk at each one that we pass by. They reach out to her too, their trumpeting twined into the sound of scraping branches and whistling stalks. Her ears flap at them, her eyes watch every form. *I am coming*. One among the trees is smaller than the others. It flits repeatedly among the lower shrubs … She sees him but doesn't slow. *One who was lost too soon; I am coming*. I say it out loud into the heat and I don't know whose voice it is. I'm lost in the haze but my feet keep plodding on, on to glory and home.

Noon breathes into late afternoon when he appears. There's no warning. My companion simply stops, and I look up from my feet towards the long way to go. The hyena is grinning, a mad laugh already on the edge of his lolling tongue. His dark eyes seem to flash as he pads carefully towards us.

We watch his approach. I look to the Matriarch. There's a practised calmness about her, though her eyes are brown burning coals. She examines him and he watches her, and me. I'm shaking, the bushwillow branch trembles in my hand. Then comes the shackle-raising laugh and snap of ridiculous teeth and I wish that I was by the jeep or back in the tent or anywhere else. He paces from side to side in front of us.

I want to go back, I need to go back, and I slowly retreat. There's a sudden warm firmness that holds me in place. A trunk. Her trunk. I look up to see her looking at me. *There is only ahead.* She doesn't push me, not exactly, but there's a new pressure, a wilfulness for me to take the first step. He laughs again, louder this time, and I drop the branch. *There is only ahead.* He's smiling. I agonisingly tear my foot from the ground and it hovers. Behind me, I sense the Matriarch do the same. *There is only ahead.* Our feet come down together. His laugh cuts off and turns into a growl. A second step. He snarls now, I see his saliva pooling beneath him. A third step. She still supports me, steady. We take another step. He begins to whine.

I see him now for what he is: desperate, emaciated, alone. Insane. He whimpers again. My companion trumpets and it's a war cry. It billows outwards and strikes him as I take one more step. The hyena screams and scampers off, tail between his legs. I sway but don't fall. She's holding me in place.

Sunset. The Matriarch suddenly moves off the road, turning into the scrub. I follow, by her side, my arm brushing against her front leg. There's no clear path but she picks her way through the vegetation with the same angular familiarity of the road. Twilight hastens away the heat of the day, and shadows begin to envelop us. We've been traversing this way for almost an hour when, pushing past a lush mopane tree, we reach the graveyard. It's a clearing scattered with those that had long come before; they're thrown into sharp clarity from the blood red light. There's a spot just for her, beside her mother, and she finally succumbs to her body's ravaged demands of peace. I sit by her in the growing twilight. Her trunk finds me and rests in my lap, the bristle of her hair pokes the skin through my shorts. Brown eyes, fringed with wet lashes, hold my gaze. I tell her I'll be right here until you go. *I know.*

I leave with the dawn. My head swims with tiredness, my throat begs for water. I find my way back to the road and begin the journey to the jeep. Despite the weariness, there's a vigour, a renewal that is both alien and resolute. It's windy this morning. The trees embrace the wind and whisper. I look up. I knew he'd come for me, and sure enough there he is. Walking in that way I know too well. I stop. He increases his gait, his eyes hidden by shadow and his flexing limbs ready. I see his grimace; I see his tongue curled ready to laugh or scream. He halts and beckons me. I take one step and the earth shakes.

How to Care for Flowers

Eleanor List

In the weeks following the heartbreak, you blame him. It's easier that way.

You dash home, heels colliding with the concrete path. The Friday summary meeting ran overtime. Again. No one says it, but you know it's all thanks to the big bosses. Always turning up late from their lunch, crumbs still speckling their heavy moustaches. Apparently, croissants are more important than running a tech company.

It's alright, though. Their arrogance won't impact anyone else. Because you won't let it. Despite your three-inch heels, you pelt towards home where a quick makeup and outfit change awaits. You'll show up to dinner with the girls as expected—on time and orderly.

And then you stop, halted by a strange sight. The flower has wilted, slumped on the steps leading into your apartment. You sit down beside the tear-stained Daisy and wrap an arm around her. Her eyes are downcast, so she doesn't notice you staring. In all the years, Daisy's never been like this. Not even when you were kids and her dad screamed at you two for cracking the TV.

She cries on your shoulder for a while, literally. You don't ask questions. Not yet. The words only come after the storm passes.

And finally, the rain softens to a light sprinkle, and Daisy can breathe out the words that kill her.

'I cheated on Alex.'

Shock holds your tongue. It's no secret Alex had been messing with her heart, but you didn't expect her to mess with his. Not like this. He is—was—the beloved boyfriend, star of her every Instagram post and conversation.

'It just happened,' she sobs. 'He's away all the time, and when he actually comes home, Alex is just so mean. I know he's under a lot of pressure ... There's just this nice guy from work who always looks at me … Alex made me feel like he—'

Another wave of sobs envelops her. Although you hold still, your internal being shudders, just like the trembling Daisy. Internally, you fracture, torn between a rigid moral compass and the Daisy you know. She'd never do that. But she did, so you can only assume Alex really drove her crazy.

Despite this internal conflict, you tell Daisy everything she needs to hear while still holding her tight. A few snotty sniffs later and Daisy wobbles to her feet. She waves without looking back and stumbles to her lemony yellow car—to go nowhere.

She'll just zombie around for a few weeks, processing the whole deal. But then, after a little while, she'll bloom. Just like you.

Bloody cheats—well, bloody men. You can't say you like anyone cheating on anyone, ever. But no matter who actually committed the action, it's always men at the centre of cheating. The key offenders. Perpetrators who make your world spin. The world you've fought every day for the past eight and a half weeks to be rid of. But it's not as though you're counting. Not anymore. You're over it.

But the girls aren't. Not by a long shot. At dinner, their explosive anger at Ren thankfully smothers any questions about Daisy's absence.

'Girl, I am so sorry,' Lila scoffs. 'Ugh. Men.'

'Can we just round up all the cheats and cut off their balls?' Mel adds delicately.

'They're all just stupid. You know they don't care about real relationships, right? Only getting laid,' Riley laughs.

'Or they just get mad when you're not home to cook dinner. I'm sorry. Am I not allowed to work late?'

You sip your champagne while the girls cackle, hyenas feasting upon scraps of gossip. Ravenous, and totally unfazed by the number of onlookers staring at the loud females in the corner of the restaurant.

'Sadly, I can confirm it's true. Ren used to complain whenever I worked late.'

You take another sip.

As the night darkens and the champagne takes hold, your attention flickers. Your gaze is drawn to the vibrant décor on the table. From a distance, the scarlet flowers look real, displaying an Insta-worthy vibrance and intensity. But when you lean in, it's apparent how fake they are, with tacky green leaves and fabric petals. Plastic replicas of the real thing, only discernibly fake when you get close. Perhaps that was your first clue.

After dinner, the girls walk you home. They leave you by the front door forever stained by Daisy's tears. Inside, you slip off your heels, placing them on the rack just beside the door. It's far cleaner here since Ren left. He never understood the importance of keeping things neat and tidy.

It's late, but not too late. And without Ren, you can get good sleep. There's no more debate about the purpose of beds and the night. You don't have to convince him the bed is not a place to sow your seed. Instead, it's for a good night's sleep so you're productive and well rested the following day. Planting seeds is too much work at such a late hour.

Night evaporates into morning. You don sportswear, a floral crop top and shorts that cling to your body like a second skin. Other than the soft sigh of your breath as you move from one yoga pose to the next, the apartment is still. It's possible to hear your own thoughts. No longer is Saturday morning broken by those hideous horror movies Ren would make you to stay in bed and watch. No, you're free now. Free to attain the life you've always dreamed of.

A bowl of granola for breakfast and the morning routine is over. You move through your daily prep with ease, into makeup and then wardrobe, like an actor preparing for a big show. Except you won't be performing for anyone—or so you thought.

Someone knocks. Two sharp taps followed by an earthy, 'Hello?' You hastily drag the brush through your hair and smooth down your top.

The faded front door looms just beyond you. It's not Ren, you assure yourself. The voice was too deep. You'd surely recognise his voice. Plus, he wouldn't dare to show his face back here, would he? Not after you kicked him out. Unless he wants back the things he forgot, things you'd imagined burning.

Unless he wants you back.

The door opens, revealing the bright morning, and someone on the doorstep. It's not Ren, but you're not any happier to see this man.

'Alex.'

He bares his teeth in what is supposed to be a smile. 'Hey.'

'You're at my house.' It's not a question.

'Yeah … Is Dee here?' Alex shifts his weight onto the other heavily-booted foot.

'She doesn't like being called that.'

'Doesn't she?'

You wait for the punchline, the part where Alex laughs at his terrible sarcasm. But it doesn't come. He just keeps staring.

'No. She doesn't like being called Dee.'

Alex's eyes wander over the door mat, conveniently avoiding your gaze.

'What do you want?'

'Is D—Daisy here?'

'Why?'

'Because she won't answer my calls and I'm worried.'

'You two broke up.'

'Yeah, but …'

You put one hand on each hip, a cowgirl ready for the final showdown.

'But what? She cheated on you, Alex. Daisy clearly doesn't want to be with you anymore.'

Alex bites his lip.

You sigh. 'She cheated, Alex.'

He looks up at you. His nervousness has been replaced by something else. Something a whole lot sadder.

Something he needs to say.

You shut the door. His words echo through your mind, metaphorical fragments of something you don't quite understand. Like the feeling that has overcome you. Maybe you're just feeling sorry for Daisy and her failed relationship. Maybe you're guilty you haven't texted her since yesterday. But perhaps there's more to it than that.

The icy shower splashes onto your skin. But you stay there, freezing out the pain or whatever it is for one, two, three, four, five seconds too many. Your skin cries out, forcing you to the other end of the spectrum. Hot water splutters down, replacing the cold with a warm burn. Slightly less uncomfortable. Temperature-wise, that is.

Thorny memories prickle your skin. You take the exfoliating brush and scrub, scouring off the sensation of him. The feeling of his hands down your back, washing off the soap. The skin of his body pressed against yours. Lips to neck.

Out of the shower, you stand before the bed, naked. A strange fatigue overwhelms you. The bed beckons, promising rest, relief from the alien illness infecting your soul.

But you stay fast, unable to move. Suddenly, the bed morphs into another you know too well and you're forced to relive the moment, as if for the first time …

Pulling open the door to Ren's place and tiptoeing up the stairs. Unlocking the door as quickly and softly as you can. Dashing across the kitchen and into the bedroom. Smiling as you bask in the glory of this moment. Tingling with excitement as you prepare to surprise Ren. Pushing open the door to an even bigger surprise. Gaping as you see two bodies sleeping where there should have only been one, eagerly awaiting your return from your four-week work trip.

They slept together. In both the figurative and literal sense. And it's the latter part that makes you sick now. Maybe you could have dealt with a random hook up. Even laughed about it, in the future when the pain had faded to a dull ache.

No, what happened is worse—he let her sleep beside him, in the place reserved only for you.

The weight of reality wilts you to your knees. You thought the breakup was the revolution. Condemnation of his actions—revolutionary, a denial of the patriarchy still plaguing a world professing modernity. They praised you, even worshipped your shunning of him. After all, you are a woman and hell forbid any man do you wrong. After centuries of oppression, you could take back your power. You could banish the dirty man who didn't deserve you, a woman, a lady. A rose.

But you can't just shrug off what Alex just said. Even if you wanted to. His words absorbed, and now they're all you hear.

She said she was lonely ... thought I hated her ... just wanted my time.

You take your phone. Each hand shakes but you're willing to risk it slipping and smashing on the floor. This is worth it. You open contacts and scroll to 'R'. But his number isn't there anymore. It's empty. Save for Riley's number, but she's not the one you need to message. She's not the one you overlooked. Not the person you forgot to love. Until now.

The screen scrolls to 'B'. 'Bastard'. Of course, you'll change that in a minute. But right now, you have more important things to do. To say.

You type the three words and stare at the screen, your finger hovering above the send button. Indecision grips you. Maybe you're being crazy. The girls would call you crazy. He's crazy.

But then again, so are they. And Alex. You're all a bit crazy in the end.

You hit send and sit back. The words slip from your lips, a silent whisper to yourself.

I forgive you.

It's small, but flowers grow from the tiniest of seeds. It's how you care for them that counts.

Garden of Corpses

Nicole Schmidt

I wish I was home with my garden of corpses. The ghosts of the ones I killed gave me more comfort than the steel bars around me ever could. I am in no position to complain, to shout my innocence—I'm not innocent, I'm a murderer.

I never meant to kill the first one, and the ones that soon followed were just collateral damage. I tried to not get caught, to stop the inevitable, but I guess it's called 'inevitable' for a reason.

I am by no means a serial killer—no matter what everyone thinks, I know who I am.

I am simply an average, run-of-the-mill murderer.

But I doubt anyone cares about what my thoughts are. They see me as a monster, and no matter which way I spin the events that led me here, I understand why they believe me as such.

I killed the man I loved, the only man I have ever loved. But I had serious doubts that the police would ever believe that he walked into my knife five times. So I just buried him in my backyard.

What followed after his death was a series of severely misfortunate events, of lies, blood, dirt and death. In my honest opinion, I think the dirt was the worst part, *that shit got everywhere.*

But no matter how much of a 'monster' people believe me to be, I am still a human. Humans have emotions. Such emotions of betrayal, anger, guilt, fear and self-preservation led me to do the things I did. They led me here.

Betrayal. To be honest, it's not a very nice emotion, I have come to experience. It was simply the first domino of many that led me to this place.

My fiancé, Mark, had come to my house for a romantic dinner. I made him his favourite meal, we ate, shared funny moments of our day, and as I stood to clean up the table, he told me he cheated with a girl he met at his gym and now she's pregnant.

Of all the times to tell your fiancé that you knocked up another woman, he decides the best time is right after he's finished his meal. *Unbelievable.*

I laughed, thinking he was telling a bad joke, then I realised he wasn't laughing with me. And so I cried.

Anger. I should have learnt how to deal with my anger when I was a child, maybe then I could have controlled myself. The pain of betrayal had consumed me and the next thing I knew, the man I loved, the man I planned to spend the rest of my life with, was lying on the kitchen tiles in a pool of his own blood and I was standing over him holding a bloodied knife.

Guilt. One of the suckiest emotions in my opinion. Taking someone's life isn't easy, a realisation I have become all to acquainted with, but the guilt of taking his life made me turn the bloodied knife to myself. But before I could take that fatal step, I stopped myself.

Fear. The most unpopular emotion, one I know all too well.

All I kept thinking of was, *what would happen to me after this? Will I go to jail? Will everyone I love, hate me? Will I be branded as a jealous woman who killed the man she loved so he wouldn't leave her? What will happen to me?*

So, I stripped him of his clothes—*which, let me just say, stripping him when he's dead is nowhere near as fun as stripping him when he's alive*—and buried him in my backyard.

I'm not a complete monster, I planted over a dozen daisies over his grave and decorated it with some cute and humorous gnomes. He never did like gnomes but I'm petty. If I'm being honest, it's one of my less attractive qualities. *Pettiness and homicidal rage.*

And the rest was just acting out in *Self-Preservation.*

After killing him, I dressed in his clothes, waved to my neighbour Mr Jones when he left his home for his night shift, drove his truck with his hoodie securely over my head for any possible traffic cameras and ditched his truck just outside of town near a bus station—leaving his phone and wallet inside.

I thought of everything that would make it look like he left my house alive, except for how I would get home. I won't go into much detail, mainly because it's quite gross, but it involved following a band of drunk football fans into a men's bathroom and stealing one of the drunk's sweaty, alcohol-stained football jersey, leaving Mark's hoodie on the bathroom sink to be stolen, and fleeing with the drunks.

I stayed with them until they reached an area without camera surveillance and made a run for it into the woods, returning home at the time I usually return from my early morning jogs.

Over the next few days, I called his phone and sent him text messages asking him how he is and where he was, and because I didn't hear from him, and neither had all of his friends, I did what any concerned fiancé would do—I went to the police to file a missing person report.

What I wasn't expecting was his heavily pregnant mistress to have arrived just 20 minutes prior. Her being there wasn't only just an inconvenience in regards to my story of being the 'innocent fiancé who doesn't know the love of her life cheated on her and is now having a love child with some brunette cow he met at the gym', but it also means that he lied to me about when he cheated on me. *Which was a real asshole move.*

However, having her there ended up working in my advantage, I just had to play the victim of infidelity—which I was. I didn't even have to fake tears of being betrayed, I just let out all the emotions I was feeling when the jerk first told me he had cheated and was leaving me for some fitness instructor. Which, again, he told me right after he finished the dinner I spent hours making him. *The Prick.*

And when the detectives started questioning me, all I could say was, *'here I am, panicked out of my freaking mind because he hasn't answered a single one of my texts or calls in the past two days and when I go to the police because I'm worried he might be truly missing, I find out he has a side woman who's pregnant, and here I am with his stupid ring on my finger like some clueless idiot.'*

Best performance of my life. *Hell, for a split second I believed me.* I cried so much the detectives questioning me had to go out and bring me a new box of tissues.

Thankfully, they didn't put me through much questioning after that. However, what I learnt after my award-winning performance lifted some of the guilt.

As it turns out, Mark told Stacy, *the pregnant, fiancé-stealing, brunette cow*, that he would come clean to me that night (which he did), collect his stuff and return to his flat (which he didn't). They were to meet the next day to have lunch and discuss how they would tell their families and how they would deal with the aftermath of said families' reaction to the news.

At first, I thought having the mistress come to the police station would be my downfall, but her story, at least the start of it, had worked in my favour. I told the police that Mark came to my house, we had a lovely romantic dinner, and he left because he had to go to work early the next morning. Which was confirmed by the neighbours seeing him leave and drive off in his truck. *The one time I'm thankful I inherited my father's build.*

It took nearly a week of searching but the police found his truck, ditched outside of town where I left it. They think he chickened out of telling me of his infidelity, didn't want the responsibility of being a father and ditched town the first chance he got.

That story would have satisfied any lazy cop wanting to wrap up a case, but not Detective Harris. Detective Jean Harris was relentless in her pursuit of truth and justice. She spent her days asking around town about me, my character, and my relationship with Mark. *She was a pain in the arse.*

And as it turns out, Stacy wasn't the only woman Mark had an affair with. *For a woman all about truth and justice, she was a real hypocrite.*

So I poisoned her with an apple pie.

I killed her because she was a nuisance, not because she was Mark's other mistress. I'm not *that* petty. However, there was no conceivable way that the police, a judge, or a jury could ever believe I poisoned her by mistake. So I buried her out in the yard. Planted a hedge above her grave that I had planned to grow big enough to shape into an elephant. I dealt with her car like I did Mark's and hoped her going missing would all be swept under the rug.

I was wrong.

More detectives started showing up, more questions were asked and eventually by the time the hedge had grown big enough to be shaped into an elephant, I had several bodies buried in my backyard. Each grave was beautifully decorated and my garden was slowly becoming a masterpiece—if you ignore the rotting corpses below.

Ironically, it was the beauty of my garden that was my downfall.

My neighbour, Mrs Jenkins, started going green with how nicely my garden was starting to look compared to hers, and she thought she might have a peek over the fence to see what I was hiding. Which, unfortunately for me, was when I was burying Mr Humphries. *Of all the timing.*

Mr Humphries wasn't a detective or the police like the others, he was Stacy's grandfather who decided to have me looked into. Out of the entire town, Mark's parents included, Mr Humphries held the most doubts that Mark would leave Stacy and their baby, which she had three months prior and named Macey. *Stacey and Macey, what a pair.*

Anyway, Mrs Jenkins saw me drag his plastic-bag-wrapped body towards the newly dug hole and called the police.

To be honest, having several dozen police officers surround my house and a helicopter flying above seemed like a bit of an overkill. *So I killed a couple of people and buried their bodies in my backyard; I'm not a psychopath.* I decorated their graves with pretty flowers and humorous gnomes, that's more than you can get at some creepy, downright depressive cemetery.

I was then taken into custody, put in jail and denied bail. My trial lasted quite some time; the amount of evidence stacked against me filled up half the bloody court room. And the media wasn't very nice. I prefer my name, Grace Scott, but as far as serial killer names go, 'The Gardener' wasn't so bad.

What I hated the most were the looks of fear, hatred and pure disgust I received from the public. That didn't seem fair. They were acting like I enjoyed killing those people. For the record, I didn't. Their deaths were as inconvenient for me as they were horrible for them.

The amount of blood I had to keep washing off my hands was a hassle, and the bleach I used to clean the bloodstains seemed to have burnt out any smelling senses I had in my nose.

If only one good thing came out of all of this, it was that my backyard had never looked better. Well, that was until it was dug up to retrieve the bodies.

But before that, it looked spectacular.

Two Become Three

Anna Huang

The pollen blizzard whisked the floral dresses in the backyard. The day was filled with greenery and an array of bright colours. Women conversed and nibbled on finger foods, sipping champagne. Laughter was in the air and everyone seemed content. The curiosity on everyone's mind kept the excitement for the day. A tradition of celebrating the life of a soon-to-be newborn. Clusters of small groups seemed to merge into larger numbers. My stomach churned with anxious knots. The staged small talk and niceties were alien to me; there was no way I would fit in. Adjusting the lens, I directed my camera to faces with smiles. I was emotionally checked out; I had to be. The buzz of chittering guests threatened to heighten my anxiety. It's ironic, my task was supposedly easy. Take millions of photos, collect my pay cheque, go home. But I trembled when the ladies interacted with me through their stylised smiles; asking questions about my profession. They're strangers to me. Words jumbled in my head; sentences crumbled the minute they left my mouth. I was overwhelmed by the judgement preceding me. My palms grew clammy, my chest tightened. Heat flushed my cheeks. Eyes prickled my skin like spikes. I hid behind the beaming sun; hoping anyone who noticed would blame the spring climate. Social anxiety strikes again. My mission was clear: wear a brave face and conquer the role I had to play. I'm here to take photos, that's all.

I felt invasive weaving through the groups of women taking photos. They'd stop and reposition posing whenever they saw me. So much happening. I'd make my way past the tables of brightly wrapped gifts. Blues, pinks, yellows displayed in every direction I looked. Tables of gifts, tables of food, chairs assembled across the green grass decorated excessively with flowers. And ribbon, so much ribbon!

I knew the next few hours would be excruciating because I wasn't in the mood to be brave. Too many distractions. My mood didn't resemble the vibrant décor. How could I live up to the expectation of being good at my job? How could I blend in without drawing attention?

'Thank you for turning up on such short notice,' said the pregnant girl who waddled closer to touch my shoulder. 'The photographer who I originally organised had to cancel last minute.'

'No worries. I'm glad you came across my social media page,' I replied. 'I have such a small following. Wasn't sure if my page was getting any views.'

'I was impressed by your work! Your profile picture is artistic. We wanted someone with experience to do the job,' said the pregnant lady in her mid-twenties. 'Just take as many photos as you can! It's my first, so I want this day to be really special, and help yourself to food and drink, it'll be a busy few hours for you, you'll need your strength,' she hinted. 'By the way, my name's Abbie, sing out if you need anything.'

A woman walked onto the patio and my breath hitched. I was mesmerised by her beauty. Her face was so delicate and angel-like. I caught myself staring, but I couldn't take my gaze off her. My heart swelled with magnetic attraction.

'Photo?' I interrupted the conversation between her and the host.

'Yes, of course,' she said as she smiled and wrapped one arm around Abbie's round torso. Her smile was sensational and she smelt divine. Deliciously plump yet petite. Her high cheek bones and full lips had me hypnotised. I wasn't on her radar. It was like I left my state of fear momentarily and embodied a bubble of confidence to be close to her.

'Gather around ladies it's time,' announced the boisterous one. Everyone crowded around Abbie who sat on a white chair. Presents in boxes and bags were scattered around her pedicured feet. Beside the perfectly pruned garden; I peered beyond the outskirts of the crowd and nestled into the rose bush. I held my camera and counted down: one, two and clicked on three. I found my eyes wandering onto the beautiful angel-like woman. Gobsmacked by her effortless radiance. Captivated by her beauty all over again. She handed the gifts to the pregnant star of the day. Colourful patterned paper was shredded to reveal baby gifts. Everyone was excitable about what presents she received. Screaming and clapping. Hype around each gift seemed so unnecessary. I was exhausted just by watching.

'Ladies we have a breast pump!' said the middle-aged brunette in a psychedelic wrap dress. Her black pointy shoes with stilettos sunk into the grass like quicksand. I could see her agitation; constantly lifting her shoes that swallowed her heels. Her facial expressions were priceless. I found it amusing. 'That'll be handy when Mumma needs a wine or two. You can pump and dump, that's what I did.' Her joking words made everyone giggle, aside from me. That woman's opinionated and bossy, I thought. She was the only person who didn't adhere to the floral dress theme. She stood out like a sore thumb in all the group photos. 'Excuse me, you with the camera, can you get some shots of me and my niece?' the rude lady asked as she lopsidedly adjusted her balance, signalling to me with desperation. The stilettos dug mini ditches in the grass unapologetically. She held the breast pump on display and grinned.

'One … Two …' and I clicked on three.

I had to get a moment alone with this magical creature. I had never been so attracted to another human before. The way she moved, her smile, her voice, her aura was beyond anything I've ever seen. I briskly walked to the eatery table where Monique was standing and assembling camembert with slices of kabana. I greeted her with a nervous smile. Chunky bits of fruit bounced around the punch bowl as I attempted to pour myself a drink. My hands shook frantically and I missed the cup; the contents splashed onto the food. The raspberry-coloured beverage soaked the displayed food offerings. 'Here let me help you.' she approached me with several napkins. 'I'm Monique,' she gave me a warm smile as she introduced herself officially and handed me some napkins. My cheeks matched the hot pink napkins she used to clean up the mess. I dabbed my shirt in disarray. 'Sorry about the spillage, I'm really sorry you have to clean it, let me help you,' I said as my clumsy hands knocked the cup again spilling the remainder. The napkins danced from my shirt to the uninviting wet table. Another one bites the dust. My uncoordinated tendencies reaching a peak today. Joyful embarrassment had struck again.

I was overly apologetic. I must've repeated myself two to three times. I completely messed up my chance of impressing her.

'It's ok, don't worry about the soggy food—extra flavour!' she giggled. 'We have plenty more, your shirt is soaked though, let me get you more napkins,' said the charming blonde. 'I'm the partner of Abbie, who hired you today. We're so glad you could photograph our baby shower on such short notice.'

My face dropped; I had misinterpreted the situation. Now any chance I had with her had flown out the window. My chances of pursuing something romantically with her disintegrated like a sandcastle on the beach. Washed over and flattened again after a wave of reality crashed over my soul. Turns out I totally misconstrued the situation. Firstly, she wasn't straight and secondly, she was in a long-term relationship. Thirdly, I was a complete idiot. Unaccomplished by my hot pursuit of inevitable failure. Baffled by misconception. I was head over heels from the first encounter, but nothing progressed as per usual. I grabbed the closest beverage, a beer, and skulled it, willing away my embarrassment. It took the edge off my feelings of stupidity. And to my discretion, I excused myself from the crowd for a bathroom break.

I slipped into the bathroom, avoiding eye contact with anyone who passed. The mirror reflected the stain on my shirt as I melted deeper into a slushy of emotions. 'Idiot,' I whispered to myself. Artificial lavender soap stung my nostrils. The party was revving up; somebody put on some music. I still had four hours to go. I patted water on the pink juice stain that had saturated my white shirt. Unbelievable, I made it worse. I could die of embarrassment. I had to let go of what I couldn't control and get on with it essentially. Stained, wet shirt and emotional damage intertwined into today's business transaction. Clouded misjudgement and lusty motives had to be far removed from my radar. I brushed it off and continued with my job.

Capturing the essence of this so-called special occasion. Only speaking when I was spoken to trying not to woo girls by starting small conversations. No more friendly smiles that resulted in spillages. I had already hit my daily quota for self-destruction.

'Can I have a quick word with you?' Monique asked as she softly grabbed my hand and lead me away from taking a candid group photo.

'Do you have a thing for me?' said Monique firmly.

'What do you mean? I'm not sure what you're saying,' I replied in utter confusion.

'I keep catching you staring at me, do you fancy me or something?'

'No, not at all. I didn't mean to give you that impression,' I lied, shocked at her openness. My sweat glands worked in overdrive as a gust of wind sliced through the air, stinging my sweaty face. The floral dresses were rapidly whipped in its gusty motion. I burrowed my chin deep into the scarf.

'You're very handsome; both my partner and I agreed. We were talking about you, you're brilliant at photography,' she complimented in a seductive tone, caressing my hand.

'I don't mean to be rude but what time is it?' I mumbled taking the opportunity to change the subject. It was like an alternate universe. Was this moment real? Is she flirting with me? Me?

I withdrew my phone from my back pocket and indicated my urgency to know the time. I pointed at it like a mime character. 'Excuse me, I have to make a quick phone call.' I felt uneasy in this conversation. My underarms perspired profusely. I pretended to dial my phone. Typing an unknown number to seem like I was intentionally making a phone call. I'm in trouble. I disrespected her, didn't I? Did I? Why did I let lust drive me? I should've stayed strictly professional—what am I thinking? I was an animal, controlled by instincts. My attraction consumed me like a scrub in a fire. Building small at first, a flint of a sideways glance roaring into an unstoppable wildfire. Primal sexual heat was building throughout my body. She is a goddess among mortal men; I've never felt this way before. A desire I had never experienced before today. Was she having a go? Or was she seducing me? Abbie signalled to Monique with a small wave and smirk, they both started to walk towards me. My heart beat with each step. My chest heaved in anticipation; soundless words formed in my mouth. I freaked out and my face lost colouration, translucent like a ghost. My body went stiff, and my breathing had become laborious as my stomach twisted in knots.

'Take another photo of us, will you?' said Abbie as she clutched Monique's two hands and locked lips with her passionately. I placed my phone back into my pocket and shakingly held my camera up to eye level and adjusted the lens. I counted down: one, two and clicked on three.

'When all the guests leave, will you stay back after the parties over?' winked Monique. And they giggled.

Watery Reflections

Jade Heugh-Field

Sunrays beam up at me off the glass-coated seascape below. Orange-tinged sandstone tickles the backs of my thighs. Dangling limply, my lower legs occasionally hit the rocky cliff face. The powdery deposit sticks to my bare skin, ablaze in the humidity of summer. My eyes scale down the rugged coastal-scape and fixate on feet dancing. They dance to the rhythm of slow surging waves across carefully crafted longboards. Criss-cross, hang.

I stare at a small black and white photo. I feel the sun boring into my skin, its warmth holding me as I am transported back.

My small feet squirm in the squeaky white sand—the orange globe above responsible for the discomfort. I fumble agitatedly with my mask and snorkel, struggling to get every strand of bleached blonde hair out of the way. I visualise submerging my small body into the crystal-clear water surrounding Lady Elliot Island, the colours of the world below captivating me. Before I can live out my 10-year-old mermaid dreams, a familiar voice jolts me out of my blissful trance.

'Do you think you get to just do what you want, do you?' Steve blasts, walking hastily down the beach, face tight.

'I asked Mum if I could go for a snorkel. She said it was ok if I don't go past where the ledge drops off,' I recite matter-of-factly.

'It wasn't a question. You know it. Do you think I'm stupid or something?'

'No, I'm sorry.'

'Don't apologise. It means nothing. I just can't comprehend how selfish you are. You're not on holiday with your dad. You can teach Elly to catch and pass a ball so I can enjoy my holiday too. If and when she has learned, you can go for your snorkel.'

No, I'm not. I'm not on holiday at all.

Elly pops out from behind Steve's short, top-heavy build. I laugh internally, careful to remain as emotionless on the outside as possible. The netball she holds comes a very close second in size to her six-year-old self. *I can't be angry with her. It isn't her fault her father is mean.*

We don't move, just stand, feet planted firmly in the sand, ignoring the burning sensation shooting up through our small feet. We stare after Steve as he retreats to the cabin veranda. Elly gives me the ball.

I suppose the only way to learn is to try and catch the ball. 'Elly, put your hands in front of you like this.' I demonstrate, making a triangle with my thumbs and index fingers. 'You tell me when you're ready and I'll throw the ball.'

'I'm ready.'

I hold the ball to my chest, elbows bent, palms facing outward. My arms extend as I push the ball in Elly's direction, releasing it from my control.

Bang. Thump.

'Ow!' Elly exclaims, as the ball connects with her head and her head with the sand.

'You selfish little girl!' bellows Steve.

I stand frozen, heart thumping. Steve's angry figure leaps off the veranda like a hyena. *If there's one thing I remember from my trip to Africa with dad, it's that they're loud, ugly and unpredictable.*

'You did that on purpose!'

'I didn't. I threw the ball, and she didn't …'

'You're full of shit. You have no concern for anybody but yourself! I couldn't even get through my coffee with your mother before YOU …' Steve jabs his index finger into my bony chest … 'decided to cause a scene!'

I take a moment, noticing the island goers looking on. *This is so embarrassing.*

I bring my eyes back up to meet his stare. 'I didn't do it on purpose!' I scream, the urge to be heard winning, my temper flaring.

I run. My eyes well, tears spill over and trickle down my flaming cheeks, leaving a mildly salty taste on my trembling lips.

I know he is on my heels, chasing me, out to make sure I know my place—small, silenced and never to be trusted. My little legs don't let me down, carrying me in a haze straight up the steps and onto the porch where my mum sits. I jump into her arms, but she doesn't hug me back.

'You think you're going to get sympathy from your mum after bullying your younger stepsister to get your way?' Steve pulls me off my mum. 'I know what you're doing, and it isn't going to work. She won't believe your rubbish because she knows you're selfish.' Mum maintains a blank expression, staring past the commotion into the blue surrounding the island, letting Steve continue. 'Get inside. You can spend the day in your room. I don't care what you do, just get out of my sight. This family doesn't need your nonsense ruining a nice holiday,' Steve demands firmly, still holding onto my arm—it must be bruising—as he points his gnarly finger at the door.

I stomp through the dark-stained door frame, aware of the sterile state of the cabin. *Why doesn't she tell me what to do? Why can't it be her telling me off? He's such a monster. Holidays aren't like this with dad. I just want to go home, back to my dad.* I close the door—with a slight thud—to the unfamiliar room that I share with Elly. I throw myself face first into the white pillow, the sobs not holding back. I let it all out until it is black.

A noticeable sting has replaced the warming sensation on my back, telling me some time has passed. I make no effort to move, only blinking. Droplets splat onto the ultrasound still pressed between my fingers, bringing my attention back to it. Emotions surge through me. *I just don't understand how my mother, my blood, the woman that felt me, grew me and birthed me, could be so unloving.* A sob erupts from deep within. My self-awareness lost, unconscious of who is observing—judging. *I already feel so much for this little girl. So much more than I've felt for anyone, ever. I can't comprehend how she managed to neglect me like that. Did she strive to make me feel like a liar? Like a selfish little girl inconveniencing her new family? I didn't realise the toxicity of this dynamic. How was I supposed to know the effect it would have on my mental wellbeing when it was all I knew?*

I adjust myself on the rocky cliff face and touch my swollen belly. *I want this baby. I want to take this opportunity and do better. More love— unconditional love, not this love on condition.*

Whistles and pulse calls sound from the vast seascape before me. My eyes search. Just beyond the yellow buoys that attach to shark nets below the surface, I see them. *Whales. A sign of wisdom, of hope, of good fortune.*

Slap. The majestic marine mammals wave. I crack a small smile—uplifted. At this moment, I am assured good things are on the horizon.

Capture the Moment

Lahni Edwards

The peace was music to her ears. Her shoulders sank and her breathing relaxed. Slowly, her body succumbbed to silence. She blinked. Her trained eyes framed a snapshot of the serenity surrounding her. It was a dull beauty, tainted with rosy saturation that reflected off maple tree leaves strung across the branches like fairy lights, illuminating the filtered canopy. Fuchsia radiated from the hull of a canoe which lay dormant on a lake. The canoe was tethered around the tallest maple so tightly the chain could almost represent a growth ring on the tree itself. The water offered half a metre of transparency before concealing reeds or any other life beneath. On the horizon, shrubbery lined the water's edge, presenting a strange greyish hue in contrast to the colourful maples. The water was unnerving, yet intriguing. Her skin prickled with the conflicting sentiments. *What a mysterious place.*

There was something about the canoe that invited further inspection. She was naturally curious, so she approached without question. She knelt in front of the stern, running her finger along the smooth finish of the honey timber. They had almost painted the nursery this colour but chose a neutral yellow tone instead. *Why didn't we go this one?* Incessant crying interrupted her train of thought. *Stop. No—* High-pitch needles pierced her ears. She tunnelled her focus towards ridding the pain as the sound continued to escalate. Reaching a pinnacle of intensity, she forced her hand from the canoe. Silence. She stood up abruptly. Clammy hands and shaken, she closed her eyes. *Just breathe. It'll be gone soon.*

After moments of prolonged silence, she removed the chain that tied the canoe to the majestic maple and laid it gently on the water's edge. As she pushed the canoe towards the grey horizon her feet became submerged in the murky lake. Ripples from the canoe disturbed the glassy water and temporarily broke the tranquillity surrounding her. She splashed awkwardly, rolling her body into the narrow boat. She remained still for a moment, lying on the ribs of the canoe and staring at the sky. *So blue. Beautiful, but boring when you look at it too long.* Again, that dull beauty.

She sat up and reached for the paddle, its smooth timber handle resting comfortably in her grip. Gaining confidence, she kneeled and began to stroke the water, alternating sides to keep the bow straight. The glittering spray was mesmerising and the rhythm of the craft slicing through the stillness offered a sense of active solace. The cool breeze whispered gently in her ears and played with her hair, while small droplets of water kissed her face. In the next upward stroke her gaze moved toward the paddle's shaft. A slap of recognition brought her trancelike state to a halt. She read barely legible childlike painted words: 'Lizzy and Dad's Lakeboat'. *The old owners must have a little girl too.* A wave of heat flooded her face, a sharp contrast against the shadowed crescent moons beneath her eyes. *They'll be better off without me.*

She paddled again, now determined. The incessant crying resumed, echoing louder than before. Her temples thumped in tune with her heart. Distant trees were out of focus but drew her gaze. *Soon a world away.* She grasped the coiled anchor in the stern. *My beautiful girls ... He'll cope.* She began to loop the anchor around her right ankle, trying to strangle the relentless wailing. Small ripples and the reflection of light distorted her face. She took a long, deep breath, leaned forward and closed her eyes.

'Mum! You're taking too long.'

Her body jolted upright, electrical impulses firing across every cell.

Her head snapped towards the direction of the echoing voice.

A little girl dressed in a yellow leotard and tutu stood impatiently by the water's edge. She waved a black camera above her head like it was indestructible. *Oh Lila, why? What—what are you doing here?*

'Muuuuuum! You promised a family photo.' Lila jumped around.

She blinked twice to redirect her thoughts. Steeling herself, she yelled back brightly, 'Hey darling! Let me just come back to shore.' Slowly, subtly, she removed the chain from her ankle. The links had embedded their print. Her clammy hand gripped the timber handle. The sun tucked behind a passing cloud. She paddled back towards the maples.

The smiling ballerina splashed innocently in wait in the shallows, mud splotching the nylon netting of her skirt.

A contagious grin that even from a distance brought a fresh wave of guilt, as she smiled back. Lila's father appeared with a wailing infant in his arms. He called out, 'Lila, come here! Mum was having a bit of quiet time. She said she'd be back after her forest walk.'

He looked towards the lake, his eyes meeting his wife's. She glanced at her ankle. The little girl pointed the camera at her father and baby sister, curly blonde hair narrowly visible from behind the lens.

'Say cheeeeeese.'

Choice and Change

Ellie Cooper

Looking back, it's amazing how something so innocuous as a phone call could lead to my world turning on its head.

The day had started like any other; the sun shone down on the earth and the birds chirped outside while the kids and I scrambled to get ready. A normal start to another beautiful day. It was only after the chaos incited while the kids were getting ready to leave for school died down, that I finally had a moment of peace for myself. Sat on the balcony to watch the comings-and-goings of the neighbourhood with a warm cup of tea in hand. A content sigh joined the symphony of suburbia.

A cheerful tune cut through the quiet peace. It was a call from Kathy. Kathy was not who I thought would be ringing me, considering her recent seclusion from everyone.

At first, I had contemplated letting it ring as a bit of petty revenge for her behaviour. On one hand, I could have answered and finally gotten some awaited explanations, on the other I could have ignored it and savoured that payback as a cherry on top of the idyllic morning.

In the end, curiosity and the need for answers won the fight, and I accepted the call. Great heaving sobs were the first thing I heard as it connected.

'Jenny!' Kathy had stuttered out.

'Kathy? What's wrong?' I was alarmed as Kathy had never called me in such a state before.

'I didn't want—I can't—please, Jenny, please!'

'Kathy, what are you talking about? I don't understand. Please calm down, try to take some deep breaths. You're going to pass out at this rate!'

'You—you have to believe me, please!'

Believe what? Kathy was so distraught she barely made any sense.

'What do you mean? What happened, Kathy? Please, tell me what's going on.'

'Please, I just—can you come here, please?' she begged.

'Alright, I'm coming over. I'll be at yours in five minutes, okay? Do you think you can stay calm until I get there?'

'Yes, yes, I think … I think I can …'

Whatever was going on was so distressing for Kathy that I hadn't bothered to take the time to do anything but grab my keys and rush for my car. Worry and increasingly catastrophic ideas plagued the short ride to Kathy's home. Did someone die? In the hospital? Had something happened to Kathy herself? What happened that was so horrible it sent Kathy into such a state?

Pulling up to her house, it struck me how one person's disaster can go completely unnoticed by the masses. Inside that house, my friend was breaking down, spiralling deeper into her misery and grief. Yet just two houses down, I remember seeing children squealing and playing with their father, without a care, as if there wasn't a life crumbling into nothingness.

I only spared a short rap on Kathy's door to alert her before I burst into the house.

'Kathy? I'm here, where are you?' I called.

The house held an eery silence. The atmosphere felt heavy and tense as if it were a scene in a horror movie just before a jump scare. The knot that had formed in my stomach tightened as I sat in the bleak ambience. It only took a few seconds for a slumped form to emerge from the hallway. Hearing how upset she was over the phone and seeing it in person were completely different.

Kathy was someone who always prided herself on appearing put-together; makeup done, not a hair out of place and clothes neatly pressed. The Kathy in front of me, however, couldn't be further from the woman I knew.

Her hair was a tangled, ratty mess. In place of her usual flawless makeup were dark circles painted under her eyes, flushed cheeks decorated with tears and her nose red from friction. She was donned in worn and wrinkled clothes that hung off her frame.

'God, Kathy … you look a right mess,' I blurted out and winced immediately after. Clearly, tact had fled from me like a frightened hare.

She grimaced, refusing to meet my eyes. Silence hung between us, punctuated by Kathy's soft sniffles.

'Kath—'

'I'm pregnant,' she interrupted.

'I, what? Pregnant?' I was brought up short. Confusion halted my thoughts until what she said finally processed.

'Pregnant! Kathy, I'm so happy for you! Congratulations, how far—'

'I'm not keeping it. I … I'm going to get an abortion,' she said, hesitant but determined. My elation at her announcement quickly turned to outrage.

'What do you mean "abortion"?' I cried.

'I was raped, Jenny. That's who this is from. I can't carry any part of, of … *him* inside me.'

'I—*raped*? Kathy what—is … is that why you practically went MIA a month ago?' I asked. 'Kathy … Kathy, why didn't you *say* something? I would've been there for you; we all would have.'

'And have to deal with everyone crowding and babying me? Reminding me constantly about—about what happened? No, thank you. I do that enough myself,' she said.

'Kathy, please—' I choked back.

'Don't, Jenny. Just … don't,' Kathy sighed. 'You know I'm right. Besides, do you honestly think everyone will be sympathetic to what happened? What—what … *that man* … did to me?'

'Oh, Kathy, no,' my voice hitched. 'Come on, you know the girls wouldn't be like that … surely?'

'Do I? Do you remember what they said about the girl who went through what I did at the last meetup? Because I do. Every time I thought about coming to any of you for comfort, all of those horrible and nasty things they said would come back to me. And I just—I couldn't bring myself to go through that,' Kathy said, yanking her hands through her messed hair.

There wasn't much that I could have said to rebuke that because she was right. As much as I wanted to defend the others, some of the things they had said were as foul as rotting garbage, and I hadn't admonished them for it either. It had made sense then why Kathy never reached out to anyone … to *me*. Obviously, she wouldn't have turned to any of us in her time of need.

She had been *raped*. Violated in such a severe and traumatising manner that she had completely secluded herself from society, and we had shown her that none of us could have been trusted with her vulnerability.

Sympathy welled inside me at her confession … but … even so …

'Why? How could you?' I choked out, a lump stuck in my throat.

'What? What do you mean "how could I"?'

'I just—I don't understand how you could stand to do that to the baby! What happened isn't their fault,' I said.

'It's not a baby, Jenny, it's just a clump of cells!' she shouted back.

'But even so! How could you just wilfully get rid of such a precious miracle? I get that what happened to you was traumatic and that you might want to forget all about it. Trust me, I do! But—how could you do something like this?' I cried, shouting my voice hoarse with tears to accompany my frustration. 'Don't you see, Kathy? This baby—they're your light! A beautiful shining miracle to chase away all of the horror and pain.'

'Are you hearing yourself, Jenny? Why would I want a constant reminder of what—*happened* to me? Why would I do that to myself?' she said. 'No … no, I don't want this …

this *thing*, this *reminder*. I want it gone. From me, from my body, from my life.'

'But—even if you don't want it … why *abortion*? Surely—surely adoption would be a better option? Anything but *killing* the child!'

Kathy scoffed at my remark, derision painted across her face and a sneer on her lips.

'Adoption? You're joking with me, right? You, of all people, know what that would likely mean! Even if I could stand going through with the pregnancy, I'm not going to be so cruel as to put it into that nightmare.'

'Ironic that you say that's a cruel thing to do when you're so set on murdering a baby without a shred of mercy,' I snapped. Anger dogged at my heels, riling me up with every nip.

'Oh bullshit, Jenny. I know we have had some arguments on differing opinions, but this is a new goddamn low for you. Of all things, I never thought you would be one of those "pro-life" idiots. None of you people actually care about those babies, you don't care about the parents either. You can only bring yourself to care about the baby while it's still in the womb. Everything that happens to it after that is of no concern to you. You just want to impose your own beliefs onto others, regardless of the consequences,' Kathy snarled, her chest heaving and shoulders bristling. 'You're not pro-anything, you're just anti-choice, that's it.'

The sheer vitriol she spat at me was shocking. The arguments and counterpoints I had churned up sputtered out like a suffocated bonfire, and I was left scrambling to reply.

'That—that's not true! Of course, I care about the babies after birth! How could you even accuse me of that?'

'Oh, really? Then what do you have to say about the children who are up for adoption only to be taken in by foster families who only care for the money? Or the paedophiles? Child abusers?' she retorted.

'Not all families are like that. Some are people who are unable to have their own children, so they go for adoption instead,' I said.

'Oh so, they're just meant to be a second choice. An "I'll settle for the second-best option, even though it's not as good"? Face it, Jennifer, anything you say only proves my point. Think about it. Genuinely think about this. I don't want this child. I'm not going to take the chance they'll be left in the "care" of some unscrupulous person who will do who knows what to them. And I know I cannot go through with this … pregnancy … without it completely ruining my mental health.' She paused, taking in a deep breath and wiping away the tears that started to fall. 'I'm not going to do that to myself. Don't even try to ask me to.'

My shock silenced me as she gathered herself for a moment, cheeks ruddy with rage and gnawed lips turned red. She smoothed her hair back before continuing.

'Tell me, do you always berate the people who are going through this? I bet you also heckle and jeer women going into abortion clinics as well. I suppose, you also scream and call them murderers, scum and all other kinds of horrid things as well—'

'That's not true! You're making me out to be some kind of—'

'Shut up! You think that you have the right to force people into doing what you want, according to your worldview. Regardless of their circumstances, you think that anyone who goes through an abortion is the same. Doesn't matter if it was the product of rape, a contraception failure, or because the foetus isn't viable anymore. It's all the same to you! People like you make me sick,' she screamed.

There was nothing I could say to defend myself or my beliefs because everything that Kathy threw at me was true. I knew from personal experience the exact kind of hell the foster system could be. It had taken years of horror and fear and abuse before I was able to be with a family that was good and safe; a family that loved me wholeheartedly and gave me a real home. Even still, the scars I gathered from my time in the system still lingered—irreversible damage that had imprinted itself deep into my soul. A constant dull pain that would rear its head every so often so I would never forget.

And while I had never been one of the people who went out of their way to berate and demean the women who did this, I also never hid my disdain when such instances crossed my path. Despite the horror stories I had heard about women's experiences leading up to their abortions, I had stuck by my ignorant belief that they were committing a heinous act.

I never took the time to see it from their perspective. Never let myself. I had wrongly ignored their despair and agony over the events and labelled them as murderers.

'Okay,' I said, cutting through the silence that followed Kathy's desperate and angered rant. 'You're right. So how can I help you?'

Two-Factor Authentication (2FA) Disabled

JACQUELINE KAYE

'Ma'am, are you okay?' one man asked before turning to the other tradesman. 'I'm not sure if she's alright. She's not responding. I've called the emergency services; they should be here soon.'

'We need the firies to put out the car. They can't be far away. Gosh, did you see what happened?'

'It was quick. Is she going to be, okay? Should we drag her out of the car? She's trapped and bleeding.'

'Here's her phone. Do you think we should call someone?'

'How about the last number dialled?' The tradie pressed redial, and the phone began to ring someone.

'Where are you?' boomed a voice through the phone.

'Hello? Do you know a young woman who drives a red Mazda?' asked the tradie.

'What has Rosemary done?'

'She has been in a serious car accident, so we've called the emergency services.'

'Where are you?' The voice sounded calmer now, even concerned for the woman's welfare.

The tradesman described where on the Bruce Highway they were and hung up. 'Not sure I should have done that!'

'Oh, look, she's starting to stir.'

Rosemary opened her eyes to stare into the faces of the two concerned tradies.

'You'll be okay, love. We've called for help, and your husband is on his way too.'

Rosemary looked alarmed. She turned forward. The front of the car was burning—she was trapped and couldn't move.

'Love, it's going to be alright. We will get you out. Help is on its way.' She noticed everything was crumpled. The front of the car was pushed in through the shattered windscreen. The deployed airbags left a fine deodorising smell throughout the car and covered her in white powder. The driver's door collapsed inwards and pinned her arm—her legs were crushed by the front of the car coming in through the dashboard.

How injured am I? She never believed in signs, but maybe it was time to give in. Rosemary looked through the shattered windscreen and realised she was blocking part of the road. *She noticed* a chunk of grass on her lap and realised it was falling through the open sunroof. 'Where am I?' she implored the tradie guys.

'You are at Federal on the Bruce Highway. You've had a nasty accident, but you are going to be okay,' one replied.

Gosh, this pain is excruciating. Will I die? What on earth have I done? How had this happened? I will be in so much trouble. Charles will be furious. Maybe it is time to give in? Rosemary's mind was jumbled. She was always making mistakes, and she had screwed up here too. She heard the distant sirens.

'They are coming, love. We will be able to help you soon.'

Something had decided that it was time she changed her life by sending her this sign—after all, this was a T-intersection.

The firies pulled up first and blocked the whole road. Their big red truck sirens blaring, lights flashing. It was all surreal that this was happening to her.

One of the firies came up to her crushed vehicle. 'We will need the jaws of life here, guys.'

'No worries, boss. I'll just put the engine out first.' The firie sprayed the front of the crumpled soul of a car with an extinguisher, and the smoking subsided. It was a relief as Rosemary thought the car would go up with her trapped body inside. The device the firies used resembled massive claws.

'We are going to free you.'

Sirens screaming out of tune with the firies' truck and blue flashing lights again descended upon the scene. They pulled up, blocking the highway and the fire engine. The policeman hopped out and flagged the traffic down.

'Here comes the paramedics,' the tradie said as another siren closed in, and soon, they were upon her.

'Love, do you have any pain around your neck?'

Rosemary was pulled from her trance. 'No, I don't think so.'

'Okay.'

With that, the firies pulled the front engine off Rosemary's legs. The steering wheel with the exploded airbag was removed, exposing her crushed legs.

The paramedics had a quiet chat on the side. 'Her neck injuries appear to have happened earlier, whereas the seat belt has injured her lower down.'

The firies peeled open the driver's door and the paramedics were able to get in to assess Rosemary. Her right arm was broken, and the inside of her arms were all torn from the airbag explosion. She had broken legs—they'd have to get her into the ambulance to check for internal bleeding.

Once there, the beeping and lights in the van were harsh on her senses. A paramedic looked at Rosemary's chest—*internal bruising on her abdomen and stomach. Still, the old bruising across her torso was unexpected. The airbag should have protected her chest and cracked ribs. But it wasn't his place—if something was going on, the police and the hospital would deal with it.*

'What the heck have you done?' A man's red face appeared in the back of the ambulance.

'Who are you? What are you doing here? Rosemary, do you know this guy?' the paramedic asked.

Rosemary looked at the fellow. 'Charles is my … partner.'

'We are taking her to the hospital, so you need to get out of the ambulance.'

'Is she going to be alright? Which hospital are you going to?'

The paramedics said they didn't know at this stage, and it depended on where they could get in.

Rosemary breathed a sigh of relief when the paramedics closed the doors, leaving Charles outside.

'Rosemary, do you have someone you need to call?' the paramedics asked as they finished preparing her for the drive. Something was going on here, but it wasn't their place to get involved.

The paramedics called through to the hospital, summarising Rosemary's injuries and letting them know that they are on the way.

She heard the emergency nurse call through the radio, 'Did you say you have a social worker? Is her name Rosemary?'

The paramedics looked at Rosemary and said, 'Yes.'

'Rosemary Fenton, we are here for you,' she heard the nurse say. 'Let us help you like you have helped so many before you.'

They arrived at the Gympie General Hospital and the nurses came out to meet the ambulance. 'Rosemary Fenton, what a day you've had.' Rosemary's best friend, Fay, a nurse at the hospital, met the bed and grabbed Rosemary's hand. 'I got you, babe. You are going to be ok.'

It was the final straw for Rosemary, and she sobbed. She was so pleased to see Fay—her best friend, confidant and kindred spirit. They had worked at the hospital together for a few years and became firm friends. Fay didn't leave her side as the trolley was rushed into the assessment room.

Fay could see Rosemary's injuries from before her accident. Her fragile best friend would now be protected. Rosemary wouldn't be going home for some time. She needed to believe in the revolution of changing her life and trusting in her friends. She had been revolutionary in changing women's lives in refuges and women's shelters. Now it was her time to be revolutionary for herself.

The current social worker, Richard, grabbed Fay. 'Hey, we've had a call from the police that there may need to be a protection order and an assault charge put in place. Do you know any background?'

Fay looked at Richard. 'I think you better talk to the doctors and Rosemary about that.' Richard went into the assessment room to chat with the doctor overseeing the coordination of Rosemary's care—she was sedated as the doctors looked over her injured legs and prepared for x-rays. 'Do you see any evidence of needing a protective order for this patient? The paramedics and police at the scene said that her safety may be at risk.'

'I can tell you she has had significant injuries from the car accident, but there are other older injuries. So, there is a case there. Are the police prepared to take out the order?'

'Yes, they could put an order in place to protect this young woman if she has enough injuries to support it. If Rosemary makes a statement, we could charge him for assault as well. We need her permission, but I think her friend Fay will help convince her.'

The police summarised while Richard continued to chat with them about starting a protective order.

Rosemary woke up to see her arm and both her plastered legs were elevated. She felt relieved to see Fay sleeping on the chair beside her. *What happened?*

'Good, you are awake.' The door opened and in came the registrar. 'You have a broken arm and two broken legs. In addition, you have cracked ribs and a crack in the pelvis and an injured spleen. You will be with us for a while, to give your injuries time to heal.'

Her best friend leaned over. 'The police have put in place a protective order and prepared a statement for an assault charge against Charles, Rosemary. This accident can be a revolutionary moment for you, a reminder that life is short and that you need to be safe and live the life you enjoy. They have also asked you to move somewhere safe on discharge. It's time you took control of your life.'

Rosemary agreed, and they started to put in place a plan.

Two days later, she was lying in her hospital bed when she received an alert on her phone that her Gmail account had been signed in elsewhere.

'Hey, Fay? Have you been using my email account? I've just been notified that someone has accessed it.'

'No, I haven't for a while,' Fay, seated in the chair beside her, replied.

'Hmm, that's odd.'

Despite this intrusion, they began to plan her release from the hospital. They developed it over the next few days, as there was little else to do in hospital. Rosemary was also able complete some remote work on her laptop, albeit with only one working hand.

Fay picked her up when the day came for Rosemary to go home. They had decided Rosemary would live in a rural area in a beautiful old cottage that belonged to a speech therapist friend she had worked with, Adeline. Her friends had set up her new safehouse with a well-stocked fridge and pantry, and all the comforts she needed, with devices to make her reduced mobility easier. She felt safe in this gorgeous spot in the Noosa Hinterland and looked forward to her once-a-week visits from Fay with food and supplies as needed. Her mobility improved, and she continued to do her physiotherapy exercises.

She didn't crave company, but the catch up was just perfect. Finally, she felt safe and secure with only the police and two people—Ads and Fay—who knew her location. She emailed Ads to thank her for the house. It was such a generous gesture. About an hour later, she noticed an alert on her Gmail indicating a login from a different computer.

It happened again; who is accessing the account? Have I enabled Two-Factor Authentication or is it disabled? Rosemary's thoughts raced ahead of her.

She recalled her life before the accident. *What a horror. I never thought about it before, but Charles is just like the men who mistreated the women I work with. It's time for me to make the change, and I feel stronger. My inner spirit is flourishing.*

I am finally safe and content.

The next morning, searing pain woke Rosemary. Not from her arms, legs, or internal injuries but from her ringing ear. She looked around her. A whisper came from beside her. 'You will never leave me.'

Raid

Joshua Gannon

28 June 1969, 5.38am

Holy crap.

I can't stop my body from shaking. My eyes are locked on the rough white of the ceiling, but it isn't helping. I can't stop my mind from racing. Memories of last night are flashing through my mind faster than scenes flashing across the TV as a video cassette rapidly unspools. This has never happened before—things never went this far. They have now though, we took things further than they've been taken. We pushed back, we rioted. *I* pushed back, *I* rioted. We chanted, we threw glass bottles, we burned the building. We burned Stonewall, that place which was so safe. Was, so safe.

I've been awake too long, more than 24 hours, I need to try and process what happened if I want any chance of sleep. Okay, I just need to take a few deep breaths, slow down my mind …

27 June 1969, 10.41am

Has this stack of paperwork reduced at all this morning? It's like I finish one task and someone walks past to drop three more on me. I know I wasn't the best in my class at college but I hardly expected to still be pushing paper as I push 30. Of the two men sitting at the desk either side of me, one is fresh from college and eager to impress, the other is nearing retirement and enjoying a slower pace. Around the room nearly everybody fits one of those two descriptions,with barely a handful of people in the middle who, like me, aren't destined to be big-shot lawyers running courtrooms.

It's fine, it's a job and that's all that matters. Compared to some people I see at Stonewall on a Friday or Saturday night, I'm doing very well. Not that I'd ever share that little feel-good comparison around the office. Here, I'm in my pressed grey suit, hair slicked back, an eligible bachelor who hasn't found the right woman to settle down with. My hair isn't naturally slicked, my words aren't perfectly considered, and I'm not looking for anyone to settle down with, let alone a woman. Will there be a day where I can be that person at work as well? Who knows. I doubt I'll be alive to see it. I can't afford to spiral down that rabbit hole though, not when my pile of paperwork just keeps growing. Head down, get the work done, a few more hours and I'll be free to enjoy the weekend.

12.43pm

A sad salad and a black coffee, my staple lunch from Monday to Friday in this drab little staff kitchen. These are the things we do to get through the day and keep our bodies looking a certain way. I couldn't imagine having anything but a semi-athletic body in my community, the gay community. We all do what we need to fit in.

Thankfully my chair slides out quietly when I stand up—there's nothing worse than that horrible grating sound they're known for and everyone on their break looking up at you. No, it's easier to make sure they don't look up, easier to blend in, that's what Mattachine says anyway. So, slide out quietly, mug goes in the sink, salad bowl in the fridge and back to my desk to keep going with that paperwork.

4.11pm

Today had been going so well, at least as well as it could in this place, until now. Why did Greg have to stop and talk? No offense to anyone but my colleagues aren't the kind of people I want to talk to and be friends with, and I'm sure if they knew a bit more about my personal life the feeling would be mutual.

'Sorry, what was that?'

'Brain a bit slow since it's the end of the week?' Greg had a little chuckle to himself at that, yes very funny. 'Almost the weekend, no need to worry. Margy and I are heading up to Long Lake to visit the grandkids.'

'That'll be lovely, how old are they now?' Not that I care, but it's polite to ask.

'Four months and two years, both girls.'

'Oh lovely. Hopefully the traffic won't be too bad for you.' Please leave me alone.

'We're hoping to avoid the traffic by sneaking out of here a little early—don't tell the boss! See you Monday.'

I feel bad for being thankful to see Greg slowly waddle away—he's a nice enough man after all. But I don't have time to talk about his grandkids, not if I'm to get all this work finished. I don't want to take anything home tonight. It's Friday and I'm in the mood for a few too many drinks and a good dance.

5.46pm

The lock clicks open and I swing my door in. It's not much, but my apartment is clean, tidy and all mine. I drop my briefcase next to the table by the door and beeline for the kitchen—there's a bottle of vodka in the freezer which has been calling my name all week. Vodka is my favourite, so versatile. Tonight, I think there's only one way I want to drink it—double on the rocks with a twist of lemon. Perfect.

Being out of my business shoes and stiff grey suit feels almost as good as drinking that vodka, although satisfying in a different way. The heat and humidity of the day felt trapped beneath my buttoned collar and tightly tied tie. Now it's free and I definitely need a shower. A nice cool one to wash away the day and get me ready for the night.

How long until I'm due to meet up with Luke? Almost two hours—perfect.

7.25pm

Why is it still so humid? I hate summer, I hate being sweaty. Even in just shorts and a shirt, I'm still noticeably sweating after just a 10-minute walk. Gross. I swear Luke better have a fan on when I get there. I'm not going to be sitting in stuffy heat in his apartment.

Four flights of stairs and I can feel drops of sweat trickling down my back. Do I have to knock a third time? I swear if he doesn't open the door soon …

'Hey! Sorry, sorry, I know, don't look at me like that! I'm still getting ready.'

'Why am I not surprised?' I step into Luke's apartment, waiting as he locks the door. 'It's sweltering in here; I know you don't have AC yet but at least turn a fan on.'

'It's been broken all week! The building manager refuses to fix it—there's a shock. And how did I know you were going to complain about it? So predictable. Don't worry, I have something I know you'll enjoy to make up for it!' It better be something good.

I watch Luke bound around the corner into his kitchen, a step in the right direction at least. He really does know me; there he is holding a bottle of vodka fresh from the freezer.

'Fine. I guess I'll stay.'

'Like I said, you're so predictable! How do you want it? Never mind, just make it yourself, I need to finish getting ready. I'm so excited to go out tonight, it's been weeks! You know these feet are craving a dance right now.'

And off he bounds into the bedroom—he has so much energy it's hard to keep up sometimes. Still, I can't seem to keep a small smile from creeping onto my face.

8.34pm

Ahh, that big, beautiful sign. Stonewall. I know it's not the fanciest gay bar around, and some of its other patrons can be a bit rough, but they let us dance and I love it. There are only a few people in line too—perks of coming here a little earlier than everyone else.

It's barely five minutes before I'm standing in front of the door, just a pair of eyes looking at me through a small gap in an otherwise blank door. It's not my first time here and I've seen these eyes before, so the gap closes, the door swings open and I'm quickly shuffled inside.

'Write your name in the book.'

Sure, I'll write a name, but it won't be mine. Nobody writes their real name in this book—imagine doing that and getting caught in a raid. No, Richard Clarkson is signing in tonight. I was Clark Richardson last time. But holes in the door and fake names are fine if it means I have this place. This place to be me. This place with people like me. I walk through to the bar and the black and blue lights of the place feel comforting after a week under the fluorescent lights of the office.

11.23pm

'Another vodka on the rocks, thanks.' I have to lean over the bar and shout to be heard. The place has really filled up, the white noise of hundreds of conversations and the thumping music fills every joint of Stonewall and every crevice of my mind. I love it. I'm not sure if it's all the vodka or if I'm just in a good mood but I can't stop my body from moving while I wait for my drink. Finally, it felt like hours waiting, but that beautiful glass of vodka is in front of me. I pay, pick it up, down it, and bounce back over to where Luke is by the dancefloor.

'Where's your drink?'

'I drank it! Come on, I love this song—let's dance!' Luke doesn't take much convincing. We get out onto the dancefloor and start to jump around. In this moment I'm so happy, and probably a bit drunk too, which just makes it better. There's me and Luke and drag queens, and all different types of people loving this place.

28 June 1969, 1.12am

I'm covered in so much sweat, both mine and other people's, and I can't stop panting from all the dancing. But I still manage to stumble to the bar and ask for another vodka. I love vodka. I can't help but lean on the bar and look around—everyone looks as happy as I'm feeling. Except for those four near the door. They don't look anywhere near as happy. Oh well, my vodka is here now and I'm still smiling and bouncing around. I drink it in one gulp and it's time to dance again!

1.20am

My eyes are closed and I'm bouncing around with everyone. Except, everyone has stopped bouncing. Can I still hear music or is my head just ringing? I open my eyes and, god, everything is so bright. Why is everything so bright?

'Police! We're taking the place!'

Oh. Oh god. Oh god oh god oh god. No. I'm still panting, my eyes are all over the place, and my heart is pounding out of my chest. But it's not the vodka now, it's fear. Police. Oh god. A police raid. I can't be here. I need to get out. Everyone needs to get out. And everyone else is thinking the exact same thing.

My head isn't ringing—people are screaming.

1.29am

They're getting closer to me. Deep breaths. They're just going to look at my ID. Some people up the line have refused—should I refuse? Oh god. I need to keep breathing. That officer looking at IDs, they were in here earlier, before the raid started. I think, oh I don't know, aren't there meant to be warnings?

Oh god, he's only a few people away now. Nobody has their ID out anymore.

1.43am

I'm outside, they let me outside. I didn't get arrested. Holy crap, I feel like I can breathe again. People aren't leaving, they're angry. Some of the things police were doing inside was out of line—a woman is crying because the officer hit her when she complained about where he was touching her. People have a right to be angry. We shouldn't be treated like this.

Hang on, where's Luke?

1.47am

I can't find him. I've run the whole street and he isn't out here. Is he still inside? There are so many people out here now, hundreds, why would he still be inside?

1.51am

There he is! He's just come out the door, I need to get over there. Does he have a black eye? They've hit him—what the hell?

It's too loud out here to talk, but he smiled and he's hugging me back. He's alright.

People are yelling and chanting around us.

'Gay power!'

'We shall overcome!'

I'm yelling. I'm chanting.

2.11am

People are throwing bottles at the police cars. I have a bottle. Should I throw the bottle? One police officer just hit a woman across the back of her head with a baton.

I throw the bottle.

2.26am

They've barricaded themselves inside Stonewall. Our Stonewall. The Stonewall they're trying to take from us. They can't have it.

Someone found bricks.

2.47am

There's a fire now. The people at the front lit a garbage can on fire and pushed it through a broken window. Luke and I jumped up onto a brick wall just in time to see. His arms around me now, it's nice.

2.55am

The fire's still going inside. Some officer down the front has a fire hose but there's no water. Good, I'm glad it's burning. It's our Stonewall, if we can't be safe inside then neither can they.

The Shadows of my Memories

Sharon Sutton

It was going to be a long night. I could not help but marvel at the beauty of it. That sky! Oh Lord! It was like looking into a dazzling mirror. Memories came rushing back of nights like this when we had lay in our swag and spun dreams of our future. All that was left of those dreams was dust.

I had driven since early morning and should have reached the homestead by now. Alex, the manager's wife, had said, 'The trip from Alice Springs to the station should take around eight hours, and you will cross a running creek. The turnoff into the homestead is near the large rock formation shaped like an upside-down table. You can't miss it.' The land here all looked the same, endless expanses of red dirt covered in grey shrubby vegetation with no distinguishing landmarks. Where had I gone wrong?

I was experienced at travelling in the Australian outback and had provisioned for all eventualities. Camping for the night posed no hardship for me. I soon had a fire blazing and a billy on to boil. A cup of coffee would be very welcome after the long day. I was on my second cup of coffee after finishing dinner when, with nothing else to occupy my thoughts, all my doubts, insecurities and guilt came creeping back. I had thought when I applied for and secured this job, requiring a move to another state, I was ready to move forward and get on with my life. Was I never to be free of this burden? I know the guilt and responsibility I carry for what happened was illogical, but my brain just could not process that line of thought.

The sky was so bright I doubted being able to sleep. I was weary from the drive though, so it didn't take long to drift off. Morning came in a rush. There was no lingering transition from dark to light. After a quick breakfast and a repack of my car it was time to turn around, retrace my steps and figure out where I had gone wrong.

I travelled back for about three hours before I saw the turn-off to the right. How had I missed it yesterday? Not long after getting on the right road I came to the creek crossing. Cool clear water running over rocks, shaded by giant paperbark trees. I parked on the other side of the creek, grabbed a towel and toiletries and walked along the bank until I was out of sight of the road.

Man! that water felt good. Water, the lifeblood of the land. In this country men had died trying to find it. Cattle had perished from the lack of it when drought dried the land to parchment. Pastoralists had been lucky this year though, with good falls of rain at the right time.

I hit the road again. Next stop hopefully would be the station. I was eager to get there and start work. It had been a while since I had done jillarooing but I was confident that I could get back into the groove. Hard physical work in the outdoors was just what I needed to shake off any troubling thoughts the outback stirred up. It had taken me a long time and many sleepless nights for me to achieve some peace of mind.

I could spot the huge trees shading the homestead complex from a fair way out. It looked like an oasis in a sea of red sand. As I got closer I could see that the homestead area was neat and tidy, everything in shipshape order. Alex came out to greet me as I pulled up.

'Hi, you must be Kelly. Come in, you're just in time for smoko.'

After a welcomed cuppa and something to eat, she showed me to my accommodation.

'You're our only female employee this season, so you'll have the quarters all to yourself.'

That night, over a fabulous meal of good station beef, I met the rest of the staff. They were all very welcoming. Jack was an old hand. A craggy, tanned-leather face told me he had been doing this work most of his life. There were four younger fellows. One in particular stood out from the rest. Kevin was a first-year jackaroo, polite enough, but very cocksure. Never mind, I thought, the horses and the cattle would soon sort Kevin out. I didn't realise then how prophetic my thoughts would be. I had a good feeling about my decision to take this job so far from home. I felt that working here I could finish healing my tortured soul.

The first couple of weeks were tough going, with aches in places I didn't know I had. The days were long, but time flitted by. There was so much to do on a cattle station during the mustering season. Mustering, drafting, branding—never would I get use to the smell of burning cow-hide—loading trucks for the meat works and taking cattle back to their respective paddocks. When there was a moment to spare, horses needed shoeing, colts to be handled and breaking-in the older colts to ready for work. There were also plenty of social events to attend and the work program was organised around these.

As females were outnumbered in this male-dominated environment, I was never short of an escort to social affairs. Some of my partners may have been looking for a serious liaison but friendship and some light-hearted fun was all I wanted. My heart had been torn in two and I doubted that time could heal it.

As the months floated by, I realised I was sleeping better. No more waking in the middle of the night with my heart pounding and face drenched in salty tears. I could look at his photo that stood on my bedside table without my throat constricting and feeling like I couldn't breathe. Would he be at peace with me trying to move forward? I liked to think he would be happy for me. I hoped he knew how hard I had tried that day.

Work carried on through the cold winter months. All the paddocks had been mustered and it was time to go further out into the ranges where some old piker bullocks and cleanskins were running wild. Each year there are always some cattle that are missed in the muster and get away into the unfenced bush. They become cunning and hard to muster in the usual way. Trapping on a watering point is the most successful approach.

We packed the Toyota with all the necessary gear, foodstuff, swags and personal gear. There were three of us going out to the trap-yard—Jack, Kevin, and myself. We set out in convoy, the semi-trailer for carting the cattle back to the homestead and the Toyota, which had the two-way radio for checking in with the station each night. It was a good two-hour drive out to where we would set up camp. We would have time to go down and set up the nearest trap yard. We had to camp way back from the yard as the smallest sound would scare these wily old bullocks.

After a feed of grilled steak and slabs of homemade bread washed down with pannikins of billy tea, we went down to the trap yard and found places close to the gate where we could secrete ourselves. The waiting was the hardest part, especially for Jack who smoked like a chimney. No strange smells and complete silence were needed to get these cattle to walk into the yard for water and get the gate closed behind them.

After three nights we had about a hundred head trapped, a full load for the semi-trailer. Now came the risky part—getting the cattle out of the back yards, up the loading ramp and into the truck. Some of these cattle had never been in a yard before, never seen humans. They were wild and had no respect for man whatsoever.

Jack was a real smart cattleman, but Kevin was a 'newbie' and, as yet, had not learnt a whole heap of cattle sense. I had been around cattle most of my life except for the years I had been away from the bush doing my nurses' training. All was going well with the loading until we got down to the last dozen or so cattle. These were the dangerous ones, the desperate ones that would be completely unpredictable, that would do anything rather than go up that ramp into the truck. Jack and I knew how dangerous this last bit of loading would be. Kevin was inexperienced but keen to show us that he could 'pull his weight'. I was watching the cattle but trying to keep an eye on him at the same time when a horny old cleanskin cow came back at us. I jumped for the yard rails and flew up them as fast as I could.

I turned to look back into the yard—I couldn't move, couldn't yell out. I just froze and all the memories of that fateful day came crashing back. The cow had hit Kevin and speared one of her horns through his chest. As he hit the ground, she gored him again, this time in the thigh, opening it up like a knife gliding through butter. Jack was lightning fast in getting to Kevin and turning the cow away with his stockwhip. He got the last of the cattle out of the yard and up the ramp into the truck. I was still on the top rail, shaking and struggling to breathe as I tried and failed to shake the memories that were rendering me useless. Somewhere deep down I was telling myself that Kevin needed my nursing experience if he were to survive, but all I could think was that my experience had failed me before and it would again … I had let my love die. My soulmate. The man I was going to spend the rest of my life with. The father of the children I hoped one day to have. The person I was going to grow old with. I had watched the light go out of his eyes as I tried to stem the blood gushing from the puncture wounds the bull had torn in his chest and stomach.

'Kelly! Kelly! What are you doing? Help Kevin,' Jack shouted.

It was no use. I could not make myself get down and go to Kevin's aid. Jack realised that something was wrong. He climbed up the rail next to me and started shaking me, 'Kelly, Kevin needs your help. Snap out of it!'

He could see I was traumatised. He just kept repeating that Kevin needed me. After what seemed like forever, his voice penetrated the wall I had put around my mind. It was like coming out of a trance. Suddenly, I could see that if Kevin was to have any chance of surviving it was up to me.

'Jack, hurry, fetch the first aid kit from the Toyota. Then get on the radio to the station and tell them what's happened and bring Kevin's swag back here. We'll need it to load him onto the back of the Toyota.'

Kevin was unconscious. I dressed the wounds as best as I could. The kit was basic and had no strong painkillers in it. It was going to be touch and go getting him back to the station for the Flying Doctor to pick him up. Jack and I got him loaded into the back of the Toyota and started for the station. I rode in the back with Kevin while Jack drove. Alex came out and met us with more medical supplies and a morphine needle. The doctor was on the station airstrip when we arrived. Kevin was still alive.

The news came through the next morning that Kevin had survived the surgery and was in a critical but stable condition.

I sat on the verandah of my quarters going over in my mind everything that had happened. I felt ashamed that I had reacted the way I did when the accident happened, that I needed Jack to shake me out of my daze. I could remember the day I lost my love. I understand now that I couldn't have saved him. His injuries had been too horrific. I had been punishing myself for too long. It was time to let him go. I would love him forever but I needed to face life and open myself up to whatever the future might hold. It just might bring me another chance at love.

Drowning

CHLOE DOVER

Would you be brave in your last moments? I distinctly think I would not. I've dreamt of myself drowning. At first, I was a lifeboat. Mostly I was a sailor, alone in rough seas. Once, I was a lighthouse. But now, now I am swimming.

'June, the weather says it's gonna be crazy out there,' Annie says.

'I've sailed in worse, Annie Banannie,' I say in a childish tone.

I throw the last of my things into the small sailboat. It's seen better days, but since Dad left it to me I haven't been able to part with it, as much as my sister nags that I should. She stands on the dock now, looking at me with searching eyes.

'You just don't want to come. You'd literally rather risk your life than come,' she

crosses her arms and frowns.

It's funny that even in our twenties we still act like kids around each other.

'It's not that,' I roll my eyes. She stares.

'Okay,' I give in, 'you know I don't want to go. Why are you even fishing when you know what I'll say?'

'Because I want to hear you say it.'

'I don't want to go.'

'Who knows how many more birthdays Grandad is gonna have, you can't make just this one? Are we really so bad?'

'It's a room full of people who don't care about me. And they don't care about you. Why should we?'

'How do you know they don't care? You've written them off so quickly.'

'Quickly? Annie, it's been years, and you think I didn't want it to work? I did. But they weren't there for Dad when Mum left, and they weren't there for us when Dad died. They want nothing to do with anything that isn't to do with them.'

'It's family, June. We have no one else. It's up to us …'

'It's not!'

We stare at each other as her pale cheeks grow red. Even though it's dawn, people have begun to gather on the shore. A sailing town wakes up with the tide.

'I'm sorry,' I finally say, 'but it's not up to us. We can't fix what doesn't wanna be fixed. Just give it up, Annie.'

'Fine. Sail.' She storms off and I watch her drive away.

I move a few things around in the boat, throwing rope out of the way and slamming down an esky full of water, sandwiches, and snacks. It hits the floor and the lid slides off, water bottles rolling out all over the place.

'Fuck.' I roll my eyes.

The taste of sea salt pricks my tongue, making my jaw tingle. The rough breeze tells me Annie was right, though

I'd never admit it to her face. It's nothing I haven't handled before, but today Dad's boat seems to be feeling it more than usual.

'Come on old girl,' I say to her.

I adjust the sails, but she doesn't seem to be listening. A wave hits and the boat rocks, throwing me on my side. I land on my arm, feeling a shooting pain as I stand up again.

'Shit.'

Nothing I haven't handled before. Nothing I haven't—

Another heavy wave rocks the boat, causing me to stumble like a baby giraffe learning to walk. Desperately I reach out for anything to grab onto, anything to help me ground myself in the middle of the sea. Only, there's nothing. The small boat can't take wave after wave crashing into her side. I fall to my knees and brace myself for each attack. I close my eyes and in seconds I'm submerged in cold, raging waters. I frantically look around as the boat is carried on the waves in the opposite direction.

You must decide whether you should die or carry on. I feel myself being sucked under by a wave. Another one crashes over, then another, not giving me a moment to breathe. My lungs are on fire, a drumming louder than thunder beats in my ears. Or maybe it is thunder. I see the waves that rolled in tower over me, their heavy rainfall trapping me between water and a wet place.

Over the crashing waves, a small boat approaches from the east.

'We have to save the penguins!' Annie screams.

I can barely hear her over the roaring sea, the water filling up my ears.

'What?' I scream.

'We have to save the penguins.'

Annie, only seven or eight, runs into my room. The look on her face would make you believe she'd witnessed real tragedy but I, eleven at the time, know better.

'What?'

'We have to save them,' she repeats, running over to my bed and sitting in front of me.

'What are you saying?'

'They're going to die. The ice is melting, and they'll die.'

'We can't do anything; one person can't save the world.'

'We're not one person. We're two.'

'Well, each of us is one. You're born alone and you die alone. Just you. One,' I say, waging a lone finger in her face.

'Well, you were there when I was born. And you're the oldest so you die first, and I promise I'll be there when you die.'

I didn't have the heart to tell her what I really meant. If I even knew myself. Most likely it was something I'd heard an adult say or seen in a movie. It didn't really matter because, honestly, I believed her. We were sisters. We were not one, but two, and I so needed to believe neither of us could be alone.

Though, I have never been more alone than I am now. Annie never liked sailing, it was always something Dad and I would do together, although I know she'd be great at it if she tried. The first time Dad took me sailing, real sailing, I capsized the boat. Looking back, I don't even know how I did it. It would've been a small mistake, something that set me off and for the rest of the sail I couldn't focus. I remember the day being hot, too hot for anyone to be nice. Annie was waiting for me on the dock.

'How'd it go?' she jumped up and down.

I just shook my head and stormed past her. She followed me down the rocky shore, persistent as always.

'I'm sure you were good. What's up? Dad seems happy.'

'Nothing, Annie. I don't want to talk about it.'

We walked in silence, her a few steps behind me. The ocean breeze bought slight relief to the heat, and when my sweat subsided for a moment, I stopped walking and looked out onto the ocean. Annie stood next to me.

'What happened?' she asked.

'I don't want to talk about it … but I capsized. How embarrassing? I've sailed every day since we were little, and he finally trusts me to take control and I fucked it up.'

'I'm telling him you swore.'

'Shut up, Annie,' I pushed her playfully.

She looked out at the waves with me for a while. They were gentle and lapped at our feet. The water was calm and blue that day, easy sailing weather.

'It's okay, June, you'll get to do it again tomorrow. And tomorrow it'll be easy because you already fucked it up once. What are the odds of it happening again?'

'Annie!'

She giggled as I pushed her again.

'Things don't really work out all the time. Things actually really never work out. I think they have to get really really bad sometimes, to be good again. This was tiny, June. You'll probably barely remember this day, looking back. It'll be like, oh that time I cried because of one mistake, how dumb.'

'It doesn't feel dumb, it feels huge.'

'I don't know. All I figure is, you're gonna make a lot more mistakes. Like a lot a lot. And it's a fact, unavoidable. Just hope they aren't earth shattering and let them happen, I guess.'

I looked over at my ever-wise teenage baby sister. She had her eyes glued to her soaking wet tennis shoes, kicking something around in the dirt. I wondered what mistakes she'd made, to make her think this way. I wanted to ask her what earth shattering would be, if not this. Now I think, will it be the time she couldn't convince her stubborn and unforgiving older sister to come to one birthday party, just one, on the day she died? Will she stay up at night, knowing she could've convinced me not to sail, but she didn't try hard enough? All the while knowing, the only relief she could ever get would be me, telling her she couldn't convince me the sky was blue if I didn't want to hear it. Knowing, of course, I'd be dead, and those would be words I could never say.

'I'm arguing with Dad,' Annie tells me over the phone.

It's a year ago, I've moved out of home and left her there, alone.

'About what this time?'

'He says that if he was on the Titanic, he'd rather be eaten by something than freeze or drown.'

'I don't think he'd have a choice.'

'I said I'd want to die from the fall. Hitting water from that high up is like hitting cement, you know?'

'I've heard that. I think I'd be okay with freezing, surely you wouldn't really feel it. Drowning would be rough, wouldn't it?'

'Maybe it would be peaceful.'

During a storm, I am swimming in thick black-blue ocean currents. Too deep to dream of my feet feeling the floor. I see a buoy, bobbing like they do in a storm. I swim faster and faster, not looking up, just swimming, arms burning, mouth filling with salty water. I take a moment to get my bearings but I can longer see the buoy, or the shore. I have no clue which way to go. Should I keep my course and risk swimming further into the deep blue death? The waves lap at my face, they move me around with such force I know fighting it is a losing battle. So, do I lose? People don't seem to give up, in their dying moments. Most people, from what I gather, would swim. They would find the buoy, a boat, land, and life. I tread water, but I can't seem to drown. Swimming further into the ocean is terrifying, but maybe I would find solace in action, any action, whether it be sealing my fate or not. Swim against the current, die of exhaustion. Let it move you and drown. Stay still, let your lungs fill with water and suffocate.

When death comes knocking at my door, do you think I would find peace? Would I accept my fate or die in denial. 'This can't be it. This isn't for me.'

'Move,' Annie says.

'Move, move, move.'

And so, I do.

STAR-SEEKERS

A Queer Brew

JAYDA FRANKS

The Inquisitor arrived at noon.

Mildred and Rhea had paused their farm work to share a kettle of cranberry tea and some plain scones. At the knock on the front door, Mildred grumbled and peeked through the cotton curtains to see who stood at the doorstep. She stiffened when she saw the ivory robes emblazoned with the royal crest.

The notice had arrived a week ago, and while Mildred had ample experience in such affairs, Rhea's anxiety had been steadily mounting. 'It's him, love,' Mildred said in a low voice. Rhea's eyes widened. 'I'll handle introductions,' Mildred added. 'Ye reheat the tea.'

The Inquisitor knocked again. Three short raps.

The fear swimming in Rhea's eyes made Mildred's stomach squirm. Mildred planted a peck on Rhea's salt and pepper hair. 'Deep breaths, love. It'll be fine,' she said and gingerly rose from the tea table to greet their guest.

Mildred opened the cottage's front door. Standing on the welcome mat was an older lord with a rotund middle and a receding hairline. A sagging satchel stuffed with scrolls was slung across his shoulders. He stood a good foot shorter than Mildred, and the royal emblem gleamed on his pristine robes. Behind him, his horse nibbled on a clump of weeds, the coat stark against the rippling, heather-smeared moor.

'Mornin', milord!' Mildred chirped. 'We've been expectin' ye!'

The Inquisitor's face contorted like a trodden plum. 'Good morning, madam.' His voice was tight and reedy. 'Where is your husband?'

'He's under the orchard,' Mildred said brightly. ''Fraid he won't be much help today. Meself and Rhea will answer any questions y'have.'

The Inquisitor's squashed face purpled further. 'No lord of the house? That is ... quite unconventional.'

'Aye,' Mildred said. 'Unconventional times, though.' She gestured to the cottage behind her. 'Come on in for some tea. Rhea's reheating a brew from this mornin'. A real stinker.'

Before the Inquisitor could protest, Mildred dipped back into the cottage, leaving the door ajar.

Rhea bustled about in the kitchen. Her silvern brows looked fit to escape into her hairline and her lips were pressed tightly together. Mildred passed under the sagging arch into the cluttered kitchen. Small crates filled with flasks of pickled frog liver and pouches of lemongrass were strewn across the shelves. Rhea had shifted the steel kettle atop a sputtering flame.

Mildred murmured an incantation to unlock the bottom drawer. She drew out a miniscule milky vial and slipped it into Rhea's palm. 'Add this to 'is tea, love,' she whispered. 'A few drops, go on. It'll loosen 'im right up.'

Rhea frowned, but before she could protest, the Inquisitor crossed into the room.

His eyes widened as they roamed across their hulking supply cabinet jumbled with jars of herbs and pastes, the smouldering sage stick and the kitchen broom. Despite the inky pit expanding in her chest, Mildred almost cackled. She'd flown pigs smoother than that old thing.

Rhea's knuckles were white. She stared at the Inquisitor's podgy frame, in ware and wait, as he gawked around the cabin. He seemed at a loss for words. If this is how he reacted to some jars of rosemary, Mildred thought he'd probably croak at the sight of their basement.

Mildred sat at the tea table. The Inquisitor dragged his gaze from the cabinets and crumpled into the chair furthest from Mildred.

'Rhea will join us in a mo',' Mildred said, and a bulbous vein in the Inquisitor's forehead swelled.

'She is not permitted to remain here for this,' he said tersely. 'Only residents.'

'Aye, she's a resident,' Mildred said. 'Dear Rhea's been a close companion since me late 'usband's abrupt departure. She's as much a resident as meself.' The kettle whistled. Rhea topped up the teacups and took her seat beside Mildred.

The Inquisitor blinked his beetle eyes. 'But … what of her husband?'

'Gone with the fires, milord,' Rhea spoke from the kitchen, with her best approximation of grief.

'May Lady Day bless them both,' said Mildred. 'We shan't remarry, milord. Too devastated.'

The Inquisitor's face swelled. 'Very well,' he relented. 'I am Inquisitor Perble, the designated Inquisitor for the Western Wallows.' The wings of each word he spoke were clipped. He removed a scroll from his bag and cleared his throat. 'You, Madam Mildred of the Old Wilbury Uplands, are hereby subject to the sixth routine inquisition of heresy, installed by …'

Mildred blew on her tea to disguise her soured smile. Six routine inspections too many, she thought. At least Rhea was here for this one. She glanced at Rhea, and her responding smile crinkled her face like fine linen. To a stranger, she would seem entirely at ease. Nothing to hide. Nothing to lose.

Mildred knew better.

'His late Majesty King Phylrr V,' Inquisitor Perble warbled on, 'decreed a kingdom-wide inquisition to exterminate the *scum* that taints our great lands.'

'Such noble work, milord,' Rhea gushed, her flattery a blade.

The Inquisitor blinked in surprise, then his ruddy face deepened to a mottled puce.

'Indeed, my lady!' he exclaimed. 'The noblest work to protect the rightful order!' With a purse of his lips, he added, 'You should know that the Wallows are of particular concern to His Majesty. No famine? No plague?' Perble shook his head. 'Many wise men suspect that heretic filth are behind this strange prosperity.'

Mildred's guts plunged into a frosty fjord. Rhea sat in silence, staring into her tea. 'In the Uplands?' Mildred said, feigning polite disbelief. 'We 'aven't heard nothing since that old hag in the east was strung up with 'er friends.'

Rhea was still. Neither she nor Mildred was likely to forget that tale. A royal scout had discovered the witch and her clients, and the entire village participated in their stoning. Mildred and Rhea spent months wracked with dread that they would be next.

'There ain't no chance of such things here, milord,' Mildred said with finality.

Perble harrumphed. 'I shall be the judge of that,' he said. He flourished a scroll and squinted.

'Have you sworn fealty to His Majesty King Polus?' he began, glancing up from the scroll at Mildred and Rhea. They nodded, and he continued. 'Would you be willing and able to travel to the nearest temple to renew fealty at the turn of the season?'

To Mildred's wonder, Rhea's eyes filled with tears, and her bottom lip quivered in a glorious display of theatrics. 'Milord,' she choked out, 'there is nothing I long for more in this world than further chances to prove my devotion to His Majesty.'

'She is … very devout,' Mildred lied, fighting a bubble of nervous laughter.

Inquisitor Perble blinked furiously, eyes shining, and leant closer over the table. 'My dear,' he said to Rhea in a voice compact with emotion, 'I feel *exactly the same*.'

The fabricated connection eased Perble enough that he took a sip of the tea. His eyebrows perked, and he swallowed and exclaimed, 'Madams, this tea is delicious! It tastes just like a tart my wetnurse used to make!'

Rhea beamed. 'Thank you, milord!' she gushed. 'This brew's a bestseller.' She exchanged a performative glance with Mildred and continued, 'We source herbs for our tea from all 'round the kingdom.'

'Why, that explains the cabinet!' Perble said, relief splintering across his face. He drank another mouthful, and Mildred cracked a genuine smile; this was child's play! 'Now, where was I … Do you have any financial records I could examine?'

Perble perused and praised Rhea's rigorous financial archives records. His unwary eye found nothing of note. Perhaps that is why he did not question further the curious notations scrawled in the margin corners, such as *find new source of pig's blood* and *frog liver shipment delayed.*

Instead, Perble said, 'I certainly marvel at the efficacy of your enterprise, madams. I mean, these dividends! My own manor runs scarcely as smooth as this.'

'Ye're too kind!' Rhea cried.

'If it weren't for dear Rhea to count the coins,' said Mildred, 'I'd prolly have joined me 'usband under the orchard long ago.'

Perble guffawed, and Mildred and Rhea exchanged a victorious smile. They disguised each of their lies in a cocoon of truth; they landed on Perble like dandelions carried on a gentle breeze.

Perble queried the layout of the homestead, and Mildred pulled another tome that contained the blueprints. She had modified it years ago to conceal their underground workshop and was confident there would be nothing suspicious. But Perble studied it and frowned. 'One sleeping chamber?' he said, almost to himself. 'For … two dames?'

The shock that shot through Mildred was so potent that her vision rippled. Rhea floundered, eyes darting around the room, so Mildred said, too quickly, 'Our winters are cold, milord. We do what we gotta do to get by. I'm sure ye understand, ownin' land an' all.'

Perble's frown creased his forehead, and he looked between the two women.

They held their breath.

Then he smiled, a laceration across his plump and pasty face. 'Your bond is powerful. Like sisters, blood. I am so pleased you ladies have each other.'

Mildred nodded her agreement. Her heart eased its wild thump.

'Next is … ah. Yes.' Perble gulped down the last of his tea, then leant closer and studied them both. 'The prosperity of the Wallows astounded me,' he confided. 'I have visited these parts before and found it overrun by plague, famine, all manner of gruesome diseases. The sudden departure of such issues …'

He trailed off, eyes flicking between the two women. Mildred could feel her pulse in her throat, like a toad perched just behind her tongue, set to leap. 'I must ask … do you ladies know of any concerning individuals in the area? Apothecaries or medicinal consultancies? Any healers, herbalists? Spinsters?'

Mildred swallowed the toad and smiled. 'Other than us, milord? None at all.'

Perble beamed. 'Well, is that not good fortune! I doubt I could face such a beast. And the executions are always so gruesome, no? Old Wilbury's cobbled square would never recover from such bloodshed.'

Neither woman could muster a response. Thankfully, Perble hadn't seemed to expect one. He gave a decisive flourish of his quill and announced, 'That does look like the end of it, madams. On behalf of His Majesty, I do thank you for your compliance. And the tea!' Perble brandished the empty teacup. 'I must admit, I thought the worst when I took in your collection of spices,' he added, 'but I see now that was folly.'

''Course, milord!' Rhea said. 'We are humble servants of the king.'

'Brewin' tasty teas with all the spices we can find,' Mildred added.

The buoyant conviction in Perble's beady eyes was almost pitiful. 'That you are, madams. I shall be on my way now. I wish you both the most bountiful of harvests.'

'And we wish ye safe travels 'cross the moor, Inquisitor, sir,' Mildred replied. Rhea helped Perble roll the scrolls up and pack them into his bag, then he wobbled out the door.

The two women waved him off as his horse trotted back down the hill of their homestead. It wasn't until he was ambling along the pale trail across the moor that Rhea turned to Mildred, flummoxed. 'Not saying I don't approve, but what in the Grey Dame's name was in that damned potion?'

Mildred gave a weak smirk. 'Certainly not tea leaves, that's sure and certain.'

Rhea chuckled, then laughed, and kept laughing. Mildred couldn't help it and cackled along. Tendrils of relief bled into her, steeping her soul with the promise of security. She gazed at Rhea through teary eyes, and the realisation settled over her like a freshly sheared fleece—it was over. They did it. They were safe.

'Whatever was in it,' Rhea murmured, 'I reckon I'll need somethin' even stronger to forget all that.'

Mildred pulled her into her arms. 'Suit yerself. I've got all I need right here.'

Dawnshaper

Courtney Jordan

Diana's pulse hammered away, and she peeked at the man closest to her, thinking he could hear it. Her stomach dropped as they made eye contact, and she gulped down bile as she tried to compose herself—she could be executed for this.

The sun blazed onto the training arena, with only their shadows as shade on the gravelled dirt, hazy with heat. In one corner, next to a stack of dulled swords, were odd-looking straw dummies in a clumsy mess. An archery range was on the other side, with targets that needed to be replaced.

A man with an unnaturally straight posture stood facing the recruits. His grey moustache curled slightly at the tip but did nothing to hide the dismayed curl of his lips.

'I am Sir Albert Foulk. You are here today because you think you have what it takes to be a Knight of the Zimirith Kingdom. I will only train the best; today, we will see who that is with a test of strength and stamina.' The man meticulously pronounced each word, and several people shifted uncomfortably.

Fifty-two men and Diana lined up as Sir Albert Foulk strode down the line with his hands behind his back. Diana stood next to some men with smaller builds to blend in. She could only hope her sooty, scruffy disguise didn't come under the scrutiny of Sir Albert Foulk. She had stolen a ragged old tunic and leather pants from her merchant father and while everyone seemed to be wearing their finest clothes—Diana stood out like a pirate ship. She assumed they would be relentlessly training and thought these were better than ruining some of her father's finer clothes. Diana felt the uneven edges of her black hair prickling her shoulder blades—she had cut it earlier that morning—she would have done it sooner, but she wanted to avoid her father's suspicion.

Sir Foulk walked past Diana and paused. 'You there—step forward and state your name.'

'Daniel, sir.' She had practised deepening her voice for weeks. Still, under the revered Sir Albert Foulk's scrutiny, she had trouble maintaining her pitch.

'How old are you, soldier?'

'Nine—' her voice broke awkwardly, and she cleared her throat, 'nineteen, sir.'

'Nineteen? You are a bit scrawny. I will not tolerate liars.'

'Sir Albert Foulk, I really am nineteen.'

'Is that so? Drop and give me fifty. ALL OF YOU.' The sudden increase in volume caused everyone to flinch back.

Diana dropped and started doing push-ups. After nine, two men on her left had collapsed.

'Disqualified.'

The harsh assessment filled everyone with a new vigour while the two men were ushered off to the side.

Sixteen, seventeen, Diana could see the trembling arms of the men next to her, but not her; she had trained for this day. Three more were disqualified.

Thirty-four, thirty-five.

Only twenty-one men were still going. Diana felt giddy that her hard work was paying off. Finally, by outlasting the burly men, she had a better shot.

Forty-nine, fifty. Diana slowly lowered herself down to rest—

'Keep going until I tell you to stop,' Sir Albert Foulk barked.

Diana pushed back up as someone down the line flopped to the floor.

Sixty-one, sixty-two. She felt the strain starting to seep in and sweat formed on her brow. *Seventy-four*. Her arms were trembling now. She risked a quick glance and was pleased to see only four others still going—she only needed to outlast them—they would not be able to refuse her. Her hands had turned white and clammy and sweat trailed down her nose, splashing on the ground lightly. Diana froze for a moment. The sweat was dripping black—the soot she had put on her face was coming off. She pressed on.

Eighty-eight. Diana was in a tie.

Thud.

'Disqualified,' called out for the last time.

'Get up, champion.'

Diana shakily pushed herself up to stand. She felt like she was on fire, trembling down to her toes. She kept her head down, acutely aware her disguise was falling apart. The sweat made her tunic cling to her body, and she tried to pull it away from her figure discreetly.

'Raise your head, soldier.'

Diana reluctantly looked up at Sir Albert Foulk, trying with all her might to not cower in the sharpness of his glare.

'A ... woman? A *woman* bested all these men?' a man said.

'Not a woman. *Witch*,' Sir Albert Foulk spat. 'Seize her.'

Two men quickly grabbed her arms.

'What? I'm not a witch! Please, I haven't done anything,' Diana cried.

'How else? How else could a girl beat all these men in a test of *strength*? Girls are weak! You must have cast some foul enchantment to steal the strength of those around you.' The man's loud over pronunciation of each word riled the trainees up, and they quickly formed a crowd around Diana and the men holding her in place.

'Please, I did noth—' Diana's voice was drowned out by the crowd calling her wretched names.

'So, you deny they were the first to fall? Take her away.' The men started dragging her away as a small path cleared in the crowd.

'We should be offered a second chance. The witch stole our strength!' one man cried out and was met with cheers of agreement from the rest.

'Wait! I have trained for this. I deserve a chance too.'

'You would dare admit that you have planned treason?' The captain's voice rang out clearly, and the men holding her paused and turned her around to face him.

'Treason?' Diana shrieked.

'Did you think you could get close to the King if you became a knight? Lies, treachery and treason.' The captain's voice was mirthful. He gestured them away.

'NO. Stop putting words in my mouth. I did nothing,' Diana shouted over her shoulder. 'I AM NOT A WITCH!'

The men's bulkier frames made it tricky to hold onto her as they descended the narrow staircase, guffawing when Diana stumbled down several steps.

'No. This is a misunderstanding. Please. I am not a witch.'

The cell they shoved her into was small and dark. Still, despite the lack of sunlight—apart from a tiny window in the uppermost corner—the room was unbearably hot. Sharp little rocks dug into the palm of her hand as she fell.

The guards locked the cell door, and with one last 'filthy witch' spat at her, they walked back up the narrow staircase. Diana scrambled up and painfully turned on her knees to grasp the cell doors.

'Let me out. I am innocent,' she yelled at the sniggering men.

Diana sighed and moved back from the door. One corner of the cell was darker, but she dismissed that as being out of the light's reach and continued her assessment of her foreseeable living arrangements. Diana tried not to think of the squeaking and scurrying of the rats, the stench of bodily fluids, or the death and decay. As much as she did not want to think about her fate—she wondered what method they would use—would she be burned? Hung? Beheaded? Drowned? Or would she rot in this cell? All for dreaming of a life as more than someone's wife.

The corner moved.

Diana's hazel eyes darted back to the corner, and she waited … nothing happened. It was a trick of the light.

'Witch, eh?' a raspy voice crackled out.

Diana flinched into the bars of the cell behind her. 'Who are you?'

The dark shape crawled into the light, revealing a woman grinning widely, flashing a golden tooth. Her laugh lines were exaggerated by her weathered skin. She had numerous braids running through her hair, pinned back by a blue scarf. Her outfit was like Diana's, yet she made it look purposeful. Diana was fascinated.

'Cap'ain Medusa Madley. Oo are ye?' Her voice was raspy from disuse and dehydration but marginally better than before.

'Oh, you are a pirate,' observed Diana, shuffling her feet. Meekly, she introduced herself. 'I am Diana.'

'And yere a witch. Mind cas'ing a fancy spell and boo'ing us out o'here?'

'Ugh.' Diana dragged a hand over her face. 'I am NOT a witch. And it is simply ridiculous to accuse me of such.'

'Got some'ing against witches, girly?' Medusa frowned.

'No. No, of course not. I am just not a witch myself. Ma'am.'

'Why they call ye a witch then?'

'Because I did something they did not like,' Diana muttered.

'Go on.'

'Well, I want to be a knight.'

Medusa screwed up her face like she tasted something foul. 'What ye want ter be a knight fer?'

'I don't just want to be someone's wife. Or someone's daughter. Or mother. I want to be me. I don't want a mundane life.'

'And ye thought becoming a knight would help ye? But they found ye out.'

'Only after I had bested them in a test of strength and stamina.' Diana smiled, still proud of her accomplishment despite the turn of events.

'So, ye beat the boys in raw strength, and ye are now to be executed for witchcraft?'

'Yes. That's right.'

'What did ye expect?'

'What?'

'Listen up, young un. A man's ego is a very fragile thing. You put em all in a group together like that and shatter their egos? Ye lit a fuse in a puddle of gunpowder.'

'I always wanted to be a knight since one saved my mother when I was a child. I want to go on adventures and save people. I want to wield a sword and I want ... *I want to be respected*—'

'There'd be better ways to escape from the mundane, girly. Ye do not need to be a knight to do any o' those things. I do all that an' more as a pirate.'

'You mean steal things?' Diana scrunched up her nose.

'Don't ye be looking at me like that, girly. I don't think those clothes belong to ye, now do they?'

Diana shifted a bit and moved away from the uncomfortable bars of the cell. 'Well, no. But it was all part of my disguise.'

'Eh? Needs work,' Medusa smirked.

'So,' Diana averted her eyes, 'how would one go about becoming a pirate?'

'Well, for a girly like you, a better disguise,' Medusa paused to consider Diana before adding, 'or a welcoming crew.'

'And where would someone find—'

'No need to draw it out. Ye already know a captain, and my crew will be here any moment.'

'Really? We are getting out of here?'

'Aye! Don't be daft.' Medusa turned her head and muttered, 'We'll need to work on that.'

'I'm sorry, did you say something?' a confused Diana said.

'Nothing, of course. First thing, ye'll need ta name ye new ye.' Diana's eyes widened, and the captain smirked. 'Ye didn't think me name was really Medusa Madley, did ye?'

'Dawnshaper,' Diana whispered out. Medusa thumped the side of her head twice and leaned forward.

'What was that? I didn't hear ye.'

'My name from now on is Diana Dawnshaper,' she spoke confidently.

'What's it mean?'

'It means from now on, every day I get to shape my own destiny. Every morning I wake up, I am in control of my life.'

'That's … unique. But we will need to teach ye how to speak properly,' Medusa grinned.

'I am speaking proper—'

'Exactly. Proper. We don't like that on our ship. Ye'll learn.'

'Oh. Will I get a sword? Do we get to save people? Will we go looking for treasure? Do you think I will get seasick? I've never been on a boat before,' Diana rambled out.

'Don't be calling my ship a boat,' snapped Medusa defensively. 'Ye'll be swabbing the deck ter start.'

BOOM!

The cell shook slightly, and Diana shrieked, grabbing onto Medusa tightly.

'Well, that'll be me crew and a puddle of gunpowder.'

The Psygodons and I

ELSHA FORREST

Henry always told me the monsters were outside the dome, but I soon learned the real ones were on the inside. Grey, grey, grey. Grey robes, grey walls, grey chains. I remember when my life was bursting full of colour, the crimson curls of my daughter. It comes back to me like a dream.

'Count to 100,' Henry says.

Anastasia grins with her crooked baby teeth. I run deep into the maze, a rainbow of roses, ruby, burnt orange, gold and sapphire. The scent is almost as sweet as Anastasia's head. I hide behind the statue of a man wielding a spear and riding a psygodon. Crunch. Crunch. I peek out. And make eye contact with Henry. He winks at me.

My thoughts are interrupted by Luther's snores. I stroke his face. I remember the night I saw him.

I had hoped the night would cloak me in darkness, but it is a cloudless night. The gnarly trees touch me with their icy fingertips. There's a silhouette under a pine tree. The moon scintillates behind him, casting an ethereal glow.

'When I received your first letter, I was suspicious it was at the King's orders, but you have proved yourself trustworthy so I

can show my face. I don't understand how someone as privileged as you, who feasts on truffles and sleeps with a warm fire, would risk that to help us?' Luther says.

'I couldn't bear the executions any longer. I had to sit there and be impassive while I watched people be torn from limb to limb,' I say.

'King Henry is an evil man.'

'Violent, but not evil. He puts on a vicious façade so people will respect and obey him.'

'Well, I suppose he was raised that way. His father ordered my parents to make the dome. Both of them died. My mother fell from the top. I found her mangled body outside my school. And my father fell off the other way—I like to think he drowned peacefully, but he was probably eaten alive by the psygodons.'

'I don't want to hurt my husband. I just want to help the innocent. I will help you until an heir replaces him.'

'I must warn you; he will just be like his father. And even if he's not, a spoiled, sheltered boy is just as much an insult to the people.'

'You mean someone like yourself? What would you do?'

His eyes light up.

'Well, obviously, no more executions. The resources and prosperity would be shared equally. I would devote our efforts to getting out of the dome. Only a selfish coward would force us to live within the dome where food is scarce. There are rumours of islands near here.'

'You are a wise man.'

'Ursula,' Luther says.

Luther's emerald eyes face me. The only piece of colour in this cell. He removes his gold necklace. After a series of complicated manoeuvres, he opens it with a click to reveal a vial.

'What's this?' I ask.

'I snuck in something the revolution has been working on. It's still experimental, but it's worth a shot. It's supposed to protect you against the psygodons. You should swim to an island north of here.'

'You take it.'

'You should take it. I've devoted my life to this cause, and I can die happy.'

He hands it to me. I open the nozzle and drink it.

'You can die happy?'

'Yes, they're storming the castle tonight. Our spies have infiltrated the King's guards.'

'What will happen to my children?'

'No one will hurt them.'

'I've abandoned them.' I feel a catch in my throat.

'I am truly sorry. I should have found a way to get them out of the dome as well. No. I should have never involved you in the first place. This is all my fault.'

'It was my choice.'

The trees wear sparkling wedding dresses. I want more than anything to be Luther's bride. Luther strokes the grizzly bear resting her head in his lap.

'She's all healed now, ready to be set free,' Luther says.

'She's so fragile. Even with your help, she can't possibly survive out there,' I say.

'Creatures, like her, they're resilient, strong—after what she's been through, nothing can break her.'

'Isn't she safer and happier in your cottage?' I ask.

'No one can ever be happy if they're not free,' Luther says.

'It seems a shame to turn such a sweet creature into a ferocious beast.'

'Sometimes you must become a beast to survive this world,' Luther says, then pauses. 'You remember that.'

He gently kisses me on the forehead.

'And what about Henry?' I ask.

'Violence is against what the revolution stands for. He will be spared but imprisoned. You can't seriously still be worried about him.' Luther says.

Henry sits opposite me at the table, but there is an ocean of silence between us. The room is as dark as the ocean's depths. And I shiver in the cold. His eyes look black in the light. And his chiselled features are as cold and imposing as a statue.

'I am truly sorry I went behind your back,' I say.

He doesn't answer.

'I understand if you'd be angry' I say.

'I'm not angry,' he says.

First course. Main. Second glass of ale. Dessert. Third glass of ale. Fourth glass. I get up and pace by the window. Looking anywhere, anywhere, but him.

Crash. A glass shatters in his hands.

'Let me fix you up,' I rush over.

I must pretend I still love him. He recoils at my touch.

'It's a shame. A shame for me, I had hoped for an heir. And for Anastasia, of course, but you never cared for her.

'What's a shame?' I ask.

'You've given me no choice but to execute you.'

'You wouldn't do that. I know you're a kind man.'

'And how did that work out? I trusted you and you lied to me, betrayed me, humiliated me, hurt me.'

'I never wanted to hurt you.'

'Not just me, Anastasia, you put her in danger. Is she even mine?'

'Yes, how cou—'

'I can't listen to you anymore; you disgust me. It was all an act, you're nothing but a whore.'

It's getting harder to keep my calm, loving mask on. The tears wash it off.

'Don't cry now. You have such pretty, pretty eyes. Too pretty. I wonder how you'd look once I gouged them out of your head.'

'If you do anything to me, Luther will kill you.'

Slap. My face stings.

'Oh, I don't plan to yet; you still owe me an heir. Guards! Escort her to our room.'

A guard picks me up. I bite his hand and scratch his arms, but he ignores me and carries me into the room.

I still have nightmares.

His touch was more than cold and emotionless; it was something else. Something like the ocean. The terrifying rage and wrath of a storm. And how could I not love him when Anastasia reminds me so much of him? Tears roll down my cheeks. Luther holds me close.

Stomp. Stomp. Clang. Clash.

'It's time for your execution,' says the guard.

I stand on a stage facing an opaque barrier that looms over us, on the other side a psygodon swims in the obsidian ocean. The grey creature is the size of a house and has incisor-like teeth. It thrashes through the water towards us, it's stinger tail gleaming. An open semicircle amphitheatre surrounds us. On my right, the royal family barks like hungry sea lions, while on my left the lower class is as silent as sand. The dome has cast a shadow over the crowd. And nestled amongst them are my daughter and newborn son—as perfect as pearls. Henry stands in front of the dome, enveloped by the dome's darkness. His blue-black eyes are the same shade as the ocean behind him.

'Good morning, my subjects. To keep our civilisation free from anarchy, I present four new prisoners. May this remind you of the value of the law. Remember, anyone who looks away will have poison sprayed in their eyes.'

'A rule-breaker of the curfew,' he says, pointing to the man first-in-line. 'A thief,' he says, pointing at another man whose ribcages protrude. 'And the revolution leader,' he says, pointing at Luther. 'As an example of my fair and just ruling, I present to you my wife, Queen Ursula.' Shocked exclaims echo through the crowd. 'No one is free from the rules, not even the Queen. She has been conspiring against me and fraternising with the revolution leader!' The guards grab our shoulders. 'No, leave the Queen for last,' Henry says.

Henry unlocks the transparent door, revealing a room nestled within the dome's walls. Luther doesn't resist, but the other two prisoners cry and shake. They flail their arms and legs as the guards throw them into the room. He closes the door and presses a button. I can't tear my eyes away from Luther. A psygodon rips off his head in a single swift movement and swallows it whole. I feel bile rising in my throat. There is an explosion of crimson blood.

All the colour that left my life explodes back in my face like someone stabbed a scarlet, bloody heart, and splattered me. And I am covered in emotion and colour tenfold more than ever before. All my senses return stronger. I can smell the blood through the door, the sweat of the guard. I can hear my heart. I can taste the bitterness in my mouth. The ocean is bluer and blacker; the pygodons are bigger.

Another psygodon emerges and grabs one arm while the other grabs his leg and tears him apart. The psygodons bare their teeth and spin around each other, colliding, biting and stinging. I can barely see Luther, as the wall turns grey from the sheer number of psygodons. Every cell in my body is alive and screaming with anger, fear and despair, except one, just one, single cell of hope.

A guard grabs me by my arm. The upper class erupts into cheers.

'Mum,' Anastasia wails. Her ear-piercing cry silences the crowd.

The guard puts me inside the dome and Henry locks the door. I can't hear anything except a sucking sound, I feel myself being dragged towards.

I can't breathe. Bang. Bang.

'Let me in!' I try to scream, but I only engulf the water.

Henry looks at me, a small crease between his brows. That no one else would notice except me.

'I'm sorry,' he mouthes.

He locks the door. I kick it frantically. I feel something silky against my leg. It's a psygodon. I look deep into its mouth, filled with pointy teeth. Blackness. Pain. So much pain. I feel dizzy. Dots form at the edge of my vision.

I can breathe and see clearly again. Henry stares at me in shock. What's going on? I go to bang my hand on the door, but I see a fin. The potion! Luther must have made a mistake; it was supposed to save me, not turn me into a monster.

I would love to tear Henry's head off and taste his salty blood in my mouth. My mouth salivates at his tender flesh. He didn't just kill Luther; he killed me. The thought of my Anastasia trapped in there with Henry fills me with burning determination. I swim as fast as I can into the door, hitting it with my head. Again. And again. And again. Until they all go home, and I am all alone.

A psygodon swims towards me and waves its tail in greeting. I follow it to the surface and engulf deep breaths of salty air. The gulls dip and dive, like psygodons swimming in the water. The ocean's waves sparkle like sapphires. Like my daughter's eyes. I was drowning in a corrupt society, a cold home. A fishbowl with a monster, whom I loved and loathed. I pressed my fins longingly against the glass. And to escape the monster I had to become one? Maybe all of us have what they call a 'monster' within … What are 'monsters'? Creatures that refuse to be docile. May Anastasia find her monster.

The Atlas of Time

CHANTELLE KOCH

The *Atlas of Time* sits atop the dust-coated counter of the abandoned book shop. Tanulia stands before it, mesmerised by the glowing purple and silver colours of the cover that illuminate the shop. Too afraid to touch it again.

Jaxith's seven-foot frame towers behind her, watching the atlas just as she does. His bat-like wings encompass the space around them. 'So, are you going to open it?' he asks.

'I don't know,' Tanulia replies. 'I should, but … I don't know.' Tanulia can't look away from the book, no matter how hard she tries. She feels an invisible hand reaching out of the book and grabbing her, slowly dragging her into the pages. She wants to be dragged in, wants to fall into the atlas and travel to a time before the war began, but everyone's warnings of the dangers of time travel play in her mind.

You are disrupting the natural flow of time.

Whatever you do in the past cannot be undone.

You may want to fix the world, but you might cause such disruption that this war would seem like a paradise.

'Where will you go?' Jaxith asks, interrupting her thoughts.

'I told you, before The Uprising.'

'I know, but … If it were up to me, I'd go back to when the world began and destroy those fucking Elven arseholes.'

Tanulia doesn't respond. She had never considered going anywhere other than before The Uprising.

'You know,' Jaxith continues, 'I only decided to journey with you because you look just like my wife. You were a reminder that I need to avenge her death, or find a way to bring her back.'

'Is that why you want to go to the beginning?' Tanulia asks. 'Two thousand years ago?'

Tanulia feels Jaxith's body move away, the enclosure created by his wings disappearing with him. 'I don't want all of our efforts, the death of my wife and your brother, to be for nothing,' he says. 'You're an elf. You don't understand. I don't want to go back to how things were for us. I want to live peacefully among the elves. We can make that happen.'

'*Save us* …' Tanulia's brother's final words are like a dagger stabbing her without end. She tries to pull away from the invisible hand dragging her towards the atlas, to look at her friend and comfort him, but the hand won't let her. 'Come with me,' she says.

'What?'

'When I use the book, come with me.' She uses all her mental strength to pull out of the hand's grip, and finally looks at Jaxith. She manoeuvres through dismantled bookshelves and tattered books splayed on the floor and stops where Jaxith stands near the front door. 'We can change the world together. Please, come with me.'

'That wasn't the plan,' he replies.

'I know, but you've come all this way, and we've been through so much together. I don't think I can do this without you. Do you really just want to sit back and do nothing while I'm gone?'

He turns and looks out the dust-covered window. Tanulia follows suit, wanting to see what he sees. The dust makes the abandoned street look like an old grainy film. Moonlight streaks the town's main road, allowing Tanulia and Jaxith to view the destructive nothingness of the war.

Flames engulfing the trees, now a circular barricade.

Screams reverberating off the orange border.

Squelching of blades through flesh.

Blood splatter across her face.

'Save us …'

Jaxith's sobs pull Tanulia back to the present. She turns to him and her heart cracks. His head rests against the window and tears stream down his face.

'Jaxith,' she whispers.

'I just want her back.' He breathes deeply, trying to hold back his tears. 'I'll go anywhere with you as long as I get her back.'

Tanulia wraps her arms around his hips, her fingertips barely touching on the other side of his broad torso. Her head reaches his chest and Jaxith has to lean down to reciprocate the hug. His large wings wrap around her.

'If we go back to when the world began,' Jaxith says, 'we could stop so much from ever happening.'

Whatever you do in the past cannot be undone.

Tanulia pulls back, Jaxith's wings parting for her, and looks out the window again. 'I don't know if there's a solution where we both get what we want.'

'You're probably right.' Jaxith turns back to his window and Tanulia can feel his arm pressed against hers. 'You always are.'

'Not always.'

Tanulia sees Jaxith in her peripheral looking at her. He doesn't speak.

'The night my brother died, I had a chance to save him.' Tears drip onto the windowsill. 'He told me to save him. But I ran. I thought that if the Elven Guards saw me running, they would come after me, giving my brother a chance to save himself.' The touch of Jaxith's wing across her back sends a warmth down her spine.

'You have the chance to save him now.'

'I know, and I will, but it's not the same. I made that decision, and it will haunt me for the rest of my life.' Jaxith drapes his arm across her shoulders, and she leans into him, resting her head against his ribcage. 'Changing time won't fix what I did.'

Jaxith squeezes Tanulia's shoulders. 'Doing something is better than doing nothing.'

You may want to fix the world, but you might cause such disruption that this war would seem like a paradise.

'This isn't about me,' Tanulia says.

'What do you mean?'

'I'm an elf. I don't understand. You said so yourself.' Tanulia pulls away and stumbles through the ruins of the book shop towards the atlas. 'And you're right. The only thing I want is to bring my brother back, and no matter what we do, that will happen.' She turns to face him. 'But you … you've faced discrimination your entire life, all because of a decision that some old bastards made two thousand years ago about your race. *And* you need your wife back. This is *your* decision. Not mine.'

'You're sure about this?'

'A hundred percent.'

Jaxith walks to the *Atlas of Time* still shimmering on the counter. Tanulia watches his face, illuminated with purple and silver. His eyes are wide, lips parted, as he reaches for the spine of the book. He pulls away before he touches the coated paper. 'We go to the beginning,' he says. He doesn't look at Tanulia, and she knows the invisible hand has latched on to him, holding him in place.

'Okay,' is all she can manage. She stands beside him and another invisible hand grabs her. A twinkling can be heard from the book.

Jaxith reaches for the atlas—

'Wait,' Tanulia says.

His fingers freeze a centimetre from the book.

'You may never see your wife again.'

His eyes widen, and he asks through his now clenched jaw, 'What do you mean?'

They both stand before the shimmering atlas, arms grazing against each other. Tanulia feels his warmth radiating through her. 'When we go back, we're going to change the world. Two thousand years is a long time. Who knows what could happen. The world is never going to be the same again. For all we know, your wife may never be born because of us.'

She feels his now clenched fist hitting the back of her hand. 'You're wrong.'

'Maybe,' she whispers.

'She and I are meant to be together.' His voice rises, echoing through the shop. 'We found each other in a world where my race and her race despised one another. We will find each other again.'

'So, you really want to do this?'

'I will change the way my people are treated, and I will find my wife again.' The only sound is the twinkling of the atlas before he speaks again. 'Yes, I want to do this.'

'Then let's go.' Tanulia wraps her hand around his fist, and he opens his hand to her. They interlock their fingers. She opens the *Atlas of Time* and it automatically flips to a page documenting the beginning of the world. Their hands are guided onto the pages by the invisible hands of the atlas.

They touch the pages, and a white light illuminates the shop.

The light disperses. Tanulia strains her eyes against the harsh daylight. A colourful expanse of life greets her—grass, trees, a flowing stream, birds chirping.

The *Atlas of Time*, now closed on the ground before them, still shimmers and twinkles.

Tanulia feels a comforting squeeze on her hand. She turns and Jaxith is there, his towering frame the only familiarity in this foreign place.

'What is this?' an alien voice croaks behind them.

Tanulia and Jaxith turn, their linked hands splitting. Eight elves are watching them, wide-eyed shock across their faces. A male and female sit on thrones erected from leaves and twigs, and a smaller one, a child, sits on the ground at their feet, all three wearing sparkling crowns.

The other five, three women and two men, are scattered in front of the thrones.

'Who are you?' The male on the throne, the king, asks. His green eyes are like emeralds piercing Tanulia's soul.

'I—I'm Tanulia,' she says. She looks to Jaxith.

'And I'm—' he begins.

'Did I ask you?' the king says.

Jaxith's open hands return to fists, his jaw clenches. His wings flare out behind him, but he doesn't argue.

'How did you get here?' The king speaks directly to Tanulia.

'We used an atlas.' She turns to find the atlas still on the ground. Jaxith grabs her hand and twists her back around.

'What are you doing here?' the king asks.

'It's complicated.'

'Well, why you've come doesn't involve us. Run along, please. We're busy trying to build a peaceful world on what I assume is your land.' He waves his hand at them as though they're flies he's trying to shoo away.

'*Peaceful?*' Jaxith's veins appear more defined across his forehead and down his arms. 'What you make of this world is anything *but* peaceful!'

'What do you mean?' says the queen. 'Where did you come from?'

'Your "peaceful" world is war and destruction across the land,' Jaxith says, ignoring the queen's question. 'Across our home.'

'This is getting ridiculous,' says the king. 'Take them away.' Three of the five other elves move towards Tanulia and Jaxith.

Jaxith grabs a dagger from his belt and stabs in their direction. 'Don't even think about coming near us.' The elves step away. Jaxith steps towards the king, weapon still in hand, his wings folding behind him. 'Do you know what I am?'

The king doesn't respond. The small elf has climbed onto the queen's lap.

'Of course, you don't. You already hate me. Why would you need to know more about my species when you can just create a "peaceful" world that discriminates against us for all eternity?' His ragged breathing causes his shoulders to rise and fall. Jaxith stalks towards the thrones, dagger aimed towards the king. Tanulia sees that the elves have no weapons to fight with.

'Jaxith,' she cautions.

He ignores her. 'Your selfishness caused my species to be repelled by society.' His voice is low, so quiet that Tanulia has to step forward to hear him. 'Your selfishness caused my species to rise up against you, starting a world war between us and the elves.' Jaxith is now in front of the king, dagger pointed towards his throat. The small elf cries in the queen's lap, and Tanulia sees tears brimming in the queen's eyes. The other five elves back away, arms raised in surrender.

Tanulia moves closer to Jaxith. 'Jaxith,' she repeats.

Again, he ignores her. 'Your selfishness killed my wife.' He steps on to the throne, causing the king to lean back in his chair. 'She was an elf, just like you. And you killed her.' The dagger's tip is pressed against his throat. Jaxith's huge body towers over the king. 'And now, you're going to pay.'

He pushes the dagger into the king's throat.

The queen screams and cries, holding the child tight.

The other five elves move to run, then choose to stay and protect the queen.

Jaxith turns around. He moves to one of the male elves. His hands are on the elf's neck—

Snap! The elf falls to the ground.

'Jaxith!' Tanulia screams. She spins around, trying to find him.

Jaxith slices through an elf's throat.

His black wings flare and spin, the sharp points cutting an elf in two.

He punches through the chest of an elf, pulling their heart out.

He stabs the last elf through the eye.

All five elves are limp on the ground. Only the screaming queen and the child are left unscathed.

Jaxith moves towards them, but Tanulia runs in front of him. 'Jaxith, stop it!' Her hands are on his torso, holding him in place. He looks down to Tanulia. He turns and sees the mass of murdered elves, then looks back at the queen and the child.

Tanulia is crying. 'Jaxith,' she whispers. He puts his arms around her shoulders, squeezing her to him, and now he's crying too.

Thana and Callista

Amy Swalwell

If you were anyone, you shopped at Callista's. Thana Astor wouldn't be found dead in any other brand.

Thana's long face appeared from behind the changeroom's velvet curtain, her 50 shades of blonde bob tucked behind her ear. 'Excuse me … hello … you there.'

The young trainee attendant hurried to the curtain, her voice, shaking. 'Yes ma'am.'

'Your sizing is wrong; I am always a ten. Put this piece of cloth away,' huffed Thana.

'Yes ma'am, would you like me to fetch you the next size?'

Thana gasped. 'How rude! Are your ears painted on? I am only EVER a size ten.'

'Of course, sorry ma'am, I'll fetch another design in a ten,' said the attendant.

'Don't bother. I'll take my business elsewhere.'

Thana stormed out of the boutique, almost knocking over an elderly woman.

'Oh, I wouldn't shop in there. The new girls just push the sale, no customer service anymore,' said Thana, not bothering to apologise.

'That is sad to hear,' replied the woman, 'it is a favourite of mine.' Her large emerald eyes looked up at Thana.

Thana rolled her eyes and dismissed the woman. *Look at the time*, thought Thana, looking at her watch. *Why did I plan so long here?* Thana got out her phone and dialled her driver.

'Hello ma'am,' came a voice through the phone.

'James, forget Trevor's suits, I need to be picked up now,' demanded Thana.

'I'm sorry, ma'am, I won't be able to turn around for a while. I will be about an hour.'

'That's not good enough, James.' Thana didn't wait for a reply before hanging up the phone.

An hour, AN HOUR! Who does he think he's talking to? I can't just wait around here. I will see what cars are at the—ick—taxi rank. Thana walked to the taxi rank and waited beside a business class car. She stood there. She took out a tissue and knocked on the window.

The driver wound down the window. 'What can I do for you?'

'Why haven't you opened the door?'

'You've got hands.'

Thana turned away in a huff and walked to the lights. As she arrived the signal turned red. *Well, I'm not going to wait. These cars can wait for me.* Thana walked. Horns blared. A SUV came through the lights—

Thana lay on the bitumen, pain radiating through her body. Her laboured breathing slowed. As her eyes closed, she spied the emerald eyes of the elderly woman, head shaking in disappointment.

Thana thrashed in her bed, heart racing, sweat pouring off her.

'Tan, Tan, wake up.' Trevor shook her.

Thana sat up with a scream. 'Where am I?'

'Woah, Tan, you're at home, in bed.'

'What? But I … a car … Callista's.' Thana looked around, everything looked in its place. 'But a car hit me … how am I at home?'

'Tan, it was just a dream,' said Trevor, rubbing her back. 'Ask the kids, no car accidents have happened.'

'Your nieces are here?' asked Thana.

'What nieces?' Trevor sat up. 'I don't have any nieces. That dream really traumatised you. Our children, Grace, and—'

'We don't have—this is a terrible dream.' Thana tried to pinch herself awake, her heart beating faster every pinch. She made her way to the door and out to the mezzanine, then looked at the three remaining doors. Thana held her breath and opened the first door. It was as she had left it: Four-poster, redwood bed with burgundy curtains. Redwood furniture filled the room. Thana exhaled in relief. She opened the second door. Inside was decorated in posters of Callista models, a glass cabinet of beauty pageantry trophies and crowns. Thana walked cautiously into the room. It was the room that she had dreamt of as a child, but she never achieved further than first runner up. In the centre of the cabinet was a photo of a young girl with Thana, maybe 11 or 12, wearing the Young Miss Melbourne sash. Thana looked over to the single four poster bed, sheets sprawled over it. *Okay*, Thana took a deep breath, *we have a child's room here. Could be worse*, Thana slowly breathed out, *this child is ... acceptable.* Walking to the third door. Thana noticed black sign in the centre. KEEP OUT! *Not in my house, you don't.* She turned the handle, but it was locked. Thana began to bang on the door.

'Piss off, Grace, I'm sleeping,' called a voice from within.

'If you don't open this door, I will be knocking it down.'

The door opened just a crack. 'What.'

'Don't *what* me in my house. Who do you think you are?'

'Go away, Thana. Or should I say mother dearest.'

Before Thana could open the door further, it was closed and locked again.

Trevor's voice piped up from behind her, 'Playing with fire this morning?'

Thana turned to see Trevor on the mezzanine. 'Who does he think he is?'

'Just leave him, Geoff will come out eventually. Shouldn't you be getting ready to take Grace to Callista's this morning?'

'Not Callista's, their staff are so rude. We'll head to Giselle's,' replied Thana.

'What? Not that dollar store knock-off shop. You can't be serious. I'll be the laughingstock of Melbourne,' called Grace from the ground floor.

Thana looked over the edge. Grace was a couple of years older than in the picture, but a mini version of Thana. Porcelain skin, her face framed by long, blonde hair. 'Grace, you will go where I take you, or you will go nowhere.'

'That's not fair. You only wear Callista's. You promised,' called up Grace.

'She's not wrong,' piped up Trevor, 'and you did promise to take her to Callista's from thirteen.'

'Mum, Gabriella has beat me for the last two years. If I don't shop at Callista's she's sure to beat me again.'

Grace's words lit a fire in Thana. No one would beat this daughter.

Their car pulled up to Callista's just after ten. The exterior was no longer that of a boutique store, but of a large retailer. Posters of models hung from the ceiling, some of the same that Thana had seen in Grace's room. Ladies in high-end fashion coming in and out of the marble pillar entrance.

The driver, James, turned back to Thana. 'What time would you like me to pick you up, ma'am?'

'In an hour,' replied Thana.

'Are you serious, Mum? You take a minimum of three,' whined Grace.

'Okay, come back at one, but stay close,' said Thana.

Thana and Grace left the car and walked into the store. The clothes were sorted into the different pageant categories—swimwear, formal, cocktail—the store stretched on further than Thana remembered. The pair visited every rack in store, trying on multiple outfits, ignoring the price. A store attendant followed behind, carrying every ensemble decided upon. *Well, I don't know what has happened here, but I like this new Callista's. They have real sizing too.* Thana looked behind her to the attendant, who was barely able to see over the collection of clothing.

'That will be all. Where do we pay?' queried Thana.

'Follow me, ma'am,' said the attendant, trying hard not to drop a thing.

The pair followed the attendant to the counter. The girl serving them was a couple of years older than Grace, and Grace recognised her immediately.

'Spying on everyone's pageant outfits, Gabriella?' snapped Grace.

'No need to, I'm a sure win for the third year in a row, Miss Runner Up,' retorted Gabriella.

'Oh, is that so?' laughed Thana. 'My daughter won't be the runner up to the likes of you, you ugly girl. You wouldn't even fit into the clothing at this store. Now get me another person to serve us.'

'No can do, ma'am, it's me or no one,' replied Gabriella.

'That old lady behind you has the same uniform. Excuse me … hello … we are needing proper service here.'

The old woman turned around, her emerald eyes locking into Thana's, a knowing smile appearing on her lips. Thana's eyes widened. *Is this déjà vu? A dream?* She grabbed Grace by the arm.

'We're leaving.' Thana pointed to the old woman. 'You—you did this.'

'Mum, what's wrong with you? That's Callista, of course she did something, she created these amazing outfits,' said Grace trying to pull her arm free.

'No, she … argh … I can't explain,' Thana dragged Grace out the door onto the foot path.

'Mum, stop. Let go,' yelled Grace as she yanked her arm from Thana's grip.

Thana looked at her watch. 'The car will be here soon. Stay put.'

Thana looked towards Callista's. Callista watched them from the store window. Staring into Thana's eyes, she slowly made her way to the door, not breaking eye contact. Callista opened the door, Thana took a step back. Like a dance, every step Callista moved forward, Thana moved backward. Thana's heart raced as she tripped backwards off the curb and into oncoming traffic ...

'Thana Regina Astor,' a voice boomed. 'This is your final chance. RETURN.'

Where am I? Am I alive?

A cool breeze swept over Thana. She reached for her doona. There was no doona, there was no bed. Thana opened her eyes, there was only darkness. Thana felt around as her eyes adjusted to the lack of light. Dirt, sticks, leaves, grass, this was not her house. Thana stood and started to walk towards the small dot of light on the horizon. The dot remained in place.

'A star, I've been walking towards a blooming star!' Thana yelled out in anger. Her yell was heard by some nearby farm dogs. Thana decided to walk towards the barking.

'Shut up,' called a voice from inside.

'Yes, you mutts. Shut up,' Thana yelled.

'Who's out there yelling at my dogs?' A middle-aged man appeared from within the house with a flashlight in hand.

'Where am I?' called Thana as the man shone the flashlight in her direction. 'Get that light out of my eyes.'

'Feisty young thing, aren't you?' laughed the farmer.

'I beg your pardon? Tell your animals to be quiet.'

The man hushed his dogs as he walked over to Thana. He was quite tall in comparison, his face aged from working the land. 'Where did you wander here from?'

'That is none of your business. I just need to call my husband to collect me,' replied Thana.

'Husband, at your age? Look, you'll be safe here. I'm Henry, I have a daughter, Sarah, that you can talk to if you need.'

'I am not a child. If you aren't going to help me, just point me in the direction of your town.'

'I don't know how old you think you are, but I won't be having a child walk around at this hour. If you won't come inside, I'll have to call the police to help you look for your parents.'

'I am NOT a child. Do what you want. I will just keep following the road over here.'

Thana walked along the road, feeling every stick and stone under her foot. *Where am I? This road goes on forever.* In front, blue, and red lights flashed towards her. She kept walking as the police car turned around and drove slowly beside her.

'Are you lost?' came a female voice from the passenger's side.

'Of course, you idiot. How far is Melbourne from here?' Thana rolled her eyes as she walked.

The police turned off the engine and the policeman got out. 'Manners go a long way. Melbourne's a few hours hike from here. How about we get you back to the station and ring someone for you?' He walked around to open the door for Thana.

'Who's the child you have in there?' asked Thana, looking at the car window, moon shining from above. Thana moved towards the child; the child moved towards Thana. Thana touched her face; the child touched their face. Thana's eyes widened. With a gasp, Thana ran from the car.

The policewoman hopped out from the passenger's side to help chase down Thana.

'Young lady, stop. It's not safe out here at night.'

Tired, Thana wasn't able to get far.

'Please come with us, don't struggle. We just want to help you.'

Thana followed them, defeated. *What is going on here? I'm not a child; I'm in a child's body. How? Why?* Thana turned away at her reflection as they arrived at the car. She sat silent with her head in her hands.

'What's your story?' asked the policewoman.

'What isn't my story. At some point, I think, I had the world at my feet. My husband and I were the talk of the town. Every woman wanted to be me; every man wanted me. Then some blooming driver hits me as I cross the road. Before I knew it, I was back in bed with my husband with two kids. They materialised out of thin air.'

'That sounds like quite the life,' started the policewoman.

'That's not all. I trip off the path, shopping with the new daughter at this Callista's and BANG! I'm here in this child's body.'

'Good name that one,' said the policewoman.

'Callista's? No, that place is evil … come to think of it … both timelapses … why do you say that?'

'It's my name, though I've never heard of a store named it. Maybe I should start a store.'

'NO!'

The policewoman turned to look at Thana. Those eyes, those emerald eyes.

Harpoons Against the Skies

Brody Brock

Waves crashed against the sands, greeting the arrival of the fishermen. The men prepared their ballistae, each armed with a sizable harpoon. Those not assembling the weapons looked towards the overcast sky, where clouds folded and darkened. The marble skies growled, causing the men to question whether this was the work of an oncoming storm, or a God which they had been led to defy.

'Men!' the captain exclaimed, demanding authority over the fishermen. 'Arm the leisters! The God falls here!'

Dutiful and loyal, the men aimed the ballistae high. Missiles sprung from their mechanisms and tore through the clouds with a distinct ferocity and malice. The air grew raucous with their screech before settling upon an eerie silence as they sailed beyond earshot of the sailors. The fishermen awaited with bated breaths, longing to see the fruits of their labour.

'Has it hit, yet?' one questioned.

'Shut it, lad,' the captain barked back. 'All good things come in time, yes? We've prepared for this, we 'ave. Pull 'em back in and fire again!'

The fishermen, though apprehensive of their skipper's outlandish demand, were governed by their meekness. Any doubts of this grand mission were kept within sealed-shut mouths. Their clothes, adorned with sand, stuck to their skin and began to chafe. Blisters formed swiftly beneath the pits of their arms as they reeled back the leisters and armed them once more.

'Fire, lads!' the captain screamed alongside the fishermen's accompanying laughter, which replaced all ambient sounds and echoed through the beachside.

Not even the roaring waves would best the sound of his own amused hysterics. The harpoons launched once more into the clouds above them.

One fisherman turned to face the captain. 'How do you know it's up there?'

'Question, questions,' the captain swiftly interjected. 'How 'bout some trust, boy? The Venn Diarius is there and always has been!'

His finger followed the coils connected to the harpoons, before springing towards the clouds. The harpoons continued to travel before disappearing once more.

'It's been sitting over us since the first moment of eternity! Watching—nay *reminding* us that *we* are below it! Is it not time for us take destiny into our own hands? Down with the Venn Diarius, I say!'

The captain's words rang out across the beach as the fishermen waited for the harpoons to snare a catch. Moments passed like decades, with no seeming avail. The men stood silent, doubting their expedition.

The Venn Diarius was the name many forlorn folk had granted to this entity the captain spoke of. A large head hosting a perfect duo of humanoid faces which had conjoined bewitching beauty with abhorrent horror, devoid of any body below the neck. These faces overlapped across one another to create a trilogy; one-third man, woman and child who had laid centre. The child was nameless, representing the uncertain possibilities new life held. The woman, known simply as The Northerly Mother, was the face of compassion, speaking words of beauty to humans. The captain, however, saw these words as mere manipulation, lulling humans into docility. A message he has spread to his men. The final face was unlike these others, however. Rather, this third was known as The Father of Gall, a masculine face locked with an eternal frown. He represented the brutality of men, their pride, their need for strength and conquest.

Sensing their trepidation, the captain cried out, 'Good men, we have travelled far across Gliyw Noscal. But it *is* for a noble cause, I promise this to you! Once the Venn Diarius is struck down, all folk throughout this land will finally be free! You know what that makes us? Heroes!'

The snare tightened with a mighty clang, turning all attention to the clouds. The harpoons had struck something indeed, something large. The captain sprung forward, a deep pride washing over him.

'To arms! Reel it in gentlemen, no time to waste!'

The men cheered and rushed to their stations. Twelve men per ballista turned the crank which drew back the harpoon with great resistance. The captain, now drunk with narcissistic accolades, base all egotisms and invited all praises sung by the unbarred mouths of his men. The fishermen, continuing their work, began to sing shanties of the ocean. The so-called 'sultans of the sea' were confident of their imminent triumph over the heavens through their heresy.

The line shook violently as the men continued to reel back the harpoons. A deep moan of pain boomed from the sky, filling all ambient sounds and replacing the songs of celebration. The men swiftly stepped away from the ballistae and froze, eyes locked towards the heavens. However, the reels continued to pull down their catch, no longer needing the assistance of the fishermen. Silence settled firm upon the vast dead air, as the ambience of the ocean ceased.

Yet, the captain was confused by the sudden shift in his men.

'We've almost done it, lads! What be the problem?' The captain marched forward, attempting to grasp their attention, but to no avail.

'That noise …' a fisherman began, his voice wavering.

'The sound of our victory!' interjected the captain.

'Nay, that isn't no sound of victory, sir.'

'Well, what in the hells might the sound be then, lad?'

'That's just it,' the fisherman turned towards the captain. 'That be the sound *of* hell.'

Yet the men continued to stare upwards, paying no heed to their leader. Concern flooded the captain's mind. In the distance, the harpoons could be seen falling from the sky, detaching from their catch.

This is when the men finally saw the God they sought to destroy.

The face of The Northerly Mother emerged through clouds which barely parted, like a hand passing through water. The men covered their mouths to muffle their cries of fear, now faced with the entity they had only read about or heard word of through devout clerics. The face of The Northerly Mother, unlike that depicted within religious texts and described by zealots, was dead. Her eye, bloodshot and rolled backward, with a single tear of blood trickling along her cheek. Her mouth, which once spoke those words of beauty, was closed shut forevermore. Finally, upon her cheek was a pair of deep wounds which dug deep into her flesh and spurt forward fountains of red-stained ichor. Following her, the rest of the great head, the Venn Diarius, descended without grace.

The fishermen expected the sense of power they held to last a lifetime, yet in a moment, it had fleeted. The Venn Diarius descended towards the sea below, a small distance from the shoreline, barely making a wave as it laid to rest. The Northerly Mother's face was drowned beneath the waves, her wound staining the oceans crimson and leaving only The Father of Gall buoyant.

A burly fisherman swung around to the captain, clutching at his collar with one hand and drawing a dagger with the other.

'You've doomed us! Yer pretty words tricked us! There's no freedom found in killing it!'

Another drew his dagger in opposition of this mutiny. 'Oi! He couldn't 'ave known! Drop 'im!'

The fishermen began to argue amidst each other, within each brewing a sudden, vexing rage birthed from the disgrace of their own transient weakness. The captain, meanwhile, stood silent. The accusations swayed slowly from him as the fishermen began to blame one another.

More daggers drew forward. Spears erected. Voices rose in anger, hatred and shame, possessing them. The captain took another step backward, distancing himself from the congregation.

'Yer a fool for believing this idea to be good!'

'Stop looking at me like that … you have the eyes of a dog, traitor!'

'You're holding that dagger awful close, son. You tryin' to get yerself killed!'

The sickly sound of flesh parting erupted as a fisherman ran forward and stabbed another. Ichor spilled upon blonde sands as the fishermen began to attack each other. When their bodies crumpled, something possessed them. A lingering will drove each to endure more than what they were capable of. The fishermen had become more incarnations of violence at this indictment, blinded by their hypocritical antagonisms, fear of judgement and the fault of their arrogance.

The captain scrambled to safety, shutting his eyes as he hid behind a ballista. The bloodshed continued around of him. The sounds of steel on steel, and that same steel tearing through flesh overwhelmed him, forcing his hands to cup his ears. The men, all persistent to be the sole victor, continued still. Some laid still, gasping for air as limbless heaps, more parodies of their former selves. Some drenched in blood, slashing violently at the air. This endured, until the slashing of swords softened. The blood trickled slow, and the men's gasps deepened. Bodies collapsed to the ground. Rage subsided. All life faded, until only two were the sole witnesses to such atrocities:

The captain, and the Venn Diarius. More specifically, The Father of Gall.

The captain unshielded his ears and peered over the wooden supports of the ballista. Cautiously, he etched forward and back onto the red beachside, stepping over the bodies of his underlings. Some were still breathing but too close to death to speak words. Their eyes, the captain noticed, were full of fear, silently begging for help as they locked with his own. But it was too late. Guilt and shame weighed him down to his knees, his eyes unable to be torn from his former comrades.

'I don't understand ...' the captain spoke to the corpses. 'We could 'ave been heroes. It was my destiny. Would've been yours too if you'd all just 'ave *shut yer traps*!'

Spittle flew from his mouth, desperate to shift his own blame to his men. 'What were yer all, man or beasts?! Because before me, I see a group of *mutinous dogs*!'

He stood now, screaming at the dead.

'Go on! What are ye all?! This wasn't my doing! This was your destiny, and dogs ain't got no destiny! Only death!'

The harsh winds disturbed the bodies around the captain, and they tumbled down the sands. Perhaps humans rested within the ever-changing bosom of the absolute, with neither beast nor human beginning or concluding, fated to return to what they know. The captain thought his mission was pure, yet now before him laid an army of the dead, crimson pools foaming and ebbing from their agape mouths.

Doubt crept into the captain's conscious. Was there no reason, no reward, for slaying a god? Cold sweat and tears unified within his greying beard, and a dark fear finally seized his spine with the grip of a revived clay golem. Only now did he realise there were none left to praise him for his victory. He stood still on the water's edge, an infinite valley of dunes behind him, and felt his fleeting power over those he considered inferior sink like an anchor into the depths of his ramshackle mind.

His gaze finally shifted to The Father of Gall. His only thought was to seek an answer.

'It wasn't strength I sought,' he cried. 'And it wasn't conquest! I swears it!'

Suddenly, from a distance ahead, an eye snapped open. The buoyant God whose portion of their face remained above the red oceans peered towards the captain. The captain's own eyes responded in a deepened fear. His posture straightened and composure stiffened as he addressed his superior. His knees begged to buckle beneath the fear, yet he resisted.

'We 'ave killed the mother of the north and the bless'd child! Yet now we greet you, Father of Gall! Yer' malice reaches into a vast pool of knowledge, does it not? I bequeath thee with a question my mind cannot wish to understand, yet my curiosity requests only an answer in return … *Why*?'

The mouth of the Father of Gall moved its lips as if to speak. Yet the words it so yearned to share refused to leave the immeasurable void contained within its mouth. The monumental figure then abruptly closed its mouth, pursing its lips in a strained attempt to keep something within.

Suddenly, tufts of blackened feathers spurted forth from its mouth before giving way to the disgruntled squarks of emerging ravens. Their bodies, lacerated with open wounds and near featherless, dug their way from the dark abyss. The dozens of these creatures gave way to hundreds of the same which fell from the mouth before struggling to stay afloat within the dead air.

In the air, the conspiracy of ravens wrestled for dominance before shooting towards the Father of Gall's forehead. Upon this branch of skin, they landed and furiously pecked at the weakened flesh. In unison, they dug into large portions of flesh and peeled away useless skin to relay their message to the captain. Large lettering appeared across the head of the goliath god.

Before long, the captain realised that written before him was the answer he so wished to seek. The ravens were a macabre messenger as they carved a single rigid word into the Father of Gall. The answer to the captain's question: why he sought to pull the very gods from their heavens and stand among the rotted corpse of such a figure.

The blood-soaked message was clear.

Vanity.

It Only Takes One

Ashlee Sullivan

It's snowing again. Millions upon millions of white flakes blanket the mountainside, covering the destruction and burying the bodies. What's left of the train is strewn down the slope, the pieces looking like they'd gone halfway through a shredder before being ripped away.

There will be no survivors, and there will be no evidence.

The helicopter flies lazy circles in the air. The manipulator inside thrusts their arms through the open door, straining to control the snow so it curves around them. They wait. They watch. Still, there is no movement on the mountain.

No one had survived; no one could have survived, but when the helicopter performs a wide turn and flies back in the direction it had come—and the train had been going—a single arm thrusts up through the snow.

The train was livelier than Marilore had expected, but then not many people knew about the spy on board.

Not wanting anyone to catch a glimpse of the commanders, Mari quickly slid shut the door between the solemn command car and the roaring party. So different from the sombre lighting and whispered words in the front car; the volunteers had gone all out to try and forget why they were all there.

The carriage was filled with bright, yellow light. All of the electric lanterns hanging from the ceiling vibrated with the pulse of the thrusters, swinging haphazardly anytime a large mound of snow caused the train to unexpectedly swerve or rise further off the ground. Lifters, manipulators, electrics and oculars alike all danced and jumped to the pulse of the music, stumbling into each other and laughing. The metal bands clasped tightly around everyone's forearms glinted brightly, bouncing the lantern's light around the carriage.

Because of the secrecy of the mission—and how little metamaterial cloaking technology they'd managed to steal—when they had been retrofitting the disused train most of the compartments had been cut loose. This left one for the resistance's commanders to plot, scheme and hide in; one for the volunteers to sleep in; another that held the engine and power bay; and one for, apparently, a party.

With the windows boarded over on the inside, and the outside covered in 'Invisiglass', it was like they were in their own plane of existence. Hidden from the world outside, and the world hidden from them, they were, for once, alone and untouchable.

But they still weren't free.

Mari inwardly applauded their effort to dance and laugh the night away. Once, she might have been out there with them, but ever since she had been put in charge of recruitment her ability to ignore and let loose had been swallowed by worry and fear.

She'd handpicked the mission; she was the one who'd convinced everyone on that train and in that carriage to join—to fight back against the ones who locked a part of each of them away. It would be on her conscience if something were to happen to them while doing so.

Especially since the spy must have also been someone Mari personally recruited.

Before Mari could dive into the crowd to begin her search, her nose already sniffing through the different scents and her ears tuning in to the nearest conversations, she was jumped on by the only other percepter on the train.

'Miss Marilore!' Cassia greeted.

Mari pried the teenager loose and set Cassia down in front of her. In the hopes of not letting on the extra danger they were all suddenly in, Mari was mustering a smile for her protégé when she noticed the bright red scratch marks around the band encircling her left arm and the way the girl's nose kept wrinkling. Both were common signs for when a percepter was breaking past the ability-hindering bands—Mari could already feel the urge to scratch around her own band.

Seeing the signs on Cassia gave the older percepter an idea. Normally—for this wasn't the first time the commanders had sent her sniffing after a traitor, though it had never been someone Mari knew—she wouldn't bring anyone else into it, but with everyone crowded together like they were, she could use the help.

'Cassia, have you noticed anything odd on this trip? Strange conversations? Weird scents coming off people?'

Cassia tried to play dumb, knowing she wasn't meant to use her abilities outside of lessons or the field.

Mari cut her off before she could blurt the excuse she'd come up with. 'Don't worry about it—they're not my rules. Has there been anything weird?'

Trusting her mentor, Cassia turned slightly and nodded towards a group of lifters in the corner.

'There was a weird smell over by Tover's group.'

Glancing over Cassia's shoulder, Mari quickly observed the large group of lifters. 'Want to help me with something? I can't tell you what, but—'

'Yes!' Cassia couldn't hide her eagerness, her eyes wide and alive with energy.

A fond smile—a real smile—managed to break through Mari's tide of anxiety.

She knew who the traitor was as soon as he'd taken a few steps away from the lifters.

Oculars were often tinkerers. It was thought to be a habit left over from when their ancestors needed to constantly distract themselves from the incredible eyesight their abilities gave them. Focus on the intricacies of one thing to avoid seeing every other minuscule detail around them.

Harrithee had been sitting in the corner, behind the group of lifters, and he had been tinkering with something that hummed with electricity. Something Mari had never seen before. Harrithee was always building things, so she'd thought nothing of it and continued searching the lifters' scents.

While she had been picking something up, she couldn't pin it to anyone. The lifters were having a competition on who could do the most push-ups while people stood on their backs and the stink of sweat clung to them, helping mask the odd smell. When it disappeared suddenly and she could only smell the sweat, Mari had found it again hovering around the ocular as he hurried towards the sleeping car.

Mari called Cassia over just as Harrithee reached the sliding door separating the party and sleep cars. The teenager, caught up in the fun, had joined the pile on Tover's body, but immediately jumped off the lifter to go to her mentor's side.

Mari didn't know how Harrithee had managed to move his scent away from him and to the lifters, but it must have had something to do with the machine he'd been tinkering with. It had no longer been in his hands when he'd been hurrying to the sleeping car and Mari couldn't hear that certain buzz of electricity anymore. She didn't know what had happened to it. And right then it wasn't her problem.

She had her spy.

Pulling Cassia through the crowd, Mari bent her head close to hers and told her what she'd seen, revealing the secret mission she'd been given. Though her young protégé's eyes had widened with every word she'd spoken, by the time they'd reached the sliding door they had narrowed into slits, fury and betrayal gushing out of her in heady scents.

'Cass, duck!'

A hand-held mirror flew over the young percepter's head, smashing apart against the engine carriage wall.

Harrithee ducked away from the hole he'd made in the wall of the train car, leaving the rucksack he must have picked up in the sleeping car on the floor below it, and moved to crouch behind the main engine. Knowing the electrics had been in there when the train had left to power up the lanterns, Mari knew the hole must be a recent addition to the train.

It was Mari's turn to duck when Harrithee popped back up from behind the engine to hurl a penlight at her face. She ran for the hole, ducking her head against the snow sweeping in, and pressed her back against it, trying to keep all of the golden lantern light from leaking out into the night. With the hole about the size of her head, it was enough to keep the back of the train from acting like the bottom of a firefly, but she didn't know how long she could stand there—she was already beginning to shake from the cold.

'Cassia, go find something to cover this with!'

'Like what? All of the Invisiglass was used up!'

'Something white then!' *That would work. It would have to.*

As Cassia scrambled back into the sleeping car, Mari tried to toe Harrithee's rucksack open to see if there was anything inside that could help but had no luck. From where she stood against the wall, she could see a side portrait of Harrithee, his arm deep within the engine core and his eye spread wide in an obvious use of his abilities.

Having learnt her lesson on letting Harrithee tinker, she forgot about the hole and lunged for the ocular. She heard Cassia come back into the car, shouting something about a notebook and tape, when she rounded the corner of the engine. She saw Harrithee flatten himself to the floor.

There was a spark and a pop before a small poof of smoke mushroomed from the engine above the traitor's head.

The train stuttered, throwing Mari off balance. She heard Cassia crash against something.

Mari lashed a kick into Harrithee's side, flipping him onto his back. 'Why?' she snarled.

Winded, Harrithee took a few seconds to answer. 'I'm not going to die for some fool's dream. This way—'

'What? You think they'll let you live? They won't. They'll take any excuse to kill—'

'Miss Marilore?' Cassia's voice was high and shaking.

Worriedly looking around the engine for her protégé, she saw her leaning against the wall next to the hole, her stance a defeated slump. While the notebook was still in her hand, the tape was nowhere to be seen, but Cassia didn't make a move to find it. Instead, she stared out into the night, squinting against the snow flurrying into her face.

Mari focused back on her senses again and, hearing the whir of the helicopter blades outside through the rushing wind, she knew.

Before they'd interrupted him, Harrithee had managed to signal with the mirror and penlight he'd thrown at their heads. She was hoping they'd stopped him in time, that all he had done was make the hole, but … Mari bolted for Cassia, hurling her away from the hole and back towards the sliding door.

It'll be their first target. They'll want the train fully disabled, and they won't rely on Harrithee to do it.

She needed to get Cassia as far away as possible.

Hearing the rush of air as the explosive was launched from the helicopter, Mari jumped on top of Cassia, curling her body around her protégé's, as Harrithee and the engines were blown apart.

She struggles through the snow, dragging herself forward on her hand and knees. What's left of the engine car lays buried behind her, the small hole in the snow from which she crawled the only thing marking its position.

Cassia collapses against a large shred of the train close by, heaving in breaths before sobbing them back out.

Miss Marilore.

It keeps running through her mind. Her mentor's body hitting hers, pushing her to the floor. The carriage exploding. Her arm tearing. Miss Marilore screaming. Their bodies were thrown against the wall then the ceiling, following the motion of the train as it tumbled.

In that horrible time, her senses became clearer than they'd ever been. The shred of metal, the roar of the wind and the screams—so many more followed in Miss Marilore's wake. The air never stopped rushing, explosions swallowing the screams.

The sharp bite of snow slowly numbs her body, easing away the burn engulfing her left bicep, the rest of her arm … gone, and the band with it. With nothing blocking her senses anymore Cassia doesn't have to concentrate to hear the helicopter in the sky far above her. All she has to do was wait for the sound to begin to fade before scrabbling clumsily at the snow surrounding her, going upwards to where she can smell fresh air.

Resting with her back against the wreckage, she thinks about Miss Marilore, her body forever encased in snow and metal. Cassia listens, holding her sobs in for a few fractured seconds, but she hears only the whistle of the wind; there are no more screams, no cries nor whispers—no heartbeats except her own.

The sobs rack her body again. *What am I going to do?* She has to get back to the others. She has to warn them. If there was one spy, there could be others.

She thinks about the lessons she was taught: how to break past the barrier created by the band and access her abilities; how to control her senses so she doesn't drown in the sounds and smells of the world around her. But there was nothing taught on how to survive with only one arm on a snow-choked mountainside.

Except, maybe …

Cassia remembers one of the lessons Miss Marilore taught her. Just the once she talked about it—the creatures they could transform into before the bands were legalised and put into mass effect. It was knowledge she needed to understand herself—to understand what makes her who she is. The animal all percepters shared DNA with. The animal they were once able to become.

Cassia fights the numbness enveloping her body and pulls herself onto her stomach, her hand flopping by her head.

Focus. Concentrate.

Reach out will all of your senses, all at once.

Miss Marilore's voice rings through the percepter's head as she makes the first known transformation since the bands were tightened on their arms so many years ago.

With the fur now covering her body acting as better insulation than her clothes, Cassia finds the strength to gather her new limbs beneath her. Wobbly on her three legs, Cassia lets out a mournful howl for the people lost, losing her balance as she does and collapsing back into the snow. She waits for the echoes to die out before shakily rising again.

For all the ones she didn't know, for all the ones who were her friends, and for the one she'd looked up to, she would not let this be the end. Cassia turns and begins hobbling down the mountain, back to the rest of the rebellion.

The ones on the train are all dead, but she won't let the dream die with them.

Smoke and Mirrors

S.A. Bradbury

She smells smoke. She always smells smoke.

It's a consuming scent that lingers in every fibre of furniture, decoration, and human within its vicinity. It doesn't matter where it came from: a cigarette, burning wood, a house fire. It doesn't matter now, as she waits in line and breathes it in again. It has lingered for so long that she can't remember a time when she wasn't being suffocated.

She breathes in deeply, stepping forward in the queue. The flyer feels stark and rigid in her delicate hand. Her other hand pulls out a compact mirror from her coat pocket, gently popping it open to inspect her handiwork. Shadowed eyes stare back at her, calculative and assessing. She scans her own reflection with those eyes. Blonde curls are pinned effortlessly; her skin glows with the morning sunshine; manicured nails wipe at her non-existent eye bags. A modern Marilyn, that's what people called her. It's why she got the parts. Why she *always* gets the parts.

Still, she pulls at her skin, prodding and probing her cheeks, eyelids, forehead, and lips. When everything stays in its rightful place, she relaxes. A smile splits her lips. The doctors had done a marvellous job covering the burns.

She looks down at the flyer again. Its blue design is bright against the gold words that read: *AUDITIONS! Come one, come all to be part of the world's biggest show!*

'Today's the day,' she mutters, flipping the compact closed.

She shuffles forward again, now only a few places away from being called into the theatre. Three people stand in front, and a hundred more trail behind. They all sway from foot to foot or fidget with the twisted scripts in their hands. Not her, though. She has no need for scripts. This is her life. Performance is her heart, the very thing that keeps her alive.

And she would not be denied her life again.

The theatre feels familiar, as if it were her own house. Anticipation ignites in her chest at the thought of entering it soon, standing in the spotlight after a long break away. As she inspects the charred windowsills, her stomach suddenly churns with dread. The memory of flames licking at her skin sends chills down her spine, the scent of smoke beginning to smell all too real—

She shakes herself out of the past.

I'm ok, she reminds herself. *I made it out.*

A man steps out the door, clipboard in hand. 'Next four.'

Elation sets her feet moving, following three other women as they walked through the front doors. As she walks past the caller, he calls out again. 'I said, next four.'

'We're already inside,' she says, annoyance sharpening her words.

The caller doesn't acknowledge her. Instead, his eyes focus on the line she just escaped, pointing his gaze on a younger girl dressed in an oversized coat and glasses. *The poor girl looks as if she hasn't showered in days*, she thinks, eyes wandering over the girl's thin frame and wiry hair. *Glasses Girl looks nothing like a movie star, so why is she here at all?*

The young girl grapples with her script, lost in her rehearsal. 'Oh!' she exclaims, reshuffling the papers clumsily and running up to the front doors. 'Sorry, was off in space.'

'Clearly,' is the caller's only response as he allows her to walk in and join the others.

'Are you serious?' Blonde strands escape the pins as she storms over to the caller still waiting just outside the door. 'Are you blind or something? You think slipping in a few extra auditioners will go unnoticed?'

The caller ignores her again, his expression indifferent as he finally walks inside the doors.

She follows. 'If this cuts into my audition time, I will be letting your employer know of your *insolence* the moment I—'

She is cut off by slammed-shut doors, her perfectly powdered nose just inches away from them. On the outside.

She takes a moment to register what has happened. The scent of smoke wafts up her nose, as if her chest is a furnace and her anger the fire within.

'Unbelievable!' She turns to the next person in line: a brunette with black-painted eyelids that matched her nails. 'He just shut me out as if I wasn't there! Can you believe that?'

She waits for a reaction, but all the brunette does is look at her nails with bored indifference. She rolls her eyes. 'Never mind,' she mutters dismissively. 'Seriously, is there *anyone* here of competent mind?'

She looks back to the doors. The last group of girls that went through had taken half an hour to audition. *I'm not waiting that long.*

She leaves the line to wander down the side alley created by the theatre and the bakery next door. Flour powders her pumps by the time she reaches the steps leading up to the back door. As usual, there is no one in sight. She laughs to herself. The number of times she's snuck into the theatre this way is almost second nature. She might as well have not bothered with the front door. *If you want success, you've got to take it yourself.*

Smoke congests her lungs as she steps through the door, but not in a sickening manner. It's as if the fire within is stoked by simply being in a familiar space. It recognises the long corridor ahead of it, the many doors that lead to dressing rooms, storage spaces, and, most importantly, the stage. The floorboards shine with history and the doors are open like arms ready to embrace.

The fire recognises it all. It recognises it is home.

Distant voices draw her attention back to the present, to the stage. It is the casting crew. Perhaps the director is there, too.

This is her moment.

The corridor leads to the wings, stage left. Ropes attached to overhanging lights are tied to thick bannisters; sets from old productions stand squished into the small space behind the back curtain, dividing the stage's past from its present. A cluttered costume rack stands at the ready by the stage curtains, offering a plethora of disguises for the chameleon actor.

The fire within burns warmer, more intense. The smoke threatens to invade her every sense. She takes slow, deep breaths to calm it down. *It isn't time, yet.* She walks to side curtains and peeks at the audience. Three people sit in the centre seats close to the front, pen, and paper in hand.

She is not one to be nervous, but the fire grows as she looks from the audition panel to the empty stage, knowing she will be there again soon.

The group of girls from before stand waiting in the opposite wings, lining up behind Glasses Girl. Her bug eyes flick from side to side, scanning the script she still clutches, desperate to memorise her lines before she, *no doubt*, embarrasses herself.

The smoke is intense now. She is forced onto the stage by the specific scent of burning wood and grey ashes, if only to get a breath of fresh air.

Her heeled boots click on the stage floorboards, and she supresses her surprise when she doesn't hear a creak echo afterwards. She walks centre stage, into the spotlight they've set up. As soon as she does, the rest of the world darkens. There is just her, the stage, and the fire within.

'Hello,' she speaks into the void. 'I will be auditioning for the lead female role. As you can see from my application, I've had plenty of experience in leading roles. Do you have any questions for me before I begin?'

The silence that follows is unexpected. Usually there are questions to confirm experience, or just an 'ok' to carry on. She squints into the darkness but can't see them through the light.

It unnerves her, but she immediately slips into her performer skin. Maybe they were just not conversational people? She closes her eyes in focus. She's read the monologue enough times that she can see the words in her mind.

She begins. 'By day and night—'

'Next!'

The following words are caught in her throat at the harsh cry, ripping her out of the fictional world back into the present. To the reality. Did they just …

'B—but I've barely said anything,' she says, repressing the urge to scream. How dare they interrupt her? How *dare* she be silenced?

'I said: *next!*'

Glasses Girl stumbles onto the stage, muttering insolent apologies as she walks towards centre stage. Towards *her*.

'I'm not done!' She is angry. The fire within now only burns with rage. Her breaths are quick, and short. The angry smoke from her furnace is almost suffocating. She turns her burning gaze to Glasses.

Glasses draws closer and closer, an ever-looming threat on her spotlight.

She storms towards Glasses. 'Go back to the wings until I am finished! It is my turn, you hear? My *time*—'

The hand she raises to shove Glasses falls through her shoulder like water. Unlike water though, she doesn't feel anything as her hand passes through. She doesn't feel anything when Glasses walks *through* her, taking her place on centre stage.

'I'm sorry,' Glasses says to the panel. 'Guess I'm just a bit nervous. Haven't been here since the fire.'

What just happened? She feels, but also doesn't feel. The duality is as smothering as the smoke. As the memory of flames ignites again, much more prominently.

'That's understandable,' the director says. 'It's a little strange coming back here, knowing people died.'

Died? That couldn't be true. Everyone had survived. *She* had survived.

Glasses hums in agreement. 'It's a shame about that woman, the one people say died on this stage. They say she was the next Marilyn Monroe. They tried saving her, but it was too late.'

The world suddenly destabilises as she runs off stage towards the exit. The fire spreads through her, and it itches with an intensity that makes her want to rip her skin off.

It's not true. I survived. I was saved*!*

She runs past the doors that now gleam too brightly with fresh paint, along the floorboards that no longer squeak. What once was familiar now glares at her with caution and disgust.

She throws open the back door and trips down the stairs, landing on the pavement. However, her knees don't scrape. She feels no pain. There is only the fire, of her past and her present.

There's too much smoke; she can't breathe—

Her fingers find a puddle.

She looks into it and screams.

Her porcelain skin now shows deep burns, some deep enough to draw blood. Exposed bone flashes vibrant against the red and it makes her want to empty her stomach in horror.

She looks behind her and finds that the theatre, too, is burning. The scene feels like it's been taken out of one of the great revolutions of history. Flames burst from the windows, the sound of shattering glass piercing her ears. The flames are hungry, alive, yet she feels anything but that. All she feels is hopeless, scorched, the cold stone beneath her only accentuating the heat in her skin.

That is when she remembers.

The theatre had been painted over, given a new life. Humans weren't so easily rebuilt.

She looks up at the burning building and cries. The surrounding smoke holds her as she cries for what she has lost, the pain she now feels.

It whispers to her, ghost to ghost, 'Let it go. You are no longer part of this world.'

'But I'm not ready,' she says between sobs. 'I'm not ready to become nothing.'

'Who is to say you will be nothing after this?'

'But I'm not ready.'

The smoke caresses her cheeks, forces her to look up again. 'I think you are.'

She finds the building is no longer on fire, but as she saw it before. She takes in a deep breath. The smoke is finally gone, unlocking her chest to feel again.

She breathes in and out until it is all she hears, all she feels. The world fades away as she does, folding into the ether as she takes on her biggest role yet.

Colour Outside the Lines

KATE PARSONS

For a unified society:

- You will not murder
- You will not lie
- You will not steal
- You will not cheat
- You will not exploit yourself
- You will not make haste
- You will only convey contentment
- You will align to the right

These laws were enforced, ingrained in children from the moment they could talk. Constant surveillance monitored all who bled with the temptation of possibility. This world where indifference was removed through execution.

25/04/2046

7:54AM

Location: Fallen Ave, QLD

Flagged: Lucia Perdita Age: 25 Gender: Female

Law: You Will Not Make Haste

Layers of rain engulfed all those moving amongst the streets. Two separate groups of people walked in unison, each heading in opposite directions, scattered black umbrellas providing short-lived protection. The civilians were segregated by their intended destination, always walking on the right side of the road. A dark hue hovered over the city; the brick buildings encased the streets in everlasting shadow.

Lucia Perdita's soft steps sang out from the other steady stomps that surrounded her. She weaved between the rhythm of movement, hiding within the crowd. Eyes watched her, observing glances, words of caution whispered towards her. She chose to ignore. Her swift steps and delicate motions all to survive the cameras insatiable gaze.

Her watch sent a shock into her wrist. Pain reverberated through her arm and a message displayed on her watch face.

`LUCIA PERDITA Curfew enforced: 0600 hours until 2000 hours`

`Crime: Making Haste`

She lowered her head and under her breathe she said, 'You will only convey contentment, do not show them weakness, be a figure of serenity.' A moment passed before she muttered, 'Fuck your serenity.'

The anniversary of her mother's death was today, yet there was no mourning. Her expression remained without colour, the lines of her face unmoving.

The tin roof of Alvaro's Autobody Repairs shuddered under the heavy weight of the seemingly ever-lasting rain. Lucia took the noise as a blessing as she snuck into the workshop and planted herself behind the receptionist's desk. The pungent smell of burnt tyres and swarf permeated the shop, Lucia found comfort in the scent.

A deep voice wafted towards her, 'Lucia, you're late.'

'Only by 15 minutes, Alvaro. You don't even have any customers yet.'

Alvaro was strongly built, with dark brown hair that often fell across his face. Lucia pondered whether this was to hide the frustration often experienced when things weren't going his way. Many people had their hidden tricks and techniques to remain content, just as many people found it easier to blend in with society and align with the laws. Her mother had often puzzled over why Lucia couldn't maintain the same composure and peace.

'Lucia, it's the third time this week, we rely on you to be here on time … Do I need to send Edmond to walk with you?' Humour played in his tone, not enough to draw the attention of the monitoring gaze, but enough to emit comfort.

Hearing his name, Edmond, a sandy Border Collie with mud and grease speckled through his fur, trotted in, and landed at Lucia's feet. Without hesitation, she ran her hands through his thick wavy coat as he dropped his head to rest.

'Edmond would find himself getting just as distracted as I do,' Lucia said, her eyes incandescent with delight as she gazed down at Edmond, his slobbered tongue hanging out the left side of his mouth.

'Yeah, you're probably right,' he mused, a slight smile tempted to seep through his contentment. A moment passed before Alvaro said with silent sympathy, 'how has the morning treated you, Lucia?'

'As well as any other day,' Lucia remarked, turning away.

Alvaro hesitated and slightly furrowed his brows before walking back to the deconstructed vehicle hoisted high above the ground.

25/04/2046

10:40AM

Location: Alvaro's Autobody Repairs

Flagged: Lucia Perdita Age: 25 Gender: Female

Law: You Will Only Convey Contentment

Distracted as she rubbed Edmond's belly with her foot, she gripped her pen in her left hand and instantly let it drop. *Align to the right, Lucia.* Her mother's training had kept her alive all these years, the taught tricks that hid her from the camera's view. Her mother's instructions often echoed through her mind; *keep pace with those around you, keep your head lowered, follow the path provided.*

Her mother wasn't here anymore, her life was no longer under observation. Something inside Lucia split. Edmond sensed the change and cowered under the desk.

She peered down and asked him, 'What are they going to do? Kill me?'

She reached for the pen once more, now in her right hand, she wove it through and around her delicate fingers.

Her expression became feral. Eyes watched eyes. Her stare unbroken as she looked up towards one of the many cameras perched around the workshop. She not only saw the lens but the eyes watching behind it. They monitored her every move, every choice. Her fist clenched the pen, knuckles glowed white.

Bone.

Blood.

Snap.

She winced and peeled her eyes away from the camera.

Another sharp shock.

LUCIA PERDITA Curfew adjusted: 0800 hours until 1600 hours

Crime: Unlawful Expression of Emotion

The ink stain was a constant reminder of the observing gaze and the clock that restrained her. As it neared 3:30pm, Lucia collected her items and followed her closing routine. Alvaro had concealed his dismay when Lucia informed him of her implemented curfew and allowed her to finish early. Edmond explored the surroundings whilst walking alongside her. Lucia silently sent him away; she was to travel on her path alone.

Water bellowed through the streets that Lucia followed instinctively. She kept pace with those around her. Their rhythmic feet traced the roads of the city, always aligning to the right. Ants marching to the beat enforced by their queen, never to step foot outside their set lines, never to let colour into their lives. These people, these cookie cutter citizens, let the rain pour. Let it drench and coat their entirety until their souls were frozen and set into the moulds designed for them.

Lucia walked with her head sunk, her body a reflection of perfection in the eyes of her observers. She kept her gaze watching her clock. The countdown to being house bound.

The cameras kept a watchful eye, always facing her direction, also knowing the importance of that clock. The minutes, the seconds she had to seek safety.

3:59:59pm.

Lucia entered her home and closed the door. The cameras pivoted away.

Solitude. The only place the cameras were not willing to reside. Lucia stood, head high, shoulders back as she ran her hands through the slicked hair that clung to her face. Remnants of the torrential rain sought refuge but were deserted at the corridor.

Shades of blue mixed and intertwined along the walls and roof of her unkempt apartment. Plants on guard in every window, the vines and branches providing protection against vigilant eyes. The smell of lavender and vanilla welcomed her home. Her mother had helped design this apartment, providing her a place of choice, of freedom. Her mother chose the paint that delivered the desired sense of amenity; Lucia's first rebellion was that of layering the shades, promoting individuality.

She grasped her worn paintbrush in her left hand and dunked it into a pool of crimson. Colour soaked into the brush. She relaxed into the motion of movement as she slashed vibrant paint across her walls. Her strokes struck with purpose. Worry, caution, and fear released with every wave and smear.

Power.

Intent.

Permission.

The brush was thrown away and replaced with hands. Hands spread across her walls, across her body, across *her*. Her prints played and danced, mixing to form an entwining of colour in every direction.

She fell.

The room was static with colour and energy as Lucia lay to rest on the floor, her expression fragmented with relief and anger. Her home was the image of rebellion. Blue and red now fighting along the walls, red bleeding into the desiccated blue. The pungent aroma of creativity infused her home.

3:56:12am.

The trickle of rain echoed and bounced across the roof. The kitchen tap followed the beat slightly out of time. Lucia's eyes refused to close. Her mind played alongside the strokes and swirls of the blue and red displayed on her walls.

Her mother's day had been and gone but the clock continued to rotate. The memories of her mother had begun to fade and the image of her face, that once provided stability, slowly escaped her minds barricades.

'I want to flee,' she said to the ceiling. Her sight sparked with electricity as she envisioned an array of colours dancing.

`26/04/2046`

`4:12AM`

`Location: Furnace St, QLD`

`Flagged: Lucia Perdita Age: 25 Gender: Female`

`Law: You Will Not Make Haste & Curfew Broken`

Lucia ran. She weaved and wound between the lamp posts and bus stops that housed the gluttonous lenses. Her quick movements encouraged the sprinkle of rain to act as daggers. Although not many people wandered, those who did stopped and stared. Unblinking, their statuesque figures formed a line of observers. Their fabricated lives entangled with the restriction of truth and individuality.

Her eyes winced against the spray, yet the moisture did not affect scrutiny of the surveillance.

Impending pain.

```
LUCIA PERDITA Return to residence: House
arrest enforced
Crime: Making Haste & Breaking Curfew
Caution is advised - This is your final warning
```

Lucia stopped.

And began dancing. A ballerina in a box. She danced onto the left side of the road; she danced through the people who walked in the opposite direction. She made her own path, coloured outside the lines.

Her arms flew into the air, embracing the chill of the moving mist that landed on her skin. Each drop was motivation to move. Each drop emitted a pulse of electricity.

She laughed.

Her mouth was open, facing the sky.

She spun.

Her laughter echoed along the streets, bounding off doors, buildings, fences. Lights began to flick on, people began to circle.

Eyes.

All eyes on her.

She spun, she laughed, she embraced and finally, she fell.

Lucia awoke bound and handcuffed, on display for the city to observe. An announcement blared, 'Execution of Lucia Renata Perdita. Repeated offence of laws five through nine. Your file has been reviewed; your execution approved. Do you have any final words?'

She stood inches away from her final resting place, the anomaly that appeared long before she walked the earth, a gaping hole with no end, an abyss. The stench of cold, wet moisture penetrated the air, the smell a message sent from the hole. It was as though she was staring into the eye of stagnant lake. Formed by stink hole, the depth and contents were unknown, only that those who entered never returned. This was where the people who had committed crimes five through nine resided. Her mother was not in this pit, not in the subjected hell.

Dancers, painters, truth tellers. Individual beings thrown into a chasm of nothingness. They did not belong in society. Lucia did not belong.

As she peered out into the crowd of people, their faces achromatic and hollow, she pondered her final words, whether anyone would listen, whether anyone would care. Her eyes wandered the crowd, searching for any sign of life. A break in the congregation stood out like a missing tooth in a young man's mouth. Alvaro watched the black coated executioner hold Lucia in place. His face was barren, but his eyes overflowed with fear. A single tear escaped, slid down his cheek, and found refuge in his neatly kept beard. He subtly shook his head, not in disappointment, not in anger but in hope. He longed for it not to be true. Longed for her to be safe in his workshop, safe standing beside her. He wished for a better world.

She held his stare, willed him to know she was okay. She knew what her final words must be.

'Why have I never heard you laugh?' A smiled formed as Lucia looked to Alvaro with confidence.

He mirrored her smile and began to laugh, a deep laugh that bellowed through the crowd's silence. The last image Lucia saw before being shoved into the abyss before her. She fell towards those who had lived in truth.

She felt as though she had been falling forever. The light from her watch was the only thing to provide comfort within the darkness that surrounded her. However, there was only static displayed, removing her from the world before, leaving her in a timeless limbo. The cold seeped into her skin. She was utterly alone.

With all the time in the world, she reflected on the life lived. The people she loved, the friends she had made. The ones she never held in her arms, the ones she never laughed with, never cried with, never danced with. She found comfort in the memories with her mother. Lucia remembered the efforts her mother made to ensure she was safe, the skills she was taught that had almost allowed her to survive.

She continued to fall until a light shone towards her. A piercing streak of white that sliced through the darkness. A star alone in the abyss. She aimed her body towards the glow. Her eyes began to burn, and she raised her arms above her face, shielding herself from the impending pain.

A soft warmth embraced her. The grass beneath welcomed with open arms. The delicate heat from the star shone onto her skin, creating a blanket of comfort.

She opened her eyes.

In front of her stood a tombstone, aged with algae and overgrown grass.

Lucia Renata Perdita

12/02/2021 - 28/04/2046

Her tombstone was not alone. Other graves had found their place atop the secluded knoll. Confusion and dread painted her face as she sat on her grave. Her breathing was frantic, her eyes bouncing and scanning for anything that provided answers.

A swarm of rainbow lorikeets flew around her, drawing her attention to a nearby eucalyptus tree. Their movements were sporadic, their calls a commotion of rhythmic chaos. She observed in fascination as they weaved in between the branches.

A lonesome bird flew from the tree and towards a bustling city off in the distance. Her attention was drawn to the vertical walls that acted as mirrors, pigments from the surrounding environment were reflected in every direction.

A rainbow city.

People were laughing. People were dancing. People were living.

Lucia stood to get a better view of the city and its people. She was illuminated by the city's reflections; the colours danced and formed an embracing aura. She stared out towards the distant utopia; an array of colours found refuge in her eyes, those eyes that now observed in awe.